her little black book

also by brenda jackson

What a Woman Wants

No More Playas

The Playa's Handbook

Unfinished Business

A Family Reunion

Ties That Bind

The Midnight Hour

The Savvy Sistahs

anthologies

The Best Man

Welcome to Leo's

Let's Get It On

An All Night Man

Mr. Satisfaction

her little black book

BRENDA JACKSON

ST. MARTIN'S GRIFFIN NEW YORK

This is a work of fiction. All of the characters, organizations, and events portrayed in this novel are either products of the author's imagination or are used fictitiously.

www.stmartins.com

Design by Sarah Gubkin

Library of Congress Cataloging-in-Publication Data

Jackson, Brenda (Brenda Streater)
Her little black book / Brenda Jackson.—1st ed.
p. cm.
ISBN-13: 978-0-312-35933-1
ISBN-10: 0-312-35933-0
1. African American women—Fiction. I. Title.

PS3560.A21165H47 2008
813'.54—dc22

2007048193

First Edition: April 2008

10 9 8 7 6 5 4 3 2 1

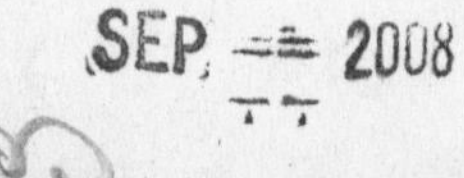

part one

1

Courtney's eyes widened just seconds before they blinked. April Fools' Day had been last week. Were her parents playing a belated joke on her?

When they had invited her to dinner, she'd expected them to announce that they'd finally decided to call it quits and get a divorce—not that they would be trying to save their marriage for the umpteenth time.

Her jaw tensed when she recalled how long her parents had been married: *too long*. They got married when Courtney's mother had become pregnant with her during her last year of college, thirty years ago, and it seemed her parents had done nothing but make each other's lives miserable ever since.

Her father frowned at her stunned expression and said, "Well, you certainly don't seem happy about it."

She decided to give him an honest answer. "I'm not. In fact, I'd think the two of you would count your losses and move on—in separate directions. Why would you continue to make each other miserable?"

"That won't happen again," said her mother.

Courtney merely rolled her eyes. That's what her mother had said the last time and the time before that—and the time before that. But the infidelity uppermost in their minds was from last year, only a month after Barbara had found out that one of her husband's students at the university was pregnant by him.

How many women was that now? Two different women pregnant in an eight-year period—when would her mother wake up and decide she'd had enough and refuse to help Ronald Andrews meet his child support payments to his illegitimate children? Her mother deserved so much better, but her father wasn't stupid. He'd realized a long time ago that his wife was more an asset to him than a liability.

Courtney sighed, picked up her cup of tea, and took a sip. Ronald Andrews was one of those men who didn't know the meaning of keeping his pants zipped. It simply never occurred to him that every time he pulled out his pecker to use on someone other than his wife he was committing adultery. And her gullible mother seemed too complacent to remind him of that fact, as well.

Most of the time.

There was that time Barbara had actually caught him in bed with another woman. A Paula somebody. Courtney had come home from junior high school and found all the dinner dishes broken, most of the furniture smashed, and her father's clothes littering the front lawn. Needless to say, her mother eventually took him back and he never learned his lesson.

"And why won't it happen again?" she asked, wondering if this time around they would give her a different answer.

Her mother smiled, and her father grinned before responding. "We're getting help."

Courtney arched a brow. "What kind of help?"

It was her mother who answered next. "From a therapist."

"You've done that before," she couldn't help but remind them.

Her mother nodded, still smiling. "Yes, but that last man only took our money. This guy will do a better job."

Not unless he's a miracle worker, Courtney thought. Maybe she was the one who needed to see a therapist. . . . What she *really* needed to do was leave before her parents gave her a monumental headache. She glanced at her watch. "I got to go," she said, sliding her chair back from the table.

"Where are you going? You just got here."

It never failed: whenever Courtney got ready to leave, the questions would start. She was twenty-nine, and they were still trying to keep tabs on their only child. She was her mother's only child, that is. No telling how many more her father could lay claim to.

"I told Sonya I would stop by to see if there's anything she needs help with before next Saturday. You haven't forgotten her wedding next weekend? The two of you are planning to attend, aren't you?"

Ronald Andrews shrugged wide shoulders. "I guess we'll be there, since it seems she's serious about marrying *that* man. I'm sure if she had looked hard enough, she could have found a nice man in her own race to marry."

Courtney rolled her eyes again. She knew her parents weren't too keen at the notion of their niece in an interracial marriage. Well, as far as Courtney was concerned, Mike Kelly was a hunk as well as a great catch. Since meeting him, Sonya had wasted too much time before accepting that true love was color-blind. And it was true love. Courtney felt it each and every time she saw Sonya and Mike together. And it was also scorching-hot love. You couldn't help but feel the heat they generated whenever they were in the same room.

"But then *you* haven't found one, so it might not be so easy after all."

Courtney's father's comment cut into her thoughts. "I haven't found what?"

"A man to marry. A black man."

She frowned. "I wasn't aware I was supposed to be looking."

"Of course you're looking," her mother jumped in to say. "You'll be thirty on your next birthday, and need I remind you that's only a few months away. You need a husband. Ron and I need grandkids."

Courtney started to say it would be just her luck to screw up and get someone like her father—and decided not to even bother. He would take that remark as a compliment. It was a good thing she didn't believe all men were like him and her uncle Joe Morrison, Sonya's dad. At least her aunt Peggy had had the good sense to finally get over Uncle Joe and move on, even if it had taken her a while to do so. She had almost driven Sonya batty in the process. Joe had destroyed his marriage of over thirty years, as well as his wife's self-esteem, when he had asked her for a divorce to marry a woman thirty-four years his junior—a woman younger than his own daughter.

"So what do you think of your mother's and my plans to improve our marriage?"

"I told you what I thought, Dad. I would feel differently if I truly thought the two of you intended to make a change, but I have no reason to think that you will."

Her mother lifted her chin stubbornly and said, "This time we're going to prove you wrong, Courtney."

She smiled sadly at them. "It would mean a lot to me if you did."

Courtney arrived at Sonya's home with a gigantic headache. Her cousin opened the door, took one look at her, and arched a concerned brow. Then she pulled her into the house and closed the door behind her.

"Another migraine?" Sonya asked, reaching out and gently pressing her fingertips to Courtney's temples.

"Yes."

"Brought on by what?"

"Another episode of Ron and Barbara Andrews trying to drive me nuts," Courtney said.

Sonya released an agitated breath. "What are those two up to now?"

"They want to make their marriage work—like such a thing can actually happen," Courtney answered, tossing her purse on the sofa in disgust. "I can't believe Mom continues to let Dad use her. If that's love, then it's abusive love."

"Calm down. If you keep this up, your head will only hurt worse. You can't let what your parents do get to you. Trust me, I found that out the hard way."

"I know you're right, but I'm tired of seeing them do each other in."

Sonya grabbed her hand. "Come on into the kitchen with me. I got just the thing for you."

Courtney allowed herself to be dragged off. "And what's that?"

"Butter pecan ice cream. Our favorite. I was about to eat a bowl, so now you can join me."

When they reached the kitchen, Courtney shook her head and grinned. "How can you indulge in a bowl of ice cream less than a week before your wedding? Aren't you afraid of gaining weight and that you won't be able to fit into your dress?"

"No. Any excess calories I take in, I'll burn off later tonight with Mike."

Courtney laughed. "You're incorrigible."

Sonya grinned as she pulled the carton of ice cream from the freezer. "Can't help it when it comes to Mike. He's the best there is, in or out of bed; however, I like our bedtime activities the best."

Courtney leaned against the counter and watched as Sonya filled two bowls. Her cousin stood five-nine, with medium brown skin, features that would make any man take a second look, a short and sassy haircut that emphasized her sophistication, and eyes so dark they almost looked black, not to mention a shapely figure. Courtney had always thought Sonya was simply beautiful. And despite a five-year difference in their ages, the two had always been close. Sonya had been the big sister Courtney had never had, and she'd always been proud of her. Sonya had always been wild and uninhibited; at least, that had always been Barbara Andrews's definition of her sister's only child. But to Courtney, her cousin's love-them-and-leave-them lifestyle had been intriguing, made her proud there was a woman who could dish it out just like a man could. Sonya had claimed there was no man alive who could make an honest woman out of her. At least that was the song she'd been singing before Mike entered the picture.

"Hey, go easy on my bowl," Courtney said when she saw how much ice cream Sonya was putting into it. "Unlike you, I don't have a Mike to help me work off any calories later, and I need to be able to fit into my bridesmaid dress."

Sonya laughed as she slid the bowl filled with ice cream toward Courtney. "Don't complain to me if you don't have a man. You and I both know why. You're too cautious; afraid you'll end up with someone like Uncle Ron or even worse, someone like my dad. Growing up watching your parents' bad marriage wasn't easy, and seeing what Dad did to

Mom is what has kept you from dating. Mom and Dad are the reason you've been so standoffish when it comes to getting serious about a man. You need to change that."

"Maybe," she said, knowing what Sonya said was true, although she never wanted to truly admit it. But turning thirty without a man had her analyzing the reason why. At the head of the list was the fact that, over the years, she *had* developed a cautious side when it came to love.

"I would date more," Courtney said, not even believing it herself, "but I'm too involved in my work to date. I'm trying to move up in my career."

Sonya waved off her words, not accepting her excuse. "No matter how hard I worked, I still made time for a social life. A little bump and grind every now and then takes the edge off. The longest period of time I went without sex was when I started dating Mike. He was determined to make me beg for it."

Courtney licked a scoop of ice cream off her spoon before asking, "And did you beg for it?"

Sonya smiled sheepishly. "Like a shameless hussy. I thought I was all savvy and would show him a trick or two, but he showed me that he already knew all the tricks in the book. The man laid it on too strong, and he was all smooth about it."

Courtney believed her. Sonya was too much of a woman, one who liked being in control. For her to give up that control to a man, that man would have had to make one hell of an impact on her senses as well as her body, but especially her senses. Over the years, her cousin had dated a number of men, but Sonya had never let one get under her skin. In fact, she went out of her way to make sure she would get under theirs with no plans of sticking around. And although more than one man had tried taming her reckless and elusive heart, each had failed miserably. "I'm glad you finally decided that race wasn't an issue and gave Mike a chance."

"I'm glad I did, too, although God knows I tried to fight it. I didn't want to get involved in an interracial affair, but I couldn't help myself. For the first time in my life, I began craving vanilla with a passion, wanted to lap it up with everything I had."

Courtney nodded. She knew the story of how Sonya had gone to the St. Laurent Hotel to confront Jesse Devereau about how he'd been treating Sonya's best friend from high school, Carla Osborne. Jesse had just found out that Carla gave birth to his son two years earlier and never told him about it, so he flew into town intent on making trouble for Carla. Needless to say, when Sonya confronted Jesse that day, she also confronted Jesse's best friend Mike, since she had interrupted them dining together.

According to Sonya, from the moment Mike laid his soulful blue eyes on her, it had been instant attraction, the hot and steamy kind. Mike was tall, hard, and had a body that would make any woman drool, so for the first time in her life, she'd wanted to find out if it was true that blonds had more fun. Sonya wanted to put Mike's smooth mouth and glib tongue to work doing something other than defending his best friend's actions.

Sonya and Mike formed a pact to straighten things out between Jesse and Carla, and their efforts eventually worked. The two were now happily married, and since Sonya and Mike were godparents to Jesse and Carla's son Craig, they began spending a lot of time with each other.

According to Sonya, at some point, she and Mike decided to stop fighting whatever was keeping them at arm's length and give in to their attraction and make things work. And they had. There was no doubt in Courtney's mind that her cousin had found her soul mate.

"It might work this time, you know."

Courtney glanced up. "What might work?"

"This thing with your mom and dad. They must have thought it through before deciding—"

"No, and that's the problem with them," Courtney said sadly. "They never think things through, Sonya. Mom refuses to analyze and accept just what an asshole Dad has been to her when she deserves so much better. I honestly think she's afraid of letting go and moving on. She's terrified that if she gives Dad up, she'll begin acting like Aunt Peggy did in the beginning."

Sonya nodded, remembering. Peggy had become a basket case when Joe dumped her for a younger woman. It had taken almost a full year for her to rebuild her self-esteem and understand that the breakup of her marriage hadn't been entirely her fault. Now Peggy had gotten herself together, joined the workforce, and was too involved with all her charities to worry about her ex these days.

Sonya's thoughts then shifted to her father. If Courtney thought her own dad was an asshole, then his brother-in-law was an A-plus asshole. What her father had put her mother through before their divorce was almost unforgivable. How could two nice-looking, highly educated blood sisters born from the same woman—a woman who'd raised them to be strong and independent—marry such heartless and untrustworthy men?

"How is Aunt Peggy handling the thought that Uncle Joe is bringing his mistress-turned-wife to your wedding?" Courtney asked.

A sad smile touched Sonya's lips. "As well as can be expected. I'm thinking she's hoping he does the decent thing and not bring her, since he knows I prefer not having her there. But we all know that he will, if for no other reason than to flaunt the fact that he has access to some young stuff whenever he wants it. I've even gone so far as to ask him to leave Suzette at home, but he refused, saying he won't disrespect his wife that way. I couldn't pass up the chance to remind him of all the times he had openly and uncaringly disrespected Mama. I doubt my words sent him on any guilt trip, so I've basically told him that if he does anything to ruin what will be the happiest day of my life, or if he allows Suzette to behave in any way to bring embarrassment to Mom, I'll never speak to him again."

Courtney nodded. She believed her. "What about Mike's family? Has he prepared them for what could happen?"

"Mike doesn't have a family. He was given up at birth and, like Jesse, got bounced around between foster homes, usually the same ones. That's why the two of them are so close and consider themselves brothers, since they were the only constant person in each others' lives while growing up. Jesse is the only family Mike has."

A part of Courtney knew that Jesse and Mike's situation was sad, but considering the parents she'd had to deal with and all their drama over the years, the thought of being raised in a foster home held some kind of appeal. Now how warped was that? "It wasn't my intent to hog your entire evening, since I'm sure Mike will be dropping by later," Courtney said, walking over to the sink to place her empty bowl into it. "But I wanted to check to make sure there're no last-minute details I can help you with before next Saturday."

Sonya smiled. "No, the woman we hired as our wedding planner is totally awesome. Carla used her when she married Jesse and was pleased with the results, and so far I am, as well. But I'm glad you dropped by—there's something I want to give you."

Courtney raised a curious brow. "What?"

Sonya's smile widened. "Wait here for a second while I go and get it." She then hurriedly raced up the stairs.

Courtney went into the living room and glanced around. She thought the house Sonya and Mike had bought together a few months ago was simply gorgeous and elegant. She'd always admired Sonya's decorating skill, and every time she visited, she couldn't help but appreciate Sonya's classic taste as well as her love for bold colors, which did so much for the gleaming oak floors and decorative tile walls. So far only Sonya had moved in. Mike wanted to officially take residence after the wedding, although Courtney was fairly certain he spent many a night here anyway.

And then there was the other home they were having

built in Los Angeles, where the corporate office for Mike's private investigating firm was located. That was where they would be spending a lot of their time. Mike's company offered professional services to law firms, prominent individuals, financial institutions, as well as major domestic and foreign corporations. Sonya would be quitting her job with a large marketing firm and would bring her marketing expertise to Mike's firm, starting with the office he had opened here in Orlando.

"I'm back and here you are," Sonya said, coming down the stairs. She walked over to her and placed a small black book in Courtney's hand. Courtney glanced up into her cousin's smiling face, confused. "You're giving me your little black book?"

"Yes."

Courtney looked down at it. This wasn't just any little black book. As far as she was concerned, it was legendary. For years she'd known it existed and had watched Sonya whip it out a few times to make a hit. She had even, on occasion, run into some of the men whose names had been plucked from the book for a date with Sonya. All the men had been tall, dark, and handsome. "Why are you giving me your little black book?" she asked.

"Because I won't need it anymore, and I can't think of another soul I'd want to have it other than you. Besides, I don't know of anyone who needs it more. You've denied yourself the chance to date as much as you could have, and now I want you to use it to get out there and have fun."

"But I've told you why I'm not dating as much."

"Yes, and you and I know there's more to it. You've never opened yourself up to anyone and we both know why. I was exposed to Uncle Ron and my dad just like you. Instead of making me cautious, it made me into a bad girl. I'm not saying that you need to become a bad girl, but I think you need to have fun. I truly believe that you want to find love but are afraid to do so for fear of what type of man you might get."

Sonya didn't say anything for a moment, wanting her words to sink in. Then she added, "Granted, you probably won't like every guy whose name is in the book, but I think there're a number of pretty good prospects. The names I've lined through are guys I've met and spent time with already. The rest are guys that I met but never got around to actually checking out, but there was definitely something about them that I found interesting enough to get their name in that book."

Curious, Courtney opened up the little black book and flipped several pages before coming to one where the names hadn't yet been lined through. The first was Harper Isaac. Mmm, the name sounded manly. She closed the book and looked at Sonya, touched. Her cousin had to care a lot about her to pass on this very special book to her.

"Like I said, Courtney," Sonya was saying, "I was once where you are now. I kept thinking, what if this man is like Uncle Ron, and when Dad left Mom I wanted to hate the entire male population. I tried convincing myself that all men were jerks, and if you couldn't beat them, you might as well join them. But even then, I longed for the man of my dreams to come into my life, take me away from being a bad girl, capture my heart, and prove me wrong. Granted, I had no idea he would be of the Caucasian persuasion, but if I had to do it all over again, the only thing I'd change is having Mike come into my life sooner. The first time he tossed one of those *I'd-like-to-get-all-into-you* looks at me, I was completely lost."

Courtney couldn't help the smile that tugged the corners of her lips. "You truly do love him, don't you?"

Sonya nodded. "Oh, yes, with all my heart," she said softly, her voice filled with emotions so deep, Courtney could actually feel them. "And I believe he won't ever do me the way your dad did Aunt Barbara or Dad did Mom. I trust Mike completely. He has shown me that all men aren't the same."

"I never said all men were the same," Courtney said defensively.

Sonya smiled. "No, but deep down you've thought it, and over the years you've operated on that theory, so have I. For me, utilizing that little black book was fun while it lasted, and now I'm passing it on to you with my blessings and best wishes. It's time for you to get out there and have some honest to goodness fun. I want you to promise me that you'll try it for at least a month—or until you meet someone that you like."

Courtney shook her head. "I don't think that—"

"No, Courtney. I won't accept any excuses. It's time for you to take the first step and I want to be the one who helps you take it. Please, let me do this for you. I don't want to feel that I'm deserting you by marrying Mike when I know the reason you're denying yourself the happiness I'm now sharing with the man I love."

Courtney thought about Sonya's words. The last thing she wanted was for Sonya to worry about her. "Okay, I'll do it."

"For at least a month or until you meet someone you like?"

"Yes."

Sonya lifted a brow. "You promise?"

Courtney rolled her eyes knowing Sonya wouldn't let up until she promised. "Yes, okay, I promise."

A relieved grin covered Sonya's face. "I'm hoping you'll find your very own Mike among some of those names in that book."

Courtney hoped against hope that Sonya was right.

2

Lake Masters leaned back in his chair, ready for the show to begin. At thirty-nine, he'd basically seen it all, and this definitely wouldn't be the first time he'd seen a display of this kind. In fact, just a couple of months ago, he'd attended his brother Shane's bachelor party and witnessed basically the same thing—a nearly naked woman popping out of a huge fake cake.

He took a sip of his beer—straight from the bottle—thinking there was nothing like a party with live entertainment. Besides, showing up for the bachelor party was the least he could do, since he wouldn't be attending the wedding. He would be leaving for Paris in a few days, where he would spend two weeks negotiating an important business deal for the advertising firm he owned.

When the woman burst out of the cake, his gaze automatically went to her plump, shapely, and well-rounded behind before drifting to the smooth lines of her bare belly. He would be the first to confess, without apology, that he was an ass man. For some reason, he would automatically seek out that part of a woman before looking anywhere else. And he had to admit that this particular stripper was well put together. A certain portion of his anatomy suddenly reminded him that it had been almost eight months since he'd slept with a woman. Expanding his advertising firm by opening the Orlando office had taken a blasted toll on his social life.

He froze within seconds of raising the beer bottle to his lips when the woman bent over, giving every guy in the room a luscious view of her backside and the barely-there thong that indecently covered it. In fact, all she was wearing was a leopard-print bra, matching thong, and a pair of matching boots. In his opinion, she was making a statement: She could get as animalistic as any male in the room. The way she was moving her body all over the place made a believer out of him.

"Your breathing has changed."

The whispered remark made him glance from the exhibition in the middle of the floor over to his brother Grey, who was less than a year his junior. "Yeah," he confirmed. It would be a waste of time to deny it, since Grey, a former FBI agent, seemed programmed not to miss anything.

"I'm surprised Brandy let you come to Mike's party tonight," Lake said. He adored his brother's wife because of the happiness she had brought to Grey's life. "I'm sure she knew what would be going on," he added.

Grey snorted. "Hell, I didn't say anything when she went to Sonya's bachelorette party last weekend. I understand some police officer showed up who bared all for the ladies. Brandy and I have this rule: We can look, but we can't touch."

Lake considered Grey's comment for a moment and then smiled. Sounded like a sensible rule, and knowing Brandy, he could buy them having made such an agreement. He shared a very close relationship with his three brothers—Shane, Grey, and Quinn—and would be the first to admit that they had hit gold when they married their wives. He considered his sisters-in-law—Faith, Brandy, and Alexia—savvy divas in their own right, although they constantly bugged the hell out of him with their reminders that he was now the last remaining single Masters brother.

"Boy, she sure knows how to work it, doesn't she?" whispered Jesse Devereau, who was sitting on the opposite side of him.

Lake chuckled. He figured that, like Grey, Jesse also had a hands-off rule in his household. Lake then looked over at the groom to see how he holding out, since the woman had her breasts all in his face. He couldn't hold back his laughter. The usual calm and collected Mike Kelly was suddenly anything but that. And although Mike's gaze had not once wavered from the tantalizing view in front of him, Lake was fairly certain that no matter how hot things got, his friend would not yield to temptation.

Lake swallowed when the stripper took a step back and

then slowly began inching her thong down voluptuous thighs before quickly yanking it back it up. She was a shameless tease who was wicked as well, if the blatant invitation she was making with her tongue was anything to go by. He could just imagine that tongue of hers wrapped around his—

"I need a cold drink of water."

He glanced over at Grey. "If you leave now, you'll miss the best part," he said.

"That's not a bad idea, and I need that damn water."

Lake grinned when his brother got up and quickly headed toward the kitchen. He figured Grey needed more than a drink of water to cool off.

"Where's Grey going?" Jesse Devereau leaned over and whispered.

"In the kitchen to cool off."

"I think I'll join him."

Lake chuckled and shook his head when Jesse got up, too. They were cowards, the both of them. That left him, Cord Jeffries—a man he'd met and become friends with through Grey—and a few other guys whom he'd met that night, friends of Mike from Los Angeles, as the remaining fearless bunch.

Pretty soon it seemed all the happily married men had deserted. Besides the groom, Lake was the only single man in the room. That meant he was the only one free to hit on the woman, make plans with her for later. He smiled at the idea.

Starting with thoughts of a potential rendezvous with the exotic dancer, stripper, or whatever title she preferred, he opened his mind to all types of possibilities, especially the ones that indicated he might finally get some sexual release after eight months. It wouldn't be his first one-night stand, and it most certainly wouldn't be his last. He was old enough to know the score, was very selective in his dealings with the opposite sex, and took the practice of safe sex seriously.

His breath caught when the stripper crouched down to remove her boots with her bare butt pointed toward him. Oh, God, he could feel his heart rate increase, his pulse getting erratic. He was convinced he was about to have a coronary. But he would enjoy every moment of it.

"So, did you and that woman get together last night after the party?"

Lake frowned as he cocked his head and looked at his clock, his eyes barely open. It wasn't even six in the morning. Why was Grey calling him this early and asking him something so obviously private? "That's none of your damn business," he growled.

He ignored the laugh that crackled in his ear. "Evidently you didn't score, since your attitude hasn't changed. Your bark is still that of a man who needs to get laid."

Lake rolled his eyes and flipped on his back in the bed, then gazed up at the ceiling.

"So, what happened?" his brother prompted.

"Nothing happened, Grey. She's married."

"Married? Shit. What kind of man would let his wife work in that type of profession?"

Lake grinned. "He's a policeman. Probably the same one who showed up at Sonya's bachelorette party."

Grey laughed. "You're probably right and they probably live in the biggest damn house there is here in Orlando, raking in all kinds of money just by exposing their bodies. Must be nice. Do you think me and Brandy are in the wrong business?"

Lake rolled his eyes again, refusing to answer that. "I know you probably have a lot to do today, but why are you calling so early?"

"Brandy wants you to come to dinner."

"Is she cooking?"

"Of course not. It's being catered as usual. My wife is too busy to cook."

Lake smiled. He knew that was Grey's nice way of sidestepping the fact that she couldn't cook. He'd heard how pampered Brandy had been while growing up. Her mother had raised her to have maids and butlers. "What time is dinner? I have to start packing since I'm flying out first thing in the morning."

"Five o'clock. I almost forgot that you won't be here for the wedding. Shame you're going to miss it."

Lake pulled himself up in bed. "There will be others."

"Your own, perhaps?"

"I'm in no rush."

"You're not getting any younger."

"I wasn't aware there was an age requirement."

"There's not, just a reminder."

"Thanks, and I'll see you at five." Without waiting for Grey's response, he leaned over and hung up the phone.

He swung his legs over the bed to get himself up and off to the bathroom, thinking in all reality he was a blessed man. He owned one of the largest advertising firms in the country, and it was growing by leaps and bounds. His company's portfolio was so broad that it included public relations, lobbying, marketing services, interactive design, and most recently he'd added media buying services. He had formed the company right out of college, and now he employed close to five hundred people in his Boston office alone, which was one of the reasons he'd made a decision to open an Orlando office.

The market here was a good one to tap into and with the city being a tourist's dream, there were a number of customer service corporations willing to pay big bucks to get their name out there before the buying public.

The St. Laurent Hotel had been one of them, and Brandy had entrusted him to take her first hotel to the next level. In less than a year, it had become the most sought-after place to stay in Orlando and boasted a five-star rating. Since then, she had built three new hotels in Atlanta, Dallas, and Los Angeles. Grey handled the security for all four hotels. The couple worked well together and made an awesome team.

Lake looked in the bathroom mirror before reaching for his razor. Why did everyone assume he should have a wife? So what if he was still single? Was that a crime? To listen to his sisters-in-law, one would think so. Maybe it was time for him to set his sights on someone who would be his perfect mate. The last thing he wanted, though, was a woman with dollar signs flashing in her eyes. He refused to become some gold digger's nugget or some young thing's sugar daddy. He wanted a woman who was pretty close to him in age and who possessed a mature mind. And she would have to be as financially stable as he was, and as emotionally balanced. He was way too old for drama.

His affair with Liz Harrison while in his late twenties had taught him a valuable lesson. There were a few things he regretted doing in his thirty-nine years, and hooking up with Liz definitely topped the list. She had been the ultimate drama queen, although he hadn't known it at first. All he'd seen was her curvaceous backside and 40D bra size. She had taken the word *clingy* to a whole other level and constantly badgered him about the time he'd spent working, trying to get his business off the ground.

The last straw was when she had moved her no-good, lazy-behind twin brother into their already crowded apartment without his permission. The man was supposedly down on his luck. Lake soon discovered that as long as he supplied Liz's brother with a roof over his head and food to eat, he was content to make no effort to find a job or move out.

Lake grimaced when he remembered the ugly scene that ensued when he'd asked Liz's brother to leave . . . and that was only after he'd caught the man going through his wallet. What erupted was more drama than he'd ever wanted to endure in his entire lifetime. The siblings teamed up against him, and in the end, Lake had been the one who left, with nothing more than the clothes on his back, vowing never to become enmeshed in a situation like that again. That fiasco had been almost twelve years ago, and he had learned his lesson well. In the years since, he found himself screening women before he dated them, but lately doing so took up too much of his time and way too much effort.

He had even gone so far as to entertain the idea of going through a dating service and would definitely check out one when he returned to the States. His firm represented a number of them, and if he were to believe his own ads, some were actually good, with high success rates.

Maybe it was time for a turning point in his life. He would consider settling down. As Gray had reminded him, he wasn't getting any younger.

A few hours later, Lake had dressed and grabbed his tennis racket on the way out the door. Thanks to his brother Shane—whom they considered the tennis pro in the family—all his siblings knew how to play the game. Today he was meeting Devin Phillips, a doctor he'd met through Grey when he first arrived in Orlando a few months back. He'd discovered Devin to be a likable guy who enjoyed playing tennis as much as he did, so they began getting together at least once a week on the courts.

He pulled into the parking area where Devin's office was located. Usually they would meet up at the country club, but today Devin had taken his car to the shop for a service check and had asked Grey if he would pick him up instead.

The parking lot was full, so he drove through slowly, mindful of all the elderly people on scooters. He smiled, remembering when his grandfather had gotten his own scooter last year. He had become as reckless with it as a kid on Rollerblades for the first time. The family soon discovered he was as dangerous driving the damn thing as he'd been when behind the wheel of a car.

Lake glanced at his watch, noting he was a few minutes early, and pulled into a parking space. He was adjusting his seat to allow more leg room when he noticed a woman walking toward Devin's medical complex. When his gaze zeroed in on her, blood rushed through his veins. He felt dizzy. And if that wasn't bad enough, intense heat settled right smack in his loins. Nothing of this magnitude had ever happened to him before. Even the woman from the striptease show last night hadn't gotten such a rise out of him, and definitely not to this degree. This was definitely lust at first sight, and it was taking one hell of a bite out of him. His libido was on full alert, red alert, hot alert.

Toting her briefcase, she was dressed in a business suit tailored to her form and emphasizing just what a curvy body she had. She was looking totally professional on one hand, and succulently luscious on the other. Who was she? he wondered. Another doctor? A patient? He seriously didn't care, just as long as she wasn't someone's wife. And from where he was parked, he couldn't see her left hand to check for a ring.

He felt a smile tug at his lips. She had the cutest shaped ass that he'd ever seen on a woman, and her legs, he thought, could be used for a lot more than just walking. His mind began envisioning them wrapped around him while they made love.

His gaze then moved upward to her face and studied it. She was definitely one stunningly beautiful woman. She had skin the color of chocolate, medium brown hair that was cut just short of hitting her shoulders, and a face with features that usually were too young for his taste. But for some reason, not today and not with her.

Damn.

She had to be about twenty-four, no more than twenty-five at the max. He couldn't remember the last time he was attracted to a woman that young. But as he continued to watch her every movement, he felt a tugging desire in the pit of his stomach. With every step she took, a part of him couldn't help but be thankful he'd been born a man.

He saw her reach the door at the same time Devin walked out. They stopped and chatted familiarly. Whatever Devin said made her smile, and simultaneously, every cell in Lake's body lit up as well. In that instant, he knew he could probably sit there and gaze at her all day. She and Devin ended their conversation, and moments later she entered the building. Devin glanced around the parking lot before noticing where Lake was parked and began walking his way.

Lake tried like hell to pull himself out of his daze. It was simply absurd that he'd spent the last few minutes lusting after a woman so young. Though anyone who knew the Masters brothers would agree that nobody could ever fault or question their taste in women.

"Sorry to keep you waiting," Devin said, opening the car door and sliding onto the seat beside him.

"Who is she?" Lake asked before Devin could fasten his seat belt.

Devin glanced over at him with a lifted brow. "Who is who?"

Lake turned the key in the ignition and began backing out of the parking space. "The woman you were just talking to."

Devin smiled now that he understood the question. "She's my drug dealer."

"What!" Lake hit the brakes.

"Whoa, Lake, calm down! It was just a joke," Devin said, laughing. "At least, it's one that she and I share. She's one of my pharmaceutical reps, but it's an inside joke between the two of us, since she sells me the drugs. And she's good at what she does. She keeps me and my staff on top of the latest advancements and breakthroughs with the medications I prescribe. I've been working with her for at least three years now."

Lake frowned. "She's kind of young, isn't she?"

Devin chuckled. "How old do you think she is?"

"Twenty-four. No more than twenty-five."

Devin shook his head. "Guess again, and add five years to the highest number."

Lake swung his head around. It was a good thing that they had come to a traffic light. "She's thirty?"

"Just about. She will be in less than six months."

"You sure?"

"Positive. The girls in the office are teasing her about reaching the big three-oh."

Lake was surprised. She was still a lot younger than

what he preferred, but there was an appeal that he just couldn't shake. "So, what's her name?"

"Courtney Andrews."

"Do you know if she's involved with anyone?"

"Now that's something I'm not sure about, but I don't think so, because my secretary has been trying to fix her up with one of her brothers. So far she hasn't been too successful. Probably because one of my nurses pulled Courtney to the side and told her what a lowlife Christine's brother is. I'm surprised that you and Courtney haven't met."

Lake glanced over at Devin before moving into the intersection. "Why would we have?"

"Because you know some of the same people. She's Sonya's cousin."

Lake's eyes showed surprise. "Sonya? Mike's Sonya?"

"Yes," Devin said, smiling. "Mike's Sonya."

Lake recalled that he and Sonya actually met sometime last year before she and Mike had become serious about each other. It had been on a day she dropped by the St. Laurent with Carla to visit with Brandy.

"Too bad you're going out of town and won't be attending the wedding on Saturday," Devin said, interrupting his thoughts. "Courtney is part of the wedding party."

"Yes, it is too bad," Lake said, but already his mind was thinking ahead to the day he would be returning to Orlando. And the one thing he intended to do when he got back was make sure he got introduced to Courtney Andrews.

When she got to the reception Courtney glanced around the exquisitely decorated ballroom of the St. Laurent Hotel. Mike and Sonya's wedding had been beautiful, and the vows they had written and recited to each other brought tears to nearly everyone's eyes.

The way Mike had stood there facing Sonya, staring deep into her eyes while pledging his love and promising to make her happy for the rest of their lives made Courtney long for a man to love her just as much.

"Hello, Courtney Diane."

She looked up at her uncle Joe. Deep wrinkles now marred a face that used to be ageless, smooth, and extremely handsome. Now it appeared that marriage to the young high-maintenance Suzette had taken its toll. The good looks were still there—if you searched real hard.

Overall, he looked tired, whipped, and a lot older than his sixty-two years. She'd recently overheard her parents saying he was routinely working additional hours since Suzette liked nice things and expected her husband to supply her with them, starting with the Porsche he had given her for her twenty-eighth birthday last year. There was also the huge monstrosity of a house he'd had built for her.

Courtney remembered how while she was growing up, Uncle Joe used to brag to everyone about his plans to retire early and not work a day past his sixtieth birthday. He would be sixty-five in three years, and thanks to Suzette, retirement wasn't in his future any time soon. At one time, she used to think the world of her uncle; he was always her favorite. She used to respect him more than she did her own father . . . until Joe discovered that, like her father, he had no intentions of adhering to his wedding vows. Although his philandering days had come later in life, still they had come, disappointing and hurting Courtney as much as Aunt Peggy and Sonya.

"Oh, hello, Uncle Joe," she said, rising slightly on her toes to place a kiss on his cheek. The gesture was more habit than affection. "How are things going?"

"Just fine. I thought the wedding was nice."

"Yes, it was," she agreed. Especially since he'd somehow convinced the sophisticated hooch he'd married to behave. Suzette was known to throw temper tantrums at any time or any place, like a spoiled child. Inwardly, Courtney was grateful Suzette hadn't made a scene, even when no one escorted her in, although it was obvious she'd felt that she should have been part of the ceremony. Why she believed that was beyond Courtney.

"I just finished talking to your parents a moment ago. They seem happy together."

Looks are definitely deceiving, she wanted to say, but instead she took a sip of her champagne and asked, not that she was really interested, "Where is Suzette?"

"She went to the ladies' room."

Courtney immediately scanned the ballroom, not seeing her aunt Peggy anywhere. She felt the hairs on the back of her neck suddenly stand up as she glanced over at Sonya. Her cousin was standing beside Mike, getting ready to cut into her wedding cake, but Courtney intercepted the silent plea in her eyes and quickly nodded. "Excuse me, Uncle Joe." She then quickly walked off.

When Courtney reached the ladies' lounge, she was about to turn around upon seeing the posted NOT IN ORDER sign on the door, but then she heard both her aunt Peggy's and Suzette's voices.

It seemed her aunt Peggy was giving out just as many insults as Suzette was hurling, and Courtney admired her aunt for finally standing up for herself. Luckily, there was no one else in the area. Their voices were getting louder and the words coming from their mouths filthier. She was glad her aunt had finally decided to fight back. Suzette would often go to extremes to flaunt her affair and subsequent marriage in Aunt Peggy's face, and today was no different.

The two women's voices rose even higher. Courtney ignored it as long as both humanly and womanly possible before deciding it was time to put the name-calling between the two to an end.

Inhaling deeply, she breezed through the door to find the women going at each other. Aunt Peggy was old enough to be Suzette's mother, something Suzette evidently didn't care one iota about. "Aunt Peggy, there you are. Mom has been looking for you," Courtney lied. She took her aunt's trembling hand in hers without giving Suzette so much as a glance.

"You're nothing but a bitch, too, Courtney," Suzette lashed out. "All of you, including the bride, are nothing but bitches. If you think you can insult me by not recognizing me as Joe's wife, then all of you are sadly mistaken."

Courtney drew a deep breath, determined to maintain her cool as well as her dignity. However, getting called a bitch for no reason tested her goodwill. "Suzette," she said, as if speaking to a sulking child. "It takes a bitch to know one, and if I remember correctly, as far as you being Uncle Joe's wife, I regret that you feel you're being overlooked, since you worked so hard for that title. I can just imagine the sores you probably still have on your back from staying in that position for so long. Trust me, everyone knows the story. They know exactly what you did to wheedle your clothes, your house, your jewelry, and that title you seem to be proud of, out of him. If you're not sure about it yourself, then try staying in an upright position for a while and see what it gets you." Courtney chuckled. "Probably nothing more than your replacement."

Before Suzette could hurl an insult that would probably blister her ears, Courtney quickly added in a voice that let the woman know she meant business, "You don't want to tangle with me, Suzette—not today and not ever. Now, if you don't mind . . . or even if you do, it doesn't matter because my aunt and I are leaving. We have more important things to do with our time than waste it exchanging insults with you."

Courtney led her aunt out of the ladies' lounge, ignoring the curse words that were spewing forth from Suzette's lips. Once they were a good distance away, she studied her aunt's face before asking, "You, okay?"

Her aunt nodded. "Yes. She followed me into the bathroom and caught me unawares. I didn't want to ruin Sonya's day," Peggy said worriedly.

Courtney hugged her aunt, whom she thought looked rather ravishing today, so much more in control than the other times she and her ex-husband had been under the same roof. "And you didn't ruin it. Knowing the situation, Uncle Joe should not have brought Suzette here."

"He's taken with her, but I refuse to let that bother me any longer. He's not worth it. Neither is she," Peggy said, blowing out a breath. "They deserve each other."

Courtney smiled sadly. "You're right, and I'm glad you finally realize that you can do better without him."

"Took me long enough."

"But at least now you have."

Peggy smiled, too. "Yes, at least now I have."

Later that night, Courtney entered her condo with a smile on her face, pleased with how Sonya and Mike's day had ended. She was one of those who had remained to see the couple off as they got into a limo that would carry them to the airport. They would be flying off tonight for a three-week honeymoon in Italy.

After dropping to the sofa, she kicked off her heels. She'd changed out of her bridesmaid dress during the evening and was glad she had. The floor-length gown had become tedious, and the stomach-cinching waistline had not expanded an inch. She was tired in a good sort of way, and she had refused to let that little incident in the ladies' lounge with Suzette ruin her day.

She wasn't sure just what Suzette had told Uncle Joe, but the two of them left right after the cake-cutting, which hadn't seemed to bother anyone, least of all Sonya. Courtney had a feeling Sonya was totally disgusted with Joe anyway, probably the same way Courtney was totally disgusted with her own father.

She sighed deeply. While she was still this keyed up, there was something she wanted to do. She padded on bare feet into her bedroom and opened the drawer where she had placed Sonya's little black book. Smiling, she pulled it out and eagerly flipped to the page she had marked and the name she wanted.

Harper Isaac.

She had done her homework this week and researched him in the city directory. Harper Isaac was six years older than she, an executive at the Sun Flower Bank, and had worked there for over five years. She'd also discovered he was a graduate from a college up north and, like most people living in Orlando, was a transplant. She was proud to have been born and raised here and always found it to be a good conversation piece.

Sitting cross-legged in the middle of the bed, she reached out and picked up the phone. Unlike her cell number, it couldn't be traced; therefore, it wouldn't ID her on the man's phone. She wanted the element of mystery to remain on her side. She inhaled again, deciding to go ahead and do this before she got cold feet. Courtney quickly began dialing the phone number and nearly held her breath when the phone began to ring.

"Hello."

She felt the bottom of her stomach drop. He sounded good, with his deep and sexy Barry White voice.

"Hello."

She decided to speak up when he repeated the greeting. The last thing she wanted was for him to get annoyed and end the call. "Hello, how are you doing?" she asked in a calm, collected, and what she hoped was a sultry tone.

"I'm doing just fine. What about you?"

"Likewise." She could just imagine his smile about now. Men were certainly different from women. If a mysterious man called her and didn't immediately identify himself, he would soon be hearing the phone slam in his ear, yet this guy hadn't even asked her who she was. "It's a beautiful night, don't you think?"

She heard his smooth chuckle. "Yes, I think so, as well." There was a pause, and then, "And who am I talking to?"

Courtney smiled. *Finally, he wants to know*. She knew the rule: first names only. "This is Courtney."

"Hello, Courtney."

Her smile spread to the far corners of her lips. The huskiness of his voice was definitely a turn-on. "Hello, Harper." *There, I've just established the fact that I know his name and haven't dialed a wrong number.*

"So, Courtney, have we met before?"

"No."

"Then when can we meet?"

Picking up a guy was just this simple. He hadn't even bothered asking how she got his number. "When do you want to meet, Harper?"

"What about tomorrow?"

Boy, he's anxious, she thought. "I've already made plans for tomorrow. What about next Friday?"

"That long?"

"Yes."

"Okay, then, Friday will work. Just name the place."

"City Jazz."

"One of my favorite places."

It was also one of hers. City Jazz at Universal City Walk was a nightclub that combined impromptu live performances and music education to create the world's foremost jazz facility. She frequented it often and knew most of the staff. Forever steering on the side of caution, she preferred getting together there with a man she would be meeting for the first time. "I can meet you there at nine, Friday night. Will that be okay?"

"Yes, that will be fine. And how will I know you from the others that will be there?"

Good question. She hadn't thought that far ahead and

had no idea what she would be wearing. Umm, except for one particular item. "I'll be wearing a dolphin heart gold anklet chain on my left leg."

"So, I take it you're a Miami Dolphins fan?"

She chuckled softly. "You take it right."

"Would you believe that I'm one also?"

He's already established something we have in common. I like that. "Yes, Harper, I think with you I can believe just about anything."

"I'm glad to hear you say that, Courtney, and I'm looking forward to Friday night."

"So am I."

Mike Kelly snagged his wife's wrist and pulled her into his arms. Their flight to Italy included a twelve-hour layover in Atlanta before flying on to Rome, where they were to spend three weeks on honeymoon. They had checked into a hotel for the layover, and he knew the moment Sonya walked out of the bathroom wearing sexy sleepwear just how they would use the next twelve hours.

Without a doubt, he'd fallen in love with Sonya the moment they met, although he'd been able to successfully keep his feelings on the back burner while working with her to get Carla and Jesse back together. Once that was accomplished, he had turned his concentration on her. It hadn't been easy, since other than his close friendship with Jesse, he was naturally a loner. He picked his friends and chose his relationships—especially those with the opposite sex—carefully. He never liked women who whined or clung to a man for support. That was probably why he'd fallen for Sonya so hard. From the first, he could tell she was tough, wouldn't take bullshit off any man. There was nothing whiny or clingy about her. She was his kind of woman. She was his.

And he could tell she was bothered by something. He combed his fingers through her hair. "What's on your mind, sweetheart?"

Sonya met Mike's gaze and inwardly cursed. He could read her so well at times. "The wedding."

He frowned slightly. "What about the wedding? I thought things went extremely well."

She nodded. "They did. But there were some behind-the-scenes things going on."

He lifted a brow. "Involving your parents?"

She nodded again. "Namely, Suzette and my mother. I didn't get a chance to ask Courtney about it, but I think Suzette may have insulted Mom . . . again." She pulled out of his arms, disgusted. "Damn it, Mike, I should have put my foot down and insisted that Dad either leave that witch at home or not come."

"But he's your father."

"Who's married to a woman young enough to be his daughter. A woman who broke up my parents' marriage and—"

He reached out and placed a finger to her lips, hushing the rest of her words. "I really don't want to hear about your parents' problems on my wedding night."

She frowned. "You're the one who asked what was bothering me."

"Now I wish I hadn't. Your parents have to work out their own issues, Sonya. Starting tonight as my wife, you'll have your hands full taking care of me."

Sonya's frown deepened, and she placed her hands on her hips. She glared up at him. "I don't think so."

Mike smiled, liking the fire that suddenly sparked to life in her eyes. "I do."

He reached out and pulled her into his arms, and although she tried protesting at first, the moment his mouth touched hers, she let out a soft, quiet, surrendering moan. He deepened the kiss, and she placed her arms around muscular broad shoulders. Some men kissed women. Mike, Sonya always thought, made it a point to do more than that. He made love to her lips with the same technique, precision, and detail that he made love to her body. The thought of what role she would play in his life from this day forward made butterflies skim through her belly. She was his woman. He was her man.

He pulled back slightly. "And what do you think now?" he asked against moist lips, his blue eyes twinkling.

She pressed her body to his, rubbed against it some, and smiled when she heard him groan. "I think it's really terrible of you to piss me off on my wedding night and then try smoothing it over with a few kisses," she said, leaning closer to nibble him on the ear.

He swept her off her feet and into his arms, quickly moving toward the bed. He gave her a look and said, "I'll have the next three weeks to make up for it."

4

Courtney looked at herself in the full-length mirror. For her date with Harper, she had chosen to wear something sleek, stylish, and seductive. Her hair was pinned up, and the outfit she had purchased last month on a shopping trip with Sonya was just the thing to wear tonight. It was a revealing black mesh dress with definite sex appeal. It had a double-V neckline that bared her shoulders and a below-the-knee hem trimmed in ruffles. And the feminine strappy sandals on her feet added the final touch.

She would be the first to admit she was nervous about tonight. This would be her first date in quite some time. For months she had been studying for an exam that would take her to the next level of her career. She was eyeing a regional sales director position—had been for the past year before finally taking the steps to achieve that goal.

Being busy for the past months had kept her parents' problems at the back of her mind. Other than studying, the only other thing she'd squeezed in time for was her responsibilities as a mentor to fourteen-year-old Jetrica Edwards.

She frowned. Jetrica had not kept their appointment today. According to the principal, she had been absent from her classes, and a call to Jetrica's house indicated she had left home that morning like she was headed to school. With anyone else, Courtney might consider possible foul play, but with Jetrica, she didn't need to. Every once in a while, Jetrica enjoyed rattling her twenty-year-old sister. The sister had basically put her life on hold to raise Jetrica after their junkie of a mother was sent to prison for knocking over a drugstore with her boyfriend. Instead of showing Bethany gratitude, Jetrica went to great pains to give her sister grief.

Courtney had been talked into becoming a mentor by Vickie, her friend from high school who had been one of Jetrica's teachers last year. Vickie was one of the few who saw beyond the teen's hell-raising antics. Courtney met with the girl every second and fourth Friday of the month at the middle school Jetrica attended. After six months, she still found the teen a challenge, mainly because the girl was determined to violate every social more that existed in the world. Sometimes Courtney figured Jetrica would deliberately test her patience to see how far she could take things before Courtney snapped. What Jetrica failed to realize or hadn't quite yet discovered was that thanks to Barbara and Ron Andrews, it took a lot to make Courtney snap.

But she wouldn't let thoughts of Jetrica ruin her night. She grabbed her purse off the table on her way out the door—it was time for her adventure to begin.

Ronald Andrews never liked repeating himself . . . especially when it came to women. And personally he didn't understand the problem he was having with Ashira Wilson. He made no woman, other than his wife, promises, and even those he made to Barbara were challenging to keep. But he would keep them this time, since he truly believed that Barbara had meant what she said: If she even *thought* he was screwing around on her again, he was out. He had too much to lose if that were to happen. He relied too heavily on the money his wife was supplying him. Child-support payments for two different women were kicking his ass, and his personal tailor wasn't cheap. He liked nice things, he liked looking nice and was used to buying the best, more than his salary as a college professor could afford.

Luckily for him, Barbara had invested the trust fund she had gotten at twenty-five. If neither of them worked another day in their lives, all was well. But she insisted they continue to work. She supported this damn belief that as long as a person had their health, they should continue to contribute to the working environment and that an idle mind was a devil's workshop. He didn't buy into all that garbage, but he'd discovered over the past fifteen years that being a college professor had its rewards even if the salary sucked. Women—especially the younger ones—were his weakness. It was easy to find a female student who'd do just about anything for a good grade. And he meant anything. He didn't mind seeing just how far they would go.

He angrily banged on Ashira's door. There were no limits with her, even when he had suggested a threesome with an old college friend of his who'd come to town a few months ago. It was a night he would remember for a long time. She was a freakin' freak. But another thing she was proving to be was a damn pain, which was why he was standing in front of her door now. He had broken off with her weeks ago. Had made it clear he was through cheating on his wife. Had asked her not to call him, especially on his private cell phone, the one Barbara had come across a few months ago. But Ashira had called earlier today, and luckily he had intercepted the call and deleted it before Barbara had found out.

The door opened, and immediately sweat popped onto his brow. Ashira stood there, eyeing him. Not in surprise but in expectation. He should have known coming here was a mistake. Knowing Ashira, it was probably a setup. She knew his weakness, and he had a feeling that tonight she planned to take advantage of it. She opened the door with only a towel around her middle. The moment she'd seen it was him, she dropped the towel, and he all but licked his lips. He was suddenly spellbound. Hard.

She had just gotten out the shower. Beads of water still clung to her body, especially on the plump breasts he love to devour, on her belly ring, and on the tattoo on her hipbone. When his gaze shifted slightly, he even saw the water glisten like sparkles on the hairs covering her femininity. He felt his erection grow harder. He needed to turn around and leave, but first he would have his say and make sure she understood. He didn't want her to call him. He wanted to be left alone to continue to work things out with his wife.

"Ronnie, I'm surprised to see you," she said, stepping aside, not caring that water was dripping to the carpeted floor. It was new carpet he'd paid for a few months ago at the peak of their affair.

Although he knew he shouldn't do so, he entered her apartment anyway, picked up the towel, and tossed it aside before turning to face her. Five feet and six inches tall, she had a body that would make any man's pecker throb. "I would appreciate it if you put some clothes on," he said in a rough tone.

She leaned back against the door in a stance that showed all: perky breasts, small waist, long legs, and a hot, wet mound. "Why?" she asked in a sultry tone. "You used to love seeing me naked. It seems like you still do."

She dropped her gaze to the crotch of his pants to zero in on the boner he couldn't hide—an erection getting bigger, especially when she licked her lips like she wanted them there. The girl had a mouth that was made for blow jobs.

He sighed deeply, refusing to let his mind and body think about that now. "Things have changed. I've told you that. Why are you deliberately trying to cause trouble?"

She pushed away from the door and took a few steps toward him and stopped. "Because I don't think you really want to end things between us. We're good together. I understand you a lot better than that woman you're married to. I bet she's never given you a blow job, has never let you get her from the back, never let you share her with a good friend. Every man needs a little kinky stuff once in a while. A good wife would know that and indulge her man. There's a reason you seek others out. There's something you're not getting at home."

He would not agree with her aloud, although everything she'd said was true. He did enjoy the kinky once in a while and would never ask Barbara to indulge him. His wife was born and bred to be a lady, not a luscious pecker-loving man-eater. Hell, he would admit his lovemaking sessions with Barbara lacked creativity. He came. She came. But they had to put a lot of work into it. But still, he knew what side of his bread was buttered . . . and by whom. "My wife is all the woman I need."

"Since when?" she asked with a smirk on her face. "If that was true, why were you screwing my brains out until a few months ago?"

"You were available."

Her smile meant she took that as a compliment. "Yes, and I'm still available. I'm also hot and wet tonight."

He shook his head. In his pockets, his hands were shaking. His erection was throbbing and aching. He could pick up her scent. He could almost taste it on his tongue. She liked to smear some of that fruity stuff inside her, and he enjoyed licking it away.

The next thing he knew, she had moved and was standing right in front of him, deliberately pressing up against him. He could feel her hot naked flesh through his clothes. "Do you really want me to believe that you don't want me, Ronnie?"

He knew he needed to step back, put some distance between them, get out of the range of her heat. But he couldn't do it. Her hot sex could home in on his shaft like radar. This woman above all others was destined to be his downfall. At times she could be overbearing, demanding, excessively jealous, and more often than not, she towed an uncivilized line, especially when she got her freak on. And he hated admitting that those were the times he enjoyed her the most because she would do just about anything to please him, excite him.

"Do you, Ronnie?" Her hand had slid down to his crotch and was cupping him, holding firm to his hard erection that was still growing under her hand. "Do you really not want me? Let me prove you're wrong by freeing this. I'll wrap my tongue around it, take it into my mouth, and give you the relief you need, that I know you want."

Her erotic words, the heat of her touch—even through his pants—had him not thinking straight. Hell, he couldn't think at all. With a mind of their own, his hands wrapped around her waist. She let go of him and ground her body against his. "When you leave here tonight, you'll know just where I stand . . . just where I lay. And just who Pretty Boy prefers. Who makes him the most happy."

Pretty Boy—that was the name she'd given his pecker the first time she saw it. Said it was pretty, big, and could definitely handle a man-size job every time. At fifty-three, he'd never had a problem getting Pretty Boy up and keeping it there. Its staying power amazed him at times. He was proud of that, since some of the guys he knew his age were dependent on Viagra. But not him. Ashira was twenty-three, thirty years his junior, and she could have any young buck out there, but instead she wanted him. She had explained that older men turned her on and that age was nothing but a number. He'd loved proving her right.

She suddenly dropped to her knees in front of him, began tearing off his belt, unzipping his pants, working her way inside his briefs. Then she pulled out his engorged shaft, and her mouth immediately and greedily latched on to it. He shut his eyes, held his breath as his body came alive underneath her mouth. Sensations beginning at his groin rammed through every part of him. His heart began racing as he threw his head back and let out a deep, satisfied moan. He needed this one last time. The feel of her gobbling him up. He knew he should push her away. Instead he caught hold of her head and securely held it in place while her mouth continued its work.

It didn't take long for his already messed-up mind to begin whirling. Then his shaft exploded when a climax hit, and she still didn't let him up. Instead she took it all like she needed it to survive. She was pulling everything out of him, draining him, taking it in. Tonight she would get just what she wanted. And he would get just what he needed.

Moments later she dragged her mouth from his shaft and stood, fixed her gaze on him while licking her lips.

His shaft was throbbing. Was up again already. He tore off his shirt, kicked off his shoes, finished undressing with the speed of lightning. Then he shoved her unceremoniously down on the floor, on her stomach, and before she could move, he was on his knees on top of her. Tilting up her ass to him, he rammed his shaft into it, taking full domination of her sex. Even the gigantic orgasm he'd gotten hadn't been enough, and this was his favorite position. One where he felt in control, he could square off with her and win every time.

He continued to thrust into her, showing no mercy because he knew she was getting just what she wanted; this was the reason she'd called him to come over. She tilted her head back and cried out his name, but he kept going, refusing to let up. Then another climax struck, one that almost stopped his breathing. It also strengthened his resolve to take her again. As soon as that orgasm ended, he flipped her on her back and was ramming into her from the front.

"I haven't gotten enough yet," was the only reason he could give her for his actions.

"Good, because I want more," she said, staring up at him with that look on her face that let him know that tonight her body was greedy as hell.

A thought suddenly forced its way into his mind: He was cheating on Barbara again, after swearing on his mother's grave that he would not. But he refused to keep thinking of that now. He was between a pair of young legs and getting all he wanted, the way he wanted. He was glad this was the night Barbara and her sister Peggy were meeting for dinner. That would give him time to return home, shower, and be in the bed before she got back.

But for now, this was what he wanted to concentrate on, and he knew, just like Ashira did, that no matter what he'd said before, what claims he'd made of wanting to end things between them, he was addicted to this and he would be back.

"So, you've decided to work things out with Ron . . . again."

Barbara met her sister's gaze, saw the concern in her eyes and understood why. There was a seven year difference in their ages and Peggy had always been overprotective when it came to her sister. It would be pointless to explain why she continued to stay with a man who had made a mockery of their marriage more times than she cared to remember; especially after what Peggy had gone through with Joe.

"Yes, I've decided to work things out. It's for the best."

Peggy rolled her eyes. "For who? You don't have any little ones, and if it was left up to Courtney, you would have ended things with Ron long ago."

"It's hard to explain."

"Try. And don't use the excuse that I don't like Ron because you would be right. I don't like him. I don't like what he's done to you; what he'll do to you again if you let him. How can you even trust him?"

Barbara felt the tiny shiver that ran down her spine with Peggy's question. It *was* hard to trust him again but she felt she had to. She loved him. She had always loved him, and was determined to make her marriage work. "I understand him. He doesn't mean to hurt me."

Peggy frowned. "How can you sit there and say that when the man has two outside children, and if what I've heard is true, Melissa Langley is pregnant."

"Ron says the child might not be his."

Peggy placed her wineglass down with a thump. "Might not be his? Isn't it enough that he slept with her, even if the baby isn't his?"

"Can we change the subject, please?" She heard the anger in Peggy's voice. The last thing Barbara wanted was tension between them. She understood Peggy's concern, but Barbara loved her husband and she had to believe that he wanted to save their marriage as much as she did. He had promised on his mother's grave that he would not cheat on her again. She had to believe him because the thought of being alone actually scared her. She saw what Peggy had gone through after Joe had walked out on her; the misery and the depression. She had watched her sister go through it, and wasn't sure if she was strong enough to handle something like that herself. She would be the first to admit that Ron wasn't perfect; he had plenty of faults but then, so did she. And lately, she couldn't help but wonder what she could do to improve their marriage, to make him want her as his only woman, the way it should be.

Barbara knew that nobody understood, not her sister and not her daughter. Especially not Courtney.

"All right, we'll change subjects, but I hope you understand that I think you're making a mistake."

“For wanting to make my marriage work?”

“No, for setting yourself up for another heartbreak.”

“It won’t happen. He promised on his mother’s grave, and he loved his mother.”

Peggy looked at her for a long time and said nothing. “You love him in a way that is consuming you. For your sake, I hope Ron doesn’t screw up again.”

Barbara took a sip of her wine thinking that for her sake, she hoped he didn’t screw up again, too.

5

Courtney walked into City Jazz and glanced around. She had arrived thirty minutes early to obtain a level of comfort and get her bearings.

Harper had asked how he would recognize her, but not once did he mention how she would recognize him. Lucky for her, a photograph of him had been posted on his company's Web site. Although he was sitting down behind a desk, she could tell he was tall, well-built, and that his features were pretty nice. Clean-shaven head, coffee-colored skin, dark eyes, nice set of lips, and a smile that had reached out to her.

She walked over to the bar to say hello to Stan the bartender. They'd grown up in the same neighborhood and had attended high school together, so their friendship went way back. The room was crowded, not unusual for a Friday night, and the musicians were getting geared up on stage. This would be her first blind date, and since she now possessed the black book, it wouldn't be her last—unless she struck gold with Harper. She slid onto the stool and smiled at Stan Freemont. "Hi, Stan."

"Court, how you've been?"

"Fine. How's the liquor business going?"

"Great. And the drugs?"

"Still paying the bills."

He nodded and wiped off the counter in front of her. "I hadn't seen you around lately."

"Been studying. Trying to move up within the company."

"Good luck on that, but I'm sure you'll do fine. You were always smart in school."

"Thanks, but with age comes fuzz on the brain. How's Marla and the boys?" she asked. His wife was also a former classmate, and his two sons were just adorable.

"Everyone in the Freemont household is doing fine. So what would you like to drink? Your usual?"

"No, just cola for now. I'm meeting someone tonight, so drinks will come later. I don't want to start too early, since I need to keep a clear head."

He chuckled as he walked off to get her soda.

She turned and watched the club's entrance. Every time a man walked in alone, she felt her heart rate increase. "Okay, get a grip," she whispered to herself and waved when a couple she knew from the local spa recognized her as they were leaving.

"Here you are," Stan said, placing the drink in front

of her. "If you change your mind and want something with a little more kick, let me know. The margaritas are two for one tonight."

He knew that was her favorite drink. "Thanks, but I'm limiting myself, since I need to drive home later."

"Good decision."

When Stan walked off again, Courtney took a sip of her drink and turned on her stool toward the stage to enjoy the musicians. A short while later, she glanced at her watch. Harper was fifteen minutes late. The only thing about arriving at a place early was that it annoyed her when someone else was late. Suddenly things that she hadn't thought about earlier went flying through her mind. What if he changed his mind and wasn't coming? Not once had she considered the possibility that he might stand her up, since during their phone conversation he'd seemed so eager to connect with her.

A few minutes later—ten, to be exact—she was still watching the door. Thirty full minutes would be the max. Anything else, as far as she was concerned, was unacceptable. She was about to turn around and motion for Stan to refill her drink when a man she immediately knew was Harper walked in.

He was as tall as she'd assumed he would be, and his features were just as they were on the Internet—striking. Her annoyance with his inability to arrive for their date on time fell by the wayside when he looked at her, met her gaze, then slowly glanced down at her crossed legs. His eyes locked on her anklet, and then he looked back up at her face and blinked as if he was taken back. Apparently, he'd thought the woman he was meeting tonight was less than desirable. Blind dates, she realized, could indeed be like that. So far, she was happy with what she saw, and if the smile on his face was any indication, so was he.

He crossed the room to where she sat. "Courtney?" he asked, as if he needed to be absolutely sure.

She knew the feeling. Letting go of a small breath, she smiled. "Yes. Harper?"

He returned her smile. "Yes?"

Courtney offered him her hand. He took it, and his eyes twinkled. "Nice meeting you, and I'm in no way disappointed."

"Neither am I." For whatever reason, she got the distinct feeling she was going to enjoy his company tonight.

He slid onto the stool beside her. "I reserved a table for us." He looked at his watch. "It should be ready in a few minutes."

"All right."

He studied her curiously, and her lips twitched slightly before she looked away to where a renowned trumpeter had taken center stage. She found it amusing that he thought she was a puzzle he needed to figure out.

Slightly inclining his head, he asked. "So, would I be wasting my time asking where you got my number to contact me?"

She met his gaze. "Does it really matter?"

His eyes skimmed down her body, and then he looked back to her, smiled, and said, "No."

She looped some loose strands of hair behind her ear

and said, "Then, yes, it would be a waste of your time." He laughed, and suddenly she felt at ease with him.

He glanced at his watch. "Our table should be ready now. Would you do me the honor of joining me for dinner?" he asked, standing.

Smiling, she replied softly. "I would love to."

By the end of dinner, Courtney was convinced that she liked him. He was pleasant company who liked talking about himself and his job. But he hadn't dominated the conversation, and he seemed interested in her life and occupation, as well. He was impressed that she could speak several different languages. And it didn't go unnoticed that most of the time his gaze focused on her with laser-like concentration.

"So, tell me something in French," he leaned over and whispered huskily.

She smiled and did what he'd asked.

"What did you say?"

She took a sip of her drink before saying, "I said that I'm enjoying your company and I'm glad we met tonight."

"I feel likewise."

"Sorry to interrupt, but are you Harper Isaac?"

Both turned automatically toward the sound of the intruding voice and found two men in dark suits standing beside their table. Even from across the table, she could feel Harper suddenly tense when he said, "Yes, I'm Harper Isaac."

One of the men suddenly flashed a badge. "We're with the FBI, and you're under arrest for embezzlement."

Harper stood. "There must be some mistake."

"I'm afraid not," the other man said, and before Courtney could blink, a pair of handcuffs were placed on Harper's hands while one of the agents read him his rights.

They had already become the center of attention, and now with the string of loud obscenities pouring forth from Harper's lips, they were doubly so. She wanted to speak up in his behalf, declare there must be some mistake, but she didn't trust herself to speak, mainly because she had just met him tonight. What had the FBI agent said? Harper had embezzled his employer?

"I need you to get me an attorney."

She came out of her daze to realize Harper had spoken to her. "An attorney?"

"Yes," he all but snapped.

"What's his name, and I'll be glad to call him for you."

He was looking at her with impatience. "I don't have one. I need you to get one for me. Please do that for me, sweetheart, and when this is over, I'll repay every cent you put out to help clear my name."

Sweetheart? How had she gone from just Courtney to sweetheart? *And clear his name?* Was he insinuating that he wanted her to pay any legal fees associated with his arrest? Good grief! She glanced around, and it seemed all eyes were on them. She knew Stan, but she suddenly prayed that no one else in the establishment knew her.

She opened her mouth to say something, but it was too late. The two federal agents were dragging a loud and belligerent Harper Isaac away. Suddenly, Stan was there at her side. "Go ahead and leave, Court. I'll take care of the bill."

She again opened her mouth, but Stan's stern expression told her it was best to do what he suggested. She had never felt so embarrassed in her entire life. She bit back a relieved sigh, grateful those agents hadn't thought she was an accomplice and hauled her off to jail along with Harper.

With fluid ease and as much dignity as she could muster under the circumstances, she stood from her chair. "Thanks, Stan."

"That's what friends are for. I'll call and check on you later."

She nodded. Her knees trembled as she crossed the floor. She left the club thinking Harper Isaac's name would definitely get scratched from her little black book.

6

The city of romance . . .

Lake sipped his café au lait while eating his croissant and watching the tourists and Parisians walking by. Maybe it was his imagination, but everyone seemed to be in couples; not only that, but they were also hugged up, snuggled up close, even in the warm weather as they maneuvered through the maze of streets. Paris was a city used to celebrating love and romance. It set the mood, opened the doors to passion.

He was still thinking about Courtney Andrews. He had yet to officially meet her, but he couldn't dismiss her from his mind. The very idea that after a full week he would be sitting at a café with thoughts of one particular woman was simply startling. And so unlike him.

Of course, he was practically married to his business,

but that hadn't stopped him from seeking out female companionship when there was a need. Most of the women he dated found his personality challenging. He knew what he wanted in life, and no feminine wiles could steer him from his goal. Numerous had tried. All had failed.

The thought that he was fast approaching forty and not involved in a committed relationship didn't bother him. The fact that he was the only one of his four brothers without a wife meant nothing. He operated on a different drive, his own unique way of both doing and looking at things. If he wanted something, he got it. He didn't waste time analyzing, dissecting, or evaluating. Once he made his mind up about something, that was it. And he was not the nitpicky type. He was a person who didn't mind being tested. To his way of thinking, that only sharpened his predatory skills.

Smiling, he thought he could definitely come up with his own ideas about any given subject, which was probably why the advertisement business was his calling. Being creative, he'd discovered very early in life, was his forte. More often than not, he had to tamp down his enthusiasm and remind himself he had a very skilled and experienced team that he had groomed to take Masters Unlimited just where he wanted it to go.

But still, he enjoyed getting back into the thick of things every once in a while. Check out the market to see where it was going and to make sure his company was right there in the forefront, no matter where it led. And when it came to acquiring accounts that were as significant as Falconer Cosmetics, he couldn't help but take a personal interest, which was why he was in Paris. He glanced at his watch. It was time to take care of business.

A few hours later, he was sitting in the office of Tammi Grier, one of Falconer's top executives. Tammi was intent on mixing business with pleasure. He figured that out the moment she'd accepted his handshake. There had been something about the way she gripped his hand, hesitated in letting it go with a keen look of interest in her ebony eyes. She was about thirty-six, tall, attractive, shapely, and from all accounts, a dynamic force when it came to the cosmetics business.

There was no doubt in his mind she was an easy mark and wanted him to know it. If he were to take her up on what she was offering, he would be relieving himself of eight months of going without. And he bet she had no qualms as far as him taking care of the matter right here in this office, probably right smack on her desk if he so desired.

He didn't.

Although he had a sharp sense of the sexually charged air surrounding them, he had a rule not to mix business with pleasure. And it was a rule he stuck to. It could be costly if things didn't work out the way one of the parties thought they should. He'd rather make deals in the office, not the bedroom. Besides, with Tammi he was being hunted, and he much preferred the role of the hunter.

That made his thoughts shift to Courtney Andrews again. He had considered finding out her address and sending her flowers with a card that would simply inform her that she had a secret admirer. But instead he decided to wait until he returned to Orlando for them to be introduced properly before making his interest known.

He leaned back in the chair and turned his attention to the matter at hand. "So, what do you think of the proposal?" he asked Tammi, mainly because the room had gotten quiet. She had stopped reading the documents a while ago and had begun studying him instead with the intensity of someone trying to acquire his innermost secrets. A trace of her perfume hung on the air, a sensuous scent, and no doubt one of Falconer's own brands.

The company she represented had expanded to include a clothing line, a designer label Falconer wanted to promote worldwide. Masters Unlimited had been hired to take them to that level. Already the tone of the ad had been set for something sophisticated, edgy, and in your face. The target market was women of all ages, but the prominent hit was women between the ages of twenty-five and forty. The Falconer Woman was to become as popular as the Marlboro Man had years ago.

"I think it's more than we anticipated," she responded in a sultry voice. "But then I'm not surprised. I'd heard you were a man known to deliver."

Lake took in her meaningful expression, along with her suggestive words and shrugged. "I try. I don't believe in giving any less than one hundred percent." And to let her know he was speaking strictly of business, he added, "And I expect the same of anyone who works for me."

She nodded. "I understand you're related to Alexia Bennett-Masters."

She had shifted topics on him, which was fine, since

he intended to keep up with her. You could never let a woman of Tammi Grier's caliber think she had your mind screwed up or your reasoning twisted into knots. "Yes, Alexia is married to my brother Quinn."

"And what does he do for a living?"

He wondered why she wanted to know, but decided to answer anyway. "He's an entertainment attorney in Los Angeles. In fact, that's how they met."

Her eyes raked over him slowly, as if she was still looking for a crack in his armor. "Did you know she's here in Paris performing?"

No, he hadn't known that. Alexia was a nationally known recording artist whose songs were legendary in becoming number-one hits on the R & B charts. The last time he'd talked to Quinn, his brother had mentioned she would be doing an international tour but hadn't said in what countries Alexia would be performing.

"No, I didn't," he finally answered, and hoped she wasn't fishing to accompany him to one of Alexia's concerts on a date. And just in case she was, he added, "In that case, I need to find out what hotel she's staying at and invite her to have dinner with me."

He watched her purse her lips. Even with her boldness, she wouldn't lower her pride to include herself in a threesome. She had too much class for that.

"Can I interest you in a drink after we finish up business here today?"

Her question made him smile. She was determined not to give up, and he was just as determined that she do so. But still, to maintain a smooth working relationship and not ruffle her feathers, he decided sharing a drink with her wouldn't hurt matters. In fact, it might help them. Even with her man-eating demeanor, she was still good at what she did at Falconer. The old man was her uncle. Family ties, he knew, were what they were.

"Yes, you can interest me in that," he answered smoothly, with a smile.

A grin touched the corners of her lips, and her hot-and-heavy gaze was still intent on him. It didn't take a rocket scientist to figure out that she thought them sharing a drink would be just the beginning. She had two weeks to break down his resistance before he returned to the States. There was no doubt in his mind that she was determined to work it with everything she had.

The corner of his own mouth twitched. She could definitely take pleasure in trying.

"You were wonderful tonight, Alexia," Lake said as his eyes roamed over the strikingly beautiful woman who was married to his brother. He had been escorted backstage to her dressing room the moment she performed her last song.

"Thanks, Lake," she said, leaning up and kissing him on the cheek. "Quinn didn't mention you would be in Paris."

"Only because the last time we talked, our conversation was rushed. I think he was trying to get the boys out of the house to day-care."

Alexia laughed, and Lake thought the sound was just

as smooth and silky as what came out of her mouth whenever she performed. "Bennett and Blake are handfuls and keep us on our toes. But then Quinn is such a wonderful father. I wouldn't be able to go on tour like I do without him. It's good knowing how well he can hold things down on the home front, but I miss my guys, though."

Lake heard the profound love in her voice for her four-year-old twin sons and for his brother, as well. Considering what she did for a living, she and Quinn had a good marriage, a sturdy one. For years, long marriages never seemed to work in the Masters family. His paternal grandmother had been married three times, and his paternal grandfather was on his fifth wife. That's why his generation of Masterses had vowed not to marry until they were sure they had found the right mate. He was proud to say that his brothers had married wisely.

"So when are you coming back out to L.A.? Your nephews are dying to see you again."

Alexia knew the best way to get to him was through the kids. He was considered the fun uncle to all his nieces and nephews because he knew how to do magic tricks, something he'd picked up from one of his roommates in college who had a knack for it. "Once I've come up with a few new routines. Don't want to bore them with the old ones." He laughed. "Last time I think Bennett was on to me."

"That wouldn't surprise me," she said, her eyes twinkling. "Blake sleeps through anything, but Bennett misses nothing. Now, how about joining me in a late dinner? I'd love the company. Besides, I want to hear about all the things you've been doing since I last saw you."

"You'll be bored to tears."

She smiled and patted his arm affectionately. "I'll take my chances."

He couldn't hold back his grin. She intended to pump him for information she could pass on to his other two sisters-in-law, Faith and Brandy. The three of them thought his days as a single man were numbered—or should be, anyway. "Are you sure about that?"

"I am."

"Then I'd love joining you."

"Why me, Toni?"

Peggy Morrison stopped pacing the office of her boss and friend, Antonia Siplin, not sure she could handle what she was being asked to do.

"Because you are the logical person to do it, Peg. We both know you're here, working away in the media office, getting lost in the shuffle when your real level of expertise lies in public relations. And I need to utilize that expertise to make sure Willie Baker understands just what we're all about."

Feeling a headache of defeat coming on, Peggy dropped into a chair across from her best friend's desk. Her friendship with Antonia went back a long way, all the way to their high school days. Toni had been there for her through thick and thin, had given her a shoulder to cry on when Joe asked for a divorce to marry a younger woman, had been the one to convince her to join Dropped Wives Anonymous when her self-esteem had plummeted so low, she'd nearly driven everyone around her crazy. Now almost three years later, she had finally gotten her act together. She no longer blamed herself or everyone else for the breakup of her marriage. The fact that her husband had left her for a younger woman didn't rush her to tears and bouts of hysteria as it once had. Her support group of women who'd gone through the same thing was wonderful, and because of them she now thought of a brighter future and new beginnings.

And Toni had been instrumental in hiring her when she'd been out of the workforce for more than twenty years, to take charge of the media department for Making Dreams Come True, a nonprofit organization that granted dreams to terminally ill kids.

She turned her full attention back to Toni and said, "But everyone knows what we're about, Toni. Why is this donor being given special treatment?"

Toni flipped a mass of blond hair from her face, and her blue eyes shone with determination and dedication when she said, "Because we're not talking about the sponsorship of a dream trip for a few of our kids. I'm talking about him footing the money to build our own amusement park here in Orlando. Can you imagine such a thing?"

Peggy smiled. Yes and no. Yes, she could imagine such a park and knew how instrumental one would be for the kids. And no, because the very thought that a single person would consider solely footing the bill for such a place went beyond her level of comprehension. "That's a lot of money."

Toni nodded. "Yes, and it's either going to come to us or our sister organization in Atlanta. We want it here, and it's important that while I'm gone Mr. Baker gets a special tour and breakdown of our facilities by someone with exemplary charm, grace, and style."

Peggy rolled her eyes, knowing Toni was laying it on thick, or at least trying to. "There has to be someone else you can get."

"But there's no one else that I'd trust. My first grandchild picked the worst possible time to be born, but nothing is going to keep me from being there to see it happen, and I want to arrive in Detroit knowing everything is under control back here. So please tell me that you'll do it."

"Toni, I—"

"Please. Pretty please."

Peggy released a long slow breath and then said, "Okay, I'll do it, but you knew that I would. Didn't you?"

Toni smiled, satisfied. "Yes, I knew that you would."

Barbara locked her office door and went back to her desk to open the package that had been delivered to her. It was in a plain wrapper so she figured it was the video she had ordered a few weeks ago titled, *Improving Your Sex Performance.*

She knew she was one of those women who had sexual hang-ups. The therapist had assured her she wasn't alone. A lot of women much preferred traditional when it came to sex, but she knew she had to change her thinking about a lot of things.

One day while at the dentist's office, flipping through a magazine, she had come across an ad for the video and ordered it. Now it was here and she was determined to be open-minded. She would do whatever it took to spice up her performance in the bedroom if it would help keep Ron from straying.

After opening the package she saw the book that accompanied the video. She blushed after flipping through the book and seeing all the different positions for making love. Did couples actually try them? Well, she hoped to find out one day.

7

Could that have gone as badly as she remembered? Courtney wondered, thinking about her date with Harper and his subsequent arrest. A huge article had appeared in the newspaper the next morning about how an FBI sting operation had resulted in the arrest of five individuals, employed at three different banks, and how they had worked together to filter money from various investment accounts to a dummy one they had established.

She thought about what a nice-looking brotha he was, how articulate he'd spoken, how well educated. What a waste—what a stupid mistake. What could he have been thinking to assume he'd get away with it?

"If you're not going to pay me any attention, we can end this session."

Courtney glanced across the table at Jetrica. She was right. Courtney hadn't been paying attention.

"Sorry about that, Jetrica. My mind wandered off for a second. I apologize."

The fourteen-year-old had been sitting in the office when Courtney arrived, not in anticipation of their meeting but because she had gotten kicked out of class for disrespecting a teacher. With a mass of shoulder-length dreads on her head, Jetrica was a pretty girl, if you could look past the bad attitude she displayed most of the time. But Courtney had quickly caught on to her. All Jetrica wanted was attention, and she was willing to do just about anything to get it. She had beautiful features, although she was trying to make herself appear older and grown-up with the use of an eyebrow pencil, mascara, and lipstick. Then there was that fake beauty mole that dotted her chin, right beneath her bottom lip.

Her clothes, donated from one of the local thrift stores, were all hand-me-downs. But at least the shirt that seemed a deliberate size too small and the jeans that were somewhat too tight, were clean.

"Like I was saying before your mind began wandering," Jetrica said smartly, irritatingly poking out her lip. "Mrs. Peyton doesn't like me. She always calls on me to answer a question when she knows good and well that I won't know the answer."

"And why won't you know the answer?" Courtney asked her.

Jetrica rolled her eyes. "Because I have better things to do with my time than study."

"Not if you want to get promoted to the next grade."

Jetrica lifted her chin. "I'm not worrying about that. My grades are good."

Courtney knew that to be true, which was one of the reasons Vickie had talked her into being Jetrica's mentor. As amazing as it seemed, even with her badass attitude and deciding to skip school whenever the feeling struck, Jetrica had the ability to ace all her exams, which meant she either did study or she had this ingrained knowledge that was unreal. Courtney leaned toward believing the former. According to Jetrica's sister, the girl locked herself in her room most of the time with a book in her face. So why couldn't she come clean and admit she had a thirst for knowledge, and why did she continue to paint herself as a dummy in the classroom?

"There's nothing wrong with being smart, you know," Courtney told her.

"I'm not smart," Jetrica all but snapped.

"Oh, I tend to disagree. And you're also talented. Several people have asked me about that painting you did for me. They were impressed."

Courtney saw the flash of interest that lit Jetrica's eyes moments before she put her nonchalant mask in place and gave a sarcastic remark. "Well, they shouldn't be, and I hope you told them who did it for you was none of their damn business."

"Excuse me," Courtney said, frowning. "I thought I told you that I would not tolerate you saying curse words in front of me."

"For crying out loud, Ms. Andrews. *Damn* is not a curse word."

"It is to me, and not one I want coming from your mouth."

Jetrica rolled her eyes, which was something she did so often, Courtney figured one day they would get stuck in the top of her head. "And what if I don't want care?" she asked, crossing her arms over her chest and glaring.

Courtney was determined not to be put off by Jetrica's mood. Jetrica was trying her, which she did often enough, but considering how her weekend went, she wasn't in the mood. "You don't have a choice, at least not for this school year anyway. You're stuck with me."

The frown on the young girl's face suddenly turned soft, and she giggled. "Okay, I'm stuck with you, which means you're stuck with me, too."

Now it was Courtney's time to roll her eyes. "And I pray every day for God's strength to endure."

"Hawaii?" Ron Andrews asked in surprise.

"Yes," Barbara said excitedly as she stared over at her husband. They had just left from meeting with their marriage therapist and had stopped by a restaurant for dinner. "You heard what the therapist said. Considering everything that's happened, it will be good to get away for a while, just the two of us, unwind, relax, and rebuild that foundation for our marriage."

Yeah, he'd heard everything the therapist had said and he'd gotten pretty damn bored just listening to it. When

Barbara had given him an ultimatum—they had to seek professional help or else, he had jumped at the idea, willing to do just about anything to save his marriage. But now that Ashira was back in his bed, or rather he in hers—and on a regular basis—he wasn't all that committed.

But he was cautious. This time he wouldn't screw up. He had explained things to Ashira, and for once she hadn't whined, sulked, and complained. She was willing to get him back on any terms, even if it meant playing second fiddle to his wife. She claimed she could handle that. But what she couldn't handle or put up with was him dropping her again. She had done things for him, both in and out of bed that she hadn't done for any other man, and wife or no wife, she was in it for the long haul. She didn't mind being the other woman as long as he knew her place and provided her with the things she wanted. She liked her single life and had no desire to be any man's wife. She actually relished the thought of being a man's personal whore. Those had been her words and not his. But the more he thought about it, the more he liked the idea. His own personal whore. And a willing one. He shifted in his chair, feeling a boner coming on.

"Ron?"

Barbara reclaimed his attention. He looked up at her. His wife wasn't so bad, and she definitely wasn't bad looking. In fact, he thought she was rather attractive. And when he imagined truly loving someone, he would immediately think of her. Over the years she had kept her body pretty much in shape. She always dressed nice and looked nice. Some men, probably most, would find her sexy, even at fifty. In a way, he did, too. Until they got into the bedroom.

She was too traditional to suit his taste. At first being traditional had been fine, until he'd gotten a taste of the wild side. It had blown his mind, given his pecker a whole new perspective, and made traditional unattractive. He liked the feel of a woman stroking him first with her hands, then with her mouth. He appreciated, loved, and simply cherished a good blow job, something his wife of almost thirty years still had never performed on him. Once, years ago, he had mentioned it and he'd actually watched her almost gag at the thought. To say she wasn't adventurous in bed was an understatement. Oral sex was simply something she refused to consider. And after finding out about all his other women, not once had she considered that perhaps the reason he'd sought out others was because of her lack of being creative, spontaneous, and a little freakish.

"Baby, I think the two of us going to Hawaii is a wonderful idea, but have you forgotten I'm teaching classes this semester and finals will be coming up soon?" he asked, hoping that would be an end to it.

A little pout formed on her lips. "Surely you can take off two weeks, Ron. I bet Elijah would be glad to cover for you."

"I don't know, Barb."

"Then ask him. You do want us to spend time together, don't you?"

To say he didn't want that would start an argument, which he'd rather avoid. Lately they were getting along just great. He could play the part of the doting husband as long as he was getting some on the side. And Ashira was really laying it on thick. "Yes, of course, I do."

"And you want our marriage to work out this time."

"You know I do, sweetheart."

He saw disappointment settle in her eyes. "Courtney doesn't think that it will."

He reached across the table and took her hand in his. "Courtney doesn't know everything."

Barbara pulled her hand back and met his gaze directly. "She knows enough, Ron. Our daughter is the main person who's been suffering through our marriage, when we couldn't get our act together. That's why she's so cynical. Why she refuses to believe we can make it work this time. We have to prove her wrong."

Ron scowled down at his plate of food. It was getting cold from him having this damn conversation. He didn't want to leave town, not even for two weeks. His pecker had gotten spoiled. There were some things it needed on a regular basis, things Barbara wouldn't deliver for two weeks in Hawaii. But he didn't want to get her upset. He didn't want her thinking there was a reason he wasn't interested in leaving Orlando for a while. Surely he would be able to survive without a mouth down south on him for two weeks.

"If it makes you happy, then I'll check with Elijah to see if he can cover those classes for me."

Barbara smiled. "Truly?"

He nodded. "Yes, truly."

She reached back over across the table and took

his hand. "Thanks, Ron. I think it's a good beginning for us."

If she said so, but personally, he wasn't all that certain.

Courtney sat on her screen porch and enjoyed the mixed drink she'd prepared. It had rained earlier, but before dusk had settled, the sun peeped out through the clouds again.

She thought about her meeting with Jetrica. The girl was trying to make it unpleasant to continue mentoring her, but Courtney refused to give up on Jetrica. And then there was that extraordinary talent the girl had. She could be an awesome artist if she put her mind to it. What Courtney had told her earlier that day was the truth. That painting Jetrica had done and given her for Christmas was simply amazing.

A few moments later, Courtney got up, went into her bedroom, and pulled her little black book out of the nightstand drawer. She was determined not to let what happened on her date with Harper deter her from seeking out another name. Besides, she had made Sonya a promise. She had marked out Harper's name after that first night, and the next name listed was Don Woods.

She reached for the phone, hoping her experience with Don would be better than the one she'd had with Harper.

8

Don Woods was a brotha on the down-low.

And it was a downright dirty shame, Courtney thought, sitting across from him and sipping her drink. She hadn't picked up on it immediately, but it hadn't taken too long to figure it out. He was handsome in a manly sort of way, well built and muscular. His voice was deep and husky. His mannerisms didn't raise suspicions either . . . at first.

But when she had looked up from studying her menu and caught him giving their waiter more than a cursory glance, the hairs on the back of her neck stood up. Something wasn't right. To be fair, she hadn't wanted to jump to conclusions, so for the rest of the evening she'd had to rely on her keen sense of observation. By the end of dinner, she was convinced Don should be calling himself Dawn instead.

"You never did say where you got my number?"

Courtney met his gaze across the table. When she had called him, unlike Harper, he had asked about that. She hadn't told him then, and she had no intention of telling him now. "Why does that matter since you decided to meet me tonight anyway?" she asked, wondering what his response would be. Chances were, he wouldn't argue the point.

He smiled. "You're right, it doesn't matter. I'm here, and so are you. You are a very beautiful woman."

She scanned his face. "And you are a very handsome man."

Courtney could see that her compliment pleased him. It hadn't been a hard one to make.

From what he'd told her, he owned a limousine company that he claimed kept him pretty busy. He was an only child, and at thirty-five enjoyed a lot of outside sports, which was the reason he kept in great physical shape.

Too bad she wasn't one of those women who didn't care if her man straddled the fence. Her parents' mockery of a marriage had taught her to seek out the real thing when it came to love and relationships and to tolerate nothing less. To do otherwise was just plain ludicrous as far as she was concerned.

That was the reason she wanted to call it an early night. Hanging around would be a waste of her time as well as his. Dinner had been nice, and they had enjoyed each other's company, chitchatting about several things, but nothing of real importance.

She knew she had to come up with an excuse to end the evening and was racking her brain, trying to come up with a pretext when his cell phone rang. A part of her was a little annoyed that he had kept his turned on when she'd turned hers off.

After pulling the phone out his jacket, he quickly checked to see who was calling, then glanced over at her and said, "Excuse me, Courtney, I need to take this call." He got up from the table and headed toward the men's room.

Now she was really irritated. To take her mind off that irritation, she looked around the restaurant. It was a nice place, real upscale. She'd been surprised when Don suggested it. The food had been excellent, the—

"Excuse me, ma'am, Mr. Woods told me to let you know he had to leave."

Courtney blinked up at the waiter, a different man from the one who had served them earlier. "Excuse me?"

"Mr. Woods, the man you were dining with, told me to convey his apologies, but an emergency came up and he had to leave." The man cleared his throat when he added, "He also said that you would be the one to take care of both checks."

"What!"

"That's what he said."

Courtney breathed in deeply. In all her years, no man had ever stiffed her with a dinner check. The first thought that came to her mind was that Don Woods was an idiot to think she would cover the cost of his dinner as well as her own, but as she stared at the waiter, she knew he was expecting her to do just that. "Fine," she said as calmly as she could. "Please bring me both checks."

When the man walked away, disappointment set in. Where on earth had Sonya found these men? Granted Harper and Don were handsome, but both of them had real issues.

"Here you are, ma'am," the waiter said when he returned. He was smiling, obviously relieved. She bet he hadn't bought the story of Don's sudden emergency any more than she had. Deciding not to stress over it any longer and to accept the fact that she had gotten screwed, she pulled the charge card out of her purse.

Suddenly something clicked in Courtney's mind. She looked up at the waiter and asked, "The other waiter who was serving us, what happened to him?"

The man shrugged. "He also had to leave. An emergency came up for him, as well."

Courtney nodded. She didn't want to jump to conclusions about anything but . . .

She handed the waiter her charge card. She hoped her bad luck with the black book was a fluke and that the next name in it would be a whole lot better than the first two. He just had to be, or she would be tempted to toss that little black book right in the trash regardless of the promise she'd made to Sonya.

Peggy glanced down at herself as she stepped off the elevator. The sun was shining brightly outside, and the drive in to work had been fantastic, especially since she had joined in with Sly and the Family Stone when her favorite song, "Everyday People," came blaring on the radio.

Her mother, Lola Phelps, had never intended for her two daughters, Peggy and Barbara, to be everyday people. Especially not after Disney arrived in the late sixties and decided they needed the tract of land—over four hundred acres—that had been in the Phelps family for years.

Wanting a better life for her and her daughters, Lola hadn't thought of not selling. After all, she was the last of the Phelpses, and there was no close living relative to offer advice on whether or not she was making a bad decision.

So Lola had taken the money and basically ran, not away from Orlando but to a nice section of town where she had raised her daughters in grace and style and given them whatever she felt they would need to survive in what she saw as a harsh and oftentimes cruel world. She had educated them at some of the finest private schools, and had sent them to Atlanta to be educated at Spellman, letting them know from the jump that just a bachelor's degree wouldn't do. They would need graduate degrees. Then she had established trust funds for them, which meant that even after the last breath had left her body, they would be taken care of. And she had lived long enough to see the both of them married off to well-educated men.

Peggy always admired her mother's strength, her ability to handle just about anything in life—including men. And that is where, Peggy thought sadly, her mother had failed them. She had provided them the proper grace and breeding to carry themselves as ladies in the truest form, but Lola hadn't educated her daughters on how to deal with doggish, no-good men. Men who didn't believe in keeping their vows. Men who constantly thought with their pecker instead of their head. Men obsessed with sleeping with women more than half their age. Men who were just plain outright assholes. The exact men she and Barbara had married.

At least she had gotten Joe out of her life and finally out of her system and had moved on. Barbara, for whatever reason, was still holding on to Ron. Peggy shook her head sadly, thinking about the conversation she'd had with her younger sister over dinner a week or so ago. Barbara actually thought that Ron was through screwing around on her, and that he was actually going to keep his pants zipped. He had promised her. On his mother's grave. Yeah. Right.

"Good morning, Ms. Morrison."

She smiled at Toni's secretary. "Good morning, Sharon."

"How was the drive in to the office this morning?"

"Funny you should ask," Peggy said, grinning. "I was just thinking about how nice it was. Oh, I ran into the usual traffic snarls, but that was okay. The radio station I was listening to was belting out some of my favorites, songs I haven't heard in years, so I decided to do a singalong. It was wonderful."

"I'm glad, because Mr. Baker wants to know if your appointment with him could be moved up an hour. Something has come up, and he needs to fly out of Orlando sooner than he'd originally planned."

Peggy nodded. "Sure. How soon did he want us to meet?"

A sheepish look came into Sharon's eyes. "Umm, how about right now? He arrived unexpectedly, so I placed him in your office, thinking it would be better than having him wait in the lobby—especially when he said that he had a few private calls to make."

"Okay. Meeting him now won't be a problem."

A few moments later she was walking down the long hallway to her office. When Toni had brought her back into the workforce a year ago, her best friend had done it in style by giving her a beautifully decorated office on the executive floor, overlooking a huge lake. Toni had claimed she needed her close by to be her sounding board when things got crazy in the office. She was yet to be used that way and always figured she wouldn't be, since Toni was the most easygoing person she knew.

The door to her office was slightly ajar, but as she got near, she could hear the distinct sound of a male voice. It had a deep, husky tone combined with a smoothed silken timbre. When she got to the door and looked inside, a man stood talking on his mobile phone, his profile to her. She was about to take a step back to give him privacy when suddenly he turned and saw her standing there.

For some reason, her muscles suddenly went lax and her breathing became labored. Their eyes met, and it registered for her that Willie Baker was a very handsome man. Tall, nicely built, he had a mature look, with a sprinkle of gray at his temples. His features were sharp, and the smile that settled on his lips at that moment was lethal. If he looked this good at fifty-nine, she could just imagine what a heartthrob he'd been at twenty-nine.

Panic skidded up her spine. This was the first time she'd taken keen notice of a man's attractiveness since her marriage to Joe. Even after the divorce, she had been too bitter to do anything but consider any man with a half-decent face nothing but trouble.

"Peggy Morrison?"

That sexy voice again made her blink, and she watched him put his cell phone in his jacket pocket before crossing the room to her, coming to a stop right in front of her, and smiling.

"Yes, I'm Peggy Morrison."

He reached out his hand, gently took hers in no more than a business handshake, yet she felt the touch all the way to her toes. "Your secretary let me use your office. I hope you don't mind."

She suddenly felt light-headed. Suddenly felt so unlike the disciplined person that she was. The one that she had become, thanks to Joe. "No, of course I don't mind," she quickly found her voice to say. "If you need me to leave and come back later, then I can—"

"No, that's not necessary."

"You sure?" she asked, thinking that maybe leaving and coming back wouldn't be such a bad idea. A few moments alone were probably something she could use to screw her head back on straight.

"I'm positive. But what I do need, before we get things started, is something to eat. I should have grabbed a bite before I left the hotel this morning but didn't. Would you have something against us having a breakfast meeting?"

"No, not at all, Mr. Baker." She recalled Toni's instructions to accommodate this man at all costs.

"I prefer that you call me Willie, and I hope you'd be comfortable with my use of your first name, Ms. Morrison."

"Yes, and it's Peggy."

"All right, Peggy, now are you sure you won't mind us having a breakfast meeting?"

A teasing glint in his eyes made her smile. "Yes, I'm sure. We have a number of restaurants in the area that you can choose from."

He nodded slowly and then said, "I'm a simple man who likes simple things. In fact, from your window I noticed my favorite breakfast restaurant."

She glanced over at her window and then back at him. "You did?"

"Yes. Come let me point it out to you."

He led her over to the window, and when he pushed back the blinds and pointed to the golden arches, she couldn't help but laugh. "I haven't been to one of those in years."

His tawny brown eyes shone when he looked at her. She tried ignoring the none-too-subtle sexual pull inside her when he smiled.

"Like I said, I'm a simple man."

Simple but rich, Peggy thought a short while later when they sat across the table from each other in the

McDonald's. *Powerful but not overbearing.* On the short car ride over, she quickly discovered he was unpretentious. What you saw was what you got. Willie Baker hadn't been born with a silver spoon in his own mouth and appreciated his own humble beginnings. You couldn't help but admire a man who thought like that. And then there was his bubbly personality, something else she hadn't expected. He liked people, and acknowledging everyone's presence with either a nod or a hello seemed to come natural to him.

She glanced at his plate. He was a hearty eater, if the pancakes and sausages piled high were any indication. He'd also gotten a carton each of milk and orange juice. She had settled on a biscuit and coffee. The breakfast notwithstanding, he was also someone who believed in staying physically fit, if his body was anything to go by. He was tall, lean, and tight. She hadn't seen an inch of flab anywhere. That said a lot for a man his age.

"Whoever thinks McDonald's is just for kids needs to think again," he said, breaking into her thoughts. She inclined her head and met his gaze, and he continued talking. She was getting used to his smile, so when she saw the sadness that suddenly appeared in his eyes, she paid close attention to what he was saying.

"Although I have to admit my granddaughter was the reason I first started coming and kept coming back. Nothing would put a smile on her face more quickly than walking into a McDonald's," he finished saying.

Peggy figured the sudden poignant anecdote had to do with the granddaughter he'd lost three years ago. Toni had told her that the little girl had been born with a rare bone disease, which was one of the reasons Willie Baker was so involved in the Make Dreams Come True Foundation. It was his way of giving back and helping to make the life of a terminally ill child that much more rewarding.

"Tell me about her."

The words were out of Peggy's mouth before she realized she'd said them. Something within her that always recognized another's pain was reaching out to him.

Her gaze met his. Strong chin, gorgeous brown eyes set in a handsome and robust face that now displayed more than the faintest sign of sorrow, pain, and regret. She watched him place his eating utensils down, and the gaze staring back at her seemed to be considering and then decisive.

He began speaking softly. "My granddaughter's name was Tiara, and she was born on a beautiful day in May. Less than an hour after her birth, her parents—my daughter and son-in-law—and I were told the heart-wrenching news that she had a rare bone disease and would not live to see her fifth birthday."

A smile touched the corners of Willie's mouth before he continued, saying, "She lived to be ten. Beating the odds. But you'll be surprised what a person can do when surrounded by so much love, and God knows that she was. To us, no matter her condition, Tiara was perfect, and our goal in life was to make her life—no matter how long it lasted—a very happy one."

He paused briefly before he went on to say, "We never considered her existence in our life anything other than a blessing and made sure that she knew it. Everything we did for her we did in love, even those mornings when the two of us would do breakfast at McDonald's. Everyone got to know us, expected to see us. It was our time together, and a few of the staff who worked there even took it upon themselves to mark the place where we always sat as Tiara's Corner. She liked that. She would smile for them. They would smile for her. Then we lost her, and for a while it seemed like there was a void in all our lives that could never be filled again."

Peggy knew the feeling. After the breakup of her marriage, for the longest time she had felt her life tumbling out of control and she with it. She cringed at the thought of what she had put her only daughter through during that time. But then she had finally awakened one morning and made the decision to pull herself together, or else she would truly lose her mind. No man was worth that. All that misery was taking place in her life about the same time that somewhere a sweet little girl was losing her life. And to think that at the time Peggy had thought she was the only one on the face of the earth having troubles.

"How are your daughter and son-in-law doing? How are you doing?" she asked, not being able to imagine ever losing Sonya at any age.

Willie's mouth eased into a sparkling smile. "They're doing fine. We're all doing fine. And last year they did something I really thought they would never get the courage to do, considering everything, and that was to have another baby. Now I have a nine-month-old grandson named David."

Peggy studied the contents of her coffee cup a minute before lifting her head and asking softly, "Is he okay?"

Willie knew what she was asking and nodded cheerfully. "Yes, he was born in perfect health."

She smiled. "I'm glad."

"So am I."

They resumed eating their breakfast. In the back of her mind, she realized they had yet to discuss anything relating to business, but that fact didn't bother her. Nor did it bother her that she found a lot of pleasure being here with him. She could tell he was a man who would value anything he possessed. A man who could be trusted and who loved fiercely. She would bet anything that while his wife was alive he'd treated her like a queen, their daughter like a princess, and that the granddaughter he'd lost had taken a part of his heart with her when she died. That sort of man could cultivate only her admiration and respect.

Moments later he pushed his tray aside, chuckled, and said. "Now that my stomach is full, we can talk business." He leaned back in his chair. "So Peggy, tell me why you think that I should put that amusement park here in Orlando instead of Atlanta."

9

"This is going to be your lucky night, beautiful one."

Courtney rolled her eyes, not caring if Solomon Wise saw her doing so. There was only one word she could use to describe the latest name she had pulled from her little black book: *annoying*.

She'd decided to give the book one more try and made the initial contact with Solomon by phone a few nights ago, immediately nuking his suggestion of dinner, especially after her last two fiascos with Harper and Don. She'd decided to play it safe and came up with the idea that they meet at the movies instead.

When she'd first seen him, she had not been disappointed—he was definitely a good-looking brotha. But so were the other two. The one thing she had learned—and rather quickly—was that looks could definitely be deceiving. It was to her benefit to check out the entire package.

By the time the movie had begun, she learned something very quickly about Solomon: Not only did he think he was the wisest of men where women were concerned, but he also believed that he was the greatest gift to them.

And for some reason, he was also convinced that tonight was going to end with them sharing a bed. The way he saw it, it was obvious the two of them connected, so why waste good bedsheets? Besides, what woman in her right mind would pass up a chance to sample the Solomon Wise experience? The only thing she had to say to that was, undoubtedly she would be the first.

"So, are you sure you want to see the rest of this movie? I can think of a number of other things we could be doing right now," he leaned over and whispered close to her ear.

She sighed deeply, deciding that she'd had enough. It was evident that he had only one thing on his mind, and she had a problem with men who thought any woman they dated was there for their personal pleasure.

"You're right, there are a number of things I can be doing, and none of them involves you, Solomon." She stood and began walking out of the theater.

He got up and followed her. When they reached the lobby, he said in a peeved tone, "Hey, what's wrong with you? I thought we understood what tonight was about."

She turned around and glared at him. "I do, but evidently you don't. All evening you've made your intentions for tonight clear, and all the while pushing aside the one single thing I expect from any man I date."

He crossed his arms over his chest and glared back. "Which is?"

"Respect."

"Respect?"

"Yes, respect. Do I need to spell it for you?"

"Oh, so now you want me to call you Aretha," he said smartly.

She shook her head sadly. Evidently, too many women had given him what he wanted, and too soon. Now he expected every other female to follow suit. The man was spoiled, conceited, and arrogant. She had had three dates in less than two weeks and had found all of them less than desirable. What a disappointment. "No, to be honest with you, Solomon, I don't want you to call me anything. Our meeting tonight was a mistake. Sorry I wasted your time."

"Yeah, so am I. I had already seen that damn movie twice," he said gruffly.

"Then why did you suggest seeing it?"

His mouth formed into a deep frown. "To impress. I know how you women are all into Denzel. I figured with him on the screen and me right beside you, it wouldn't take long for you to realize the man had nothing on me. Why would you want to settle for fantasy when I was here in living color as your reality. I just can't figure it."

Courtney pursed her lips, thinking that wasn't all he couldn't do; however, she had no intention of wasting her time explaining his shortcomings. He probably thought he didn't have any. "Like I said, Solomon, tonight was a mistake. See you around."

She turned to leave and heard him say, "Hey, I want you to lose my number."

"Gladly," she muttered, and didn't bother to stop walking or turn around. Engaging in any further conversation with him wasn't worth it. She couldn't wait until she got home. The first thing she intended to do was trash her little black book. It had brought her nothing but trouble.

Ron just didn't know how to break the news to Ashira that he would be going away for a while—two weeks, in fact—and all because Barbara had convinced him they needed to go somewhere to help their marriage.

Right now he didn't want to think about it, wasn't in the mood, especially after what he and Ashira had just shared. It had to have been the most amazing sex he'd ever had, and his body still felt like it was out in space, where it had been blasted just moments ago. He actually needed to wiggle his fingers and toes just to make sure he was still alive.

"So, what did you have to tell me?"

He forced his head to move on the pillow to glance over at her. He had forgotten he had mentioned that to her. Now he wished he hadn't. But he might as well get it over with. "I'm leaving town for a couple of weeks."

She leaned up, leaned back, and exposed a pair of perky breasts. He watched, amazed at how their tips hardened before his eyes. "Where are you going?" she asked him.

He flicked his gaze back to her face. "Hawaii. Barbara wants to go." He saw the angry tilt to Ashira's lips and decided he'd better soothe her. "You know I'm going to miss you," he said quietly, reaching out and cupping her breasts, liking the feel of them and then leaning up to kiss them both.

"Then take me with you."

He pulled back and dropped his hands and stared at her. She was dead serious. "Did you not hear what I said? I'm going to Hawaii with my wife," he repeated, annoyed. It was bad enough that he had to go; he really didn't need her giving him a hard time about it.

"Damn it, I heard you," she snapped, leaning down closer to his face, too close to suit him. "But why can't you take both of us? People with kids take their nannies, so why can't you take your other woman?"

He rolled his eyes. "Damn, Ashira, it's not the same, and you know it. Barbara expects me to spend time with her."

"Then spend time with her. I'll have plenty to keep me busy while you're doing so, since I've never been to Hawaii before. But at night, when your old lady is asleep, or if she manages to give you free time to do something that men enjoy doing, like playing golf, you can always visit my room." She licked her lips. "I'll be glad to give your balls a good workout."

He felt his pecker grow hard at the thought. But he would be stupid to try something like that. "Forget it. Something like that is too risky."

"I won't forget it, and I want to go, Ronnie. Why should

I let your wife have all the fun? Don't I mean anything to you?"

"Of course you do, but what you're suggesting is crazy. If I went along with something like that and Barbara found out, she would kill me."

Ashira smiled. "Then we'll make sure she doesn't find out." She then reached out and pulled the bedcovers back and took her hand and slowly began skimming her fingers over his body. "Just think about all the fun we're going to have, Ronnie. You have to take me along. I promise to make the risk worth it."

He rubbed his hand down his face, knowing that was the problem. Of all the other women he'd had, there was something about this one that could set his balls aflame. If he wasn't careful, he could become addicted. "I'll think about it," he said.

"Oh," she said, laughing lightly as she eased her body over his. "Then I truly need to give you something to think about, don't I?"

He opened his mouth to say something, and then got distracted by twin globes dangling down in his face. And when her mouth moved from his shoulder blades down toward his stomach, whatever he'd been about to say totally left his mind.

"You can't give up on that little black book," Vickie implored. "It probably has plenty more names in it. There has to be someone in there who's going to be worth your time and effort."

Courtney and Vickie met after work for dinner at one of their favorite restaurants at the Millennia Mall. Courtney took a sip of her margarita and gave Vickie's comment some thought. But then Vickie hadn't been the one who'd been humiliated with the three guys she'd gotten from the book so far. "Maybe, but I'm not about to take any more chances. Three was enough."

"So what did you do with it? You didn't throw it away, did you?"

Courtney shook her head. "I was tempted to but changed my mind; after all, it was a gift. And then there was that promise I made to Sonya. I threw it in the bottom drawer in my nightstand. Out of sight and out of mind. The next time I meet a guy, I'll check him out for myself. I just don't know where in the world Sonya got those men from. She must have met them during an off day. It's not like her to pick out losers."

"I know," Vickie said, completely baffled and still amazed at the thought of it. "Maybe she met them during that time she was in denial and wouldn't admit she had the hots for Mike. I bet that was when her focus wasn't good."

Courtney's lips began to twitch when she remembered how hard Sonya had tried fighting the attraction. "You're probably right. I would hate to think she'd lost her touch altogether."

"So when will the honeymooners be returning?" Vickie asked, interrupting her thoughts.

"This weekend. Carla is throwing together a party for their return. You want to go with me as my date?"

Vickie chuckled into her piña colada. "Why not? I don't have anything else to do that night, since Dan won't be coming to town," she said of the guy she'd been dating for the past year. Dan lived two hours away, in St. Augustine. They had met when the two were teaching at the same high school, but a few months ago, Dan Robbins had accepted a job offer to be the principal of an elementary school in the nation's oldest city and moved away.

Courtney eased back in her chair and glanced over at her best friend. "And how are things going between you and Dan?"

Vickie shrugged. "Okay, I guess, but being involved in a long-distance romance is the pits. I liked it better when he was able to drop in at any time, stay the night. Now it's hard for him to get away for the weekend. I was the one who drove down to see him the last two times. Now it's his turn and he doesn't seem all that eager to come. I'm getting the feeling that he doesn't care one way or the other whether we see each other or not. Sometimes, I just can't figure men out."

Vickie wasn't by herself, Courtney thought, taking another sip of her drink. But she thought Vickie had Dan figured wrong. Other than Mike and Sonya, she didn't know of any other couple who was more in love than Dan and Vickie. When you saw them together, you knew they were in love, and she didn't like hearing the sound of worry and frustration in Vickie's voice. "Maybe that new school is keeping him busy?" she said in Dan's defense.

"Yeah. Whatever." Then, as if Vickie needed to change

the subject, she asked, "How did your mentoring session with Jetrica go last week?"

Courtney frowned. "Challenging. She missed a couple of our sessions when she cut school."

"She's still doing that?"

"Yes. Worried her sister to death when she didn't get home until after dark."

Vickie raised a brow. "You don't think a boy is involved, do you?"

"God, I hope not. The last thing I need to deal with is Jetrica with a boyfriend."

Vickie's eyes glittered with amusement. "Hey, you had one when you were her age. Remember Matthew Banks?"

Courtney shook her head. "How can I forget the jerk?"

Vickie smiled. "Hmm, he's a jerk now, uhh?"

"He was a jerk then, but I was too stupid to realize it."

"Not stupid, just immature," Vickie said with another smile.

"I was stupid—trust me on that one. That was one of the few times my mother was right."

"That's scary."

"Yeah, tell me about it."

"She and your dad are still trying to make their marriage work?" Vickie asked.

"So they say. Mom mentioned today they're planning a trip to Hawaii."

"Wow, that's nice. He's finally giving in and doing the things she wants to do for a change."

Courtney released a half laugh. "Don't let Dad's dedicated act fool you. He's not stupid. Mom's trust fund is what's keeping him in line . . . *if* he's really keeping himself in line."

"You don't believe that he is?"

"I wish I could say otherwise, but my answer is no. It would take a lot for me to believe he's smartened up and has straightened up his act. But my father likes taking risks where Mom is concerned. They would have done better if they'd each gone their separate ways. Some people just aren't meant to be together."

Courtney hated thinking that way about her parents and hated saying such a thing even more, but all she had to go by was their history, which wasn't good. "Are you ready to go to Macy's and hit that sale?" she asked, smiling. She wasn't about to let her parents' problems dampen her mood. The fact that she couldn't land a boyfriend was depressing enough.

Vickie's mouth tilted in a grin. "Hey, I'm ready."

Barbara checked her watched as she placed the DVD into the player. Ron was attending a staff meeting at the university so she felt confident that he wouldn't surprise her by coming home unexpectedly. She hadn't told a soul about the video and didn't intend to either. This was her secret.

She took the loveseat in front of the television. This was her third time viewing the video. The first time she'd felt like she was watching an X-rated movie, but then she began feeling comfortable with what she was viewing. The purpose of the video, in her opinion, was not for entertainment purposes, although she was sure some people would use it as such. For Barbara it was educational.

Ron was the first and only man Barbara had shared her body with. She had been a virgin until she was twenty, and had gotten pregnant that first time. Over the years she hadn't been savvy enough to develop or try any sexual techniques other than those she was comfortable with, but now she was beginning to see things differently. It wasn't just about *her* in the bedroom. It was about Ron and his wants, needs, and desires, as well.

And as Barbara settled back into the leather cushions, she believed in her heart that what she was watching would one day help to place her marriage on solid ground. No marriage was based on sex alone but for most men it was a major part, and she loved Ron enough to try a few new things.

She smiled thinking he would definitely be surprised when she did and she hoped that he would also be pleased.

part two

Above all else, guard your heart, for it is the wellspring of life.

—PROVERBS 4:23

10

"Welcome back to the States, Lake. Did you enjoy your time in Paris?"

Lake looked at the beautiful woman standing by his brother's side. Brandy Masters. He smiled, thinking how good they looked together. Brandy made Grey happy, and for that, Lake would be eternally grateful. "Yes, things went rather well, better than expected. We were able to close the deal without a hitch."

"That's wonderful. Come by the hotel for brunch tomorrow so the three of us can celebrate," Brandy said, smiling warmly.

"I'll make sure I do that." Lake then glanced at his watch. The honorees had arrived more than an hour ago, so where was Sonya's cousin? He hadn't given much thought to the possibility that she would not attend. He was tempted to ask Brandy, since he knew she'd assisted Carla in getting out the invitations. However, he didn't want to raise Brandy's suspicions about anything. The last thing he needed was for one of his sisters-in-law to know that he was interested in any woman.

"Needing to be somewhere else, Lake?"

He glanced up and met his brother's gaze. "Why do you ask?"

"Because you keep looking at your watch."

Lake frowned. Leave it to Grey to notice every single thing. "No, I'm just trying to decide how soon I can leave," he lied. "You know how I am about parties." At least that much was the truth. In his line of business, he attended enough of them, but that didn't mean he liked them. However, he had purposefully accepted the invitation to this one. He needed to see Courtney Andrews again to make sure he hadn't gone off the deep end, and that he hadn't imagined all those things about her. The woman had become too embedded in his thoughts, and he needed to remind himself why.

"So I guess you've heard Shane and Faith's good news."

Lake nodded to his brother. "Spoke to Mom this morning, and she told me. She's excited about getting another grandchild."

Grey laughed. "*Ecstatic* is more like the word. Now if she can get you married off, I'm sure she would be overjoyed."

He was about to open his mouth and say something to that remark when Brandy said, "Oh, Courtney just arrived. Excuse me, guys, I need to speak with her for a second about something."

Both men watched her walk off, and it took a second for Lake to control the rush of sensations that were trying to overtake him. "Who's Courtney?" he asked, just to see if Grey knew anything about her that Devin hadn't shared.

"Courtney Andrews is Sonya's cousin," Grey said before taking a sip of his wine.

At that moment, Lake felt it was safe to turn around. His heart almost stopped beating when his gaze did an appreciative sweep of the woman.

Her hair flowed in a silky wave around her shoulders, and she had a long, graceful neck. Beautiful. Especially her lips. They were full, inviting, the kind a man would want to nibble, taste, and devour time and time again. He forced his eyes to move lower, and they paused at her chest, taking in the delectable curve of her breasts in the sundress she was wearing before moving downward to her small waist. His gaze moved lower still, and from the flare of the dress around her hips, one wouldn't know that she possessed one spectacular-looking backside. But he had seen it before and had liked what he'd seen.

His eyes then went to her legs. Nice. Long. Shapely. And the strappy, high-heeled sandals made them look sexy. Altogether, she was one hell of a gorgeous package, just as he remembered.

"Like what you see, Lake?"

For a minute he'd forgotten Grey was still standing there. It was too much to have hoped that his intense perusal of Courtney would go unnoticed. He turned back to Grey. "And what if I do?"

He watched Grey's brow arch. "If you do, then I'm sure Brandy would—"

"No. I don't want Brandy involved. Alexia or Faith either, for that matter." He glanced back over his shoulder to Courtney before his gaze swiveled back to Grey. "I want to handle things my way without any interference."

Grey lowered his drink from his lips, studied his brother. "Sounds serious."

"Possibly, it is."

"Just from one look?"

Lake shrugged. "This isn't the first look. I saw her from a distance at Devin's office, the day before I left the country." *And she's been on my mind ever since.* That part he decided not to share with Grey at the moment. He and his three brothers were close. They knew him. They understood him. They had long ago accepted that when it came to his personal business, he liked doing things his way. And if he wanted something bad enough, he got it.

"So, you came here tonight with a plan," Grey said, not really surprised.

Lake shook his head. "I hate to disappoint you, but, no, there's no plan."

Grey chuckled. "Smart move. When it comes to a woman who has drawn the interest of a Masters man, things work better without a plan. Ask Quinn or Shane. They'll back me on that."

Lake had no reason not to believe him. He'd been out of the game too long, and after Liz, he never really cared to know how it was played. He hoped it would be like riding a bicycle. It was just a matter of getting back on and taking off . . . for what it was worth. He glanced back over his shoulder. And from where he was standing, it was worth a lot.

"She's a lot younger than what I figured you'd be interested in."

He turned back to Grey. "Yes, she is. From what I understand, I'm almost ten years older than she is."

"Umm, I remembered what you once said."

Lake frowned. He remembered what he'd once said, too. "Yes, but I might have a good reason to look at things differently now and not let age be a determining factor."

"Evidently."

"Don't put too much into it, Grey. I haven't even met her yet," he said, trying to rationalize why he felt such a desire to have the woman standing across the room. Sure, she was attractive and had a great body, but he knew a number of women with those characteristics. Simple enough. But he had a feeling that there was something about Courtney Andrews that went beyond simple.

"I've met her," Grey interrupted his thoughts by saying. "Besides being a looker, Courtney is smart, intelligent, likable, and she has a good head on her shoulders for her age."

"I take that to mean she doesn't come with drama."

Grey grinned. "Lake, every woman comes with drama to some degree. It's going to be up to you to decide just how much of it you're willing to tolerate."

Lake wasn't surprised his brother would feel that way. Considering Grey's in-laws, namely Brandy's mom, Valerie, and her dad, Victor, he could definitely understand why Grey was saying that. Valerie and Victor never married, but after over thirty-something years, they were still embroiled in a love–hate relationship. But that's where he and Grey were different. Personally, for him when it came to drama—especially of the family kind—he had a zero-tolerance level. No woman was worth it. He had Liz to thanks for his feeling that way. "Remember what I said," Lake warned. "Not a word to Brandy and the others."

Grey chuckled. "I'm married to a pretty smart woman, Lake. She'll figure out things without my help. It won't take a rocket scientist to detect that you're interested."

"Maybe not, but I don't need or want anyone's help, and I'm depending on you to convince Brandy of that."

Grey laughed. "Her intentions are good. She loves you."

"I love her, too, but I have to determine if Courtney's the one on my own. You know the vow."

Grey glanced back over to where his wife was talking to Courtney. "Yes, I know the vow."

Lake nodded. All the Masters had vowed never to marry until they were sure they had found the perfect mate, and it was about more than a beautiful face, a nice body, and a pair of gorgeous legs.

"I'm going to move around and mingle awhile," Lake said with a sigh of finality in his voice.

"And then?"

He met Grey's inquisitive gaze. "And then when I feel the time is right, I will introduce myself."

If only I could find a guy who loved me as much, Courtney thought, reflecting on her conversation earlier with Sonya and Mike. The newlyweds had had a fabulous time in Italy, and she could tell just from the way they interacted with each other that their marriage was off to a good start. They were simply perfect for each other.

And it was quite obvious to everyone that Mike adored his wife. Courtney, although she was extremely happy for her cousin, couldn't help but feel a little envy. That's what she wanted. That's what she desired most of all: for a man to cater to her every whim, and she in turn would cater to his. She wanted a man who would be her soul mate. A man who would give her a reason to look forward to the end of every workday. A man she could share her secrets with. A man who would hold friendship with the same high regard that he would hold sex. Was that too much to ask for? Evidently it was, since she was twenty-nine and still didn't have a man. But she refused to settle for just anything or anyone. She refused to think that anything was better than nothing. Instead, she was convinced that nothing from nothing left nothing, and she was a woman who wanted everything. In her heart, she felt she was more than deserving of a man who would treat her like a princess and make her his queen.

Her parents thought she was just too nitpicky. They believed she was looking for too much out of a relationship.

She totally disagreed with them. The way she saw it, at her age, why should she waste her time on someone who didn't have anything to offer her other than grief? She was too well established in her own career to want a man who needed her help in establishing his. She wanted to meet someone already on her level or above, and not someone she had to help get there.

Thinking too much about her love life—or lack thereof—was giving her a headache, so she snagged a crystal champagne flute off the tray of a passing waiter and took a sip.

She'd had a brief moment to talk to Sonya alone, but never had the heart to tell her cousin just what she thought of that little black book she'd inherited. Just as well, Courtney thought. The last person she needed to unload her problems on tonight was Sonya. This was Sonya and Mike's night, and like the others in attendance, she had come to welcome them back home.

She took another sip of her drink and inwardly smiled. Vickie was supposed to have been her date tonight, but Dan had surprised Vickie and come to town. Just as Courtney had assumed, his new job was overloading his time, and his inability to get away for the weekends had nothing to do with how he felt about Vickie. Courtney was glad all of that had gotten straightened out. Dan was a sweetheart and Vickie was blessed to have someone like him in her life.

Thinking that she would remain at the party for another half hour at the most, she was about to cross the room and chat with Amber Jeffries, someone she'd gotten to know through Sonya's friendship with Carla, when she happened to notice a man staring at her.

At first she thought it was Grey Masters, Brandy's husband, but when she looked again, she saw it wasn't Grey but a man who closely resembled him. She wondered if perhaps it was one of Grey's brothers.

Courtney stared back, totally mesmerized as a sharp tingling sensation invaded her entire body. Something indefinable was taking place between them, and she didn't understand just what. But the one thing she did know was that the man was simply gorgeous.

She wondered about his age, since even from across the room she could see the sprinkle of gray at his temples, which gave him a very distinguished look. On top of that, dressed in a polo shirt and a pair of dark trousers, the man had a build that emitted such raw physical masculinity that it almost took her breath away.

He was tall, over six feet easily, and the coloring of his skin reminded her of malted milk chocolate. Then there were his eyes—dark, impressive, and alluring. And the short, neatly trimmed beard was classic sexy and gave a look to his face that was totally sensual.

He stood leaning against a huge planter with his hands in his pockets and his focus entirely on her. She wondered if anyone ever told him it was rude to stare. But then she wasn't helping the situation by staring back. Her eyes drew together in a slight frown, and as she watched, so did his.

Okay, so he was hot as sin, sexy as all outdoors. But she'd been in the presence of good-looking men before, so what made this one so gut-wrenchingly different? As she pondered that question, he moved, and her heart began racing when she saw he was headed over to her.

Even his walk was incredibly sexy, she thought as she watched him. He strode across the room appearing powerful, in control, confident. The nipples of her breasts began tingling with every step that he took.

She shook her head, thinking she had to be losing her mind, especially after the three disappointments she'd endured within the past three weeks. She couldn't get her hopes up. She refused to assume anything. And more than that, she would not let her guard down, although the sensations flowing through her body were as intoxicating as the drink she'd taken earlier.

Her stomach tightened, and she could actually feel her navel tingle. This man was making chills and heat consume her all at once. She thought of turning and escaping to the nearest patio, but decided she'd never been a coward. No man had ever gotten this much of a reaction from her. She would handle it or die trying. And no matter what, she would not let him know the effect he was having on her. Even if it killed her. She inhaled, trying desperately to ignore the warm sensations overtaking her the closer he got.

And when he came to a stop directly in front of her, he stared at her a moment longer before extending his hand and saying in what she thought was a deep, sensuous tone, "Hello, I'm Lake Masters."

11

At no point in his lifetime had there been any doubt in Lake's mind that he could appreciate a beautiful woman whenever he encountered one. But he was pondering the impact such a woman could have on his male senses. On every nerve ending he possessed.

He knew nothing about this woman other than the little he'd gleaned from Devin and Grey. Yet, up close and personal, she was doing things to him that no other woman had ever done before. She definitely was taking the art of physical attraction and sexual chemistry to an entirely different level. The thought that he could desire any woman so fiercely, and could experience such intense emotions so profoundly, definitely had him stumped. His response to her just wasn't normal, and hadn't been from the first.

During the time he was in Paris, knowing such a thing

had bothered him. But now he assured himself that everything was all right. She had been worth every thought that had passed through his mind, every memory. He was well aware that he still needed to get to know her, but in his opinion that was a given. Ultimately, she would discover the very thing that he now knew. There was a reason the attraction between them was of the degree that it was. And whether she accepted it or not, you couldn't change what was meant to be. As he continued to hold her gaze, he couldn't help wondering just what she was thinking.

At that very moment Courtney was thinking that she'd never encountered such an attraction to any man. She took a slow, steadying breath and finally forced her lips to move. "Nice meeting you, Lake. I'm Courtney Andrews."

Speaking the words was an effort, especially when he was still holding on to her hand, and it seemed he had no intentions of letting it go any time soon. But she was enjoying the feel of his skin touching hers, the strong muscles in his fingers gripping hers in a way that sent a surge of heat through all parts of her body, while at the same time making goose bumps appear on her skin. The thought that immediately came into her mind was that although she had found Harper, Don, and Solomon attractive at first sight, none had made her think of doing naughty things with them within the first five minutes of their meeting.

Lake Masters had.

Images she couldn't control were starting to form in

her head, totally consuming her. It was as if she were being swept away by rough seas and he was the only way out of the storm. She tensed at the thought.

"Your glass is empty. Do you want another drink?"

She swallowed, thinking it would be close to impossible for any woman not to get turned on just from his voice alone. It was deep and throaty. But then, the total package was definitely worth writing home to Mom about.

She glanced down at her glass, mainly to break free from locking gazes with him. "No, thank you. I'm driving, so I believe I've had enough." She braced herself, waiting for the customary pickup line most men would readily use, saying something really asinine about it being okay to fill her tank now because they would be glad to take her home and fill her tank in a different way later.

Instead she was surprised when he leaned close, nearly brushing his lips against her ear, and said, "I admire a woman who knows her limits."

Spoken like the sophisticated and mature gentleman that he seemed to be, she immediately thought, feeling somewhat light-headed with his closeness. He was free with the compliments, comfortable with his approach. She would even go so far as to think he was sincere and wasn't just giving her a line to impress. No, this man wasn't a wet-behind-the-ears kid but a full-fledged man who probably knew how to appreciate a woman. Considering that, she was curious about his age. He had to be older than her by at least eight years.

"How old are you?" she blurted out, and immediately wished she could cut off her tongue for doing so when he lifted his brow. For a moment he held her gaze before saying, "I'm six months shy of forty. Does that bother you?"

"Should it?"

He shrugged massive masculine shoulders, and a teasing smile appeared on his lips. "You tell me, since you're the one who asked."

Which was probably a tacky thing to do, she thought, shaking her head, annoyed with herself. "No, it doesn't bother me. I'm three months shy of thirty. Does that bother you?"

His smile widened and in a low, deliberate tone, he said, "I can't think of anything about you that would bother me, Courtney."

Her guard immediately went up. This Lake Masters was a prime male, and smooth as silk. But she was determined to find any hidden wrinkles. "How can you say something like that when you don't know me?" she asked, trying not to stare at him with the heated interest she felt.

Seemingly undaunted, he smiled at her and said, "You're right. I don't know you, but I'm a man who trusts my gut feelings."

She didn't trust hers, especially when just being near him was causing supercharged emotions to run rampant within her. His smile alone caused a sizzle inside her. He had her conscious of everything about him—including the sprinkling of dark hairs on his arms, the cleanliness of his fingernails, and the way he smelled: real nice and sexy, robust. "You're Grey's brother aren't you?"

He simply kept smiling and confirmed what she'd

said. "Yes, I'm Grey's brother. And you're Sonya's cousin, I understand."

"Yes, that's right," she responded. "Are you here visiting?"

"No, I'm a resident."

"Oh." She wondered why their paths never crossed before. "Have you been living in Orlando long?"

"For about three months now. My primary home is in Boston. I recently expanded my business to open a branch office here."

"And just what type of business are you in?"

"Advertising."

"Sounds interesting."

"It is. And I understand you're a pharmaceutical rep."

"Yes," she said, wondering how he knew that.

Something in her face must have given away her thoughts, because he inclined his head toward hers when he said, "I saw you one day."

Courtney lifted a brow when it registered just what he'd said. "You saw me?" she asked to be sure she'd heard him correctly.

"Yes. Dr. Devin Phillips and I play tennis together most Friday afternoons. I picked him up one day and was sitting in the parking lot waiting for him to come out and I watched you walk into his office."

When he didn't say anything else, Courtney felt her heart start beating fast in her chest upon realizing there might be more. Something he hadn't said as he continued to look at her. That pushed her to ask, "And?"

"And I liked what I saw."

She swallowed. A part of her felt she should say something. Lake Masters was being a little too forward. He was moving a bit too fast. He was too quick-witted for her frame of mind. Yet at the same time, that deep-rooted feminine side of her liked the fact that he had secretly checked her out one day.

"I asked Devin about you."

His words pulled her thoughts back in. She tightened her fingers around her empty drink glass and met his dark gaze. She felt his heat. It was increasing her pulse rate. It had a lump forming in her throat. And on top of everything else, her breasts suddenly began feeling sensitive against the material of her dress.

"I hope he said good things," she said, watching him take a sip of his drink and thinking she liked the decadent way his lips touched the rim of the glass.

"He did say good things," he responded as his gaze circled around the room. It then returned to her, looked deeply at her, and he said, "And he also told me what I considered the most important piece of information."

With an effort she tried downplaying the wave of sensations erupting in her stomach at the intensity of his gaze. "Which was?" she asked, staring back at him.

"The fact that you're not married, and as far as he knew, you aren't seriously involved with anyone." He paused and then asked, "Are you?"

"No," she confirmed, racking her brain as to why he would consider that to be of major importance.

"That's good."

Courtney lifted an arched brow. He had said the words with such finality, with such a keen sense of decisiveness. "And why is that good?" she couldn't help asking.

He leaned in closer. She smelled his enticing masculine scent and could feel his tantalizing hot breath in her ear when he whispered, "Because, Courtney Andrews, I intend to be an intricate part of your future."

"If you say so." Courtney chuckled, evidently thinking he was teasing, giving her a line. Lake watched a smile spread across what he considered perfectly shaped lips—full, enticing, almost magnetic. The kind you wanted to connect with your own. Savor. Nibble. Get downright greedy and devour. He saw more than a trace of amusement in her eyes. The woman had no idea he was dead serious. In fact, he hadn't known just how serious he was until now. He wanted Courtney Andrews. All of her. And not just physically.

Oh, there was a high degree of lust eating at him, forcing him to keep his aroused body under control. But then there was something else, too. With spending less than twenty minutes in her presence, he'd felt emotions, the kind that were a telltale sign to a Masters. At least to those inclined to accept the inevitable. According to Brandy, Grey had tried being a hard case and hadn't accepted how things would be for them until he'd been hit right smack between the eyes. As far as Lake was considered, no one had to hit him with what he considered so totally obvious, it wasn't funny. At least it wasn't funny to him. However, Courtney found his statement amusing, since she was grinning.

He adjusted his stance to lean back against a wall, appreciating the fact that they were standing in a part of Jessie and Carla Devereau's home that afforded them privacy, right next to French doors that led to the patio. The party was crowded, so they were unlikely to be noticed or singled out for any reason. Not that he cared. As far as he was concerned, he had just staked his claim. He had told Grey earlier to keep Brandy out of his affairs. That meant it should have been smooth sailing from here on out. Not so, if the way Courtney was handling what he'd said earlier was anything to go by. Apparently she'd never had a man tell her his intentions before.

"I take it you don't believe me," he said, about to take a sip of his drink only to find his glass empty.

She simply smiled and said, "Of course I don't believe you. Why should I? You only met me tonight, so to claim that you're going to be a part of my future—an intricate part, at that—is kind of silly, don't you think?"

Personally, he didn't see anything silly about it at all. Some men go through their lifetime looking for the perfect woman, a woman destined to be their soul mate. He'd always believed that he would know the woman who would share his life when he met her. Something about her would give it away. So he had gone through life not really dwelling on such things, not caring that he was about to turn forty and wasn't in a serious relationship.

His career, his business, trying to keep his professional life on the upward swing, had taken up most of his time.

But it was time to focus on something else for a change. His future. He was a person who'd always believed family came first, which was why he shared such a close relationship with his brothers and sisters. And to him, his mother would always be a phenomenal woman. His father had died before he'd turned six, leaving his mother alone to raise seven kids. As far as he was concerned, she had done an outstanding job in making them God-fearing, law-abiding citizens.

"Lake?"

Seeing she was waiting for his response, he said, "No, I don't see anything silly about it."

He saw a frown settle on those lips. "Well, I do. Look, I expected a lot more honesty from an older man. You're past the age of playing games, so why are you?"

He wanted to throw his head back and laugh, but the irritation in her voice kept him from doing so. He was being as honest with her as honest could get, and because he was an older man—past the age of playing games—he had moved from the small stuff to going straight to the big picture, making it clear as glass for her. It seemed he would have to use another approach. "I'm not playing games, and once you get to know me better, you'll see that part of my makeup, an essential component of who I am, involves being straightforward. I don't particularly like surprises and like to extend the same courtesy to others."

"Meaning?"

"Meaning I thought of all people that you should be the one to know that I want you. For all the right reasons. I'd even be cocky enough to believe the reason you're not involved with someone is because I'm the one you've been waiting for, just like I believe you're the one I've been waiting for."

She crossed her arms over her delectable chest and tilted her head back to glare up at him. "I think you have me mixed up with someone else."

His lips quirked into an even broader smile. "Trust me, I don't."

He saw her measuring him with her eyes and immediately knew that trusting him was the last thing she planned to do, and that she didn't want to have anything to do with him. He detected her confusion, felt the guard she wouldn't let down, and knew he would have to do whatever it took for her to see things the way he saw them. "Have dinner with me. Get to know me."

When he saw her hesitation, he leaned closer and asked, "Just what are you afraid of?"

Courtney held his gaze, thinking she could answer that question in twenty-five words or less. Disappointment would head the list. After recently dating three men who'd turned out to be just that, she was reluctant to get involved with anyone else too soon. She had even come to the conclusion that she didn't need a man in her life. Just her luck to be drawn to someone with the same characteristics as her father, and she refused to go there.

Besides, she'd always heard that anything that appeared too good to be true, usually was. Lake Masters was too good to be true, and the mere thought that he could be a part of her future had her in a tailspin. Men who looked like him were involved with women who didn't look like her. She looked fairly decent, but she figured he would go for the tall, sexy, Beyoncé type. Gorgeous even on a bad day.

"Courtney?"

She zeroed her thoughts back on him and met his gaze, remembering the question still out there. "I'm not afraid of anything."

"Then have dinner with me. Get to know me. Allow me the opportunity to get to know you better."

It was on the tip of her tongue to bring to his attention that he really didn't know her at all. But still, she would be a fool not to admit she was a little intrigued, more than a bit curious as to why this man—who had the ability to make any woman drool—felt he was the man for her. And what baffled her even further was his claim that it went beyond being just a "bed thing." However, considering her dating history, she would be naïve to take any man at face value. Doing so would be bad for her peace of mind.

"All right," she heard herself saying. "I'll have dinner with you."

He smiled. "Will tomorrow night work for you?"

She frowned. He wasn't wasting any time. "Yes, tomorrow night will be fine."

"What time do you want me to pick you up?"

Now here is where she would draw the line, even if he was Grey's brother. She had a rule about never giving her address to anyone she'd just met. "You name the restaurant, and I'll meet you there."

"Lucian at six."

She nodded. Lucian was known for its elegance as well as its good food. If he was trying to impress, he was definitely doing a good job. "Okay, I'll meet you at Lucian at six."

"I will look forward to seeing you and spending time with you, Courtney."

She felt sensations flood her stomach. He'd made it sound like they would be doing something other than sharing a meal.

"I'm leaving the party now, so until tomorrow night." He reached for her hand, brought it to his lips. She watched his long brown fingers grip hers, watched his mouth touch the back of her hand in a head-swooning kiss, felt the warmth from his lips when it happened. And that same warmth was spreading all through her, making her desire things she'd never desired before. On top of everything else, the man was a romantic.

"Yes, until tomorrow," she forced the words from her lips.

He gave her one last lingering smile before walking away, and she watched as he became lost in the crowd.

12

Vickie swallowed, not sure she wanted to believe what Courtney was telling her. She had gotten a call from Courtney that morning, and since Dan had taken advantage of the membership he still had active at a local gym to go work out, she had suggested that she and Courtney meet for breakfast at their favorite café. Now she was glad they had.

"Come on, Courtney. Did he really look that good?"

Courtney didn't hesitate shaking her head. "Yes, he looked that good. You've met Grey and you know how sexy he is, then consider a man just a year or two older but even sexier."

An image flashed across Vickie's mind, and the only word she could think to say was, "Wow!"

"Now you see what I mean."

Vickie nodded as she chewed on her muffin. "And you're having dinner with him tonight?"

"Not if I can get out of it."

Vickie stared at Courtney like she'd lost her mind. "Why would you want to get out of it?"

"Because I don't believe he's true."

Vickie frowned. "What do you mean?"

Courtney sighed. "Vickie, how many men do you know who would just walk up to a woman they'd just met and declare themselves? A man of the drop-dead gorgeous kind. A man already established in a career. A man who already has it going on. One who would be every woman's dream man."

"So you think he's stringing you along?"

Courtney shrugged. "I don't know what he's doing or thinking that he's doing. And I prefer not sticking around to find out and set myself up for another disappointment."

Vickie didn't say anything for a moment while she took a sip of her coffee, thinking about what Courtney said. "Considering the fact that he's Grey's brother, and Grey's such a nice guy, don't you want to put that in Lake Masters's favor and believe he's okay?"

Courtney sipped her orange juice before saying. "Grey might be Lake's brother, but he's not his brother's keeper. I can't assume that Lake's a nice guy like Grey. Look at Charlie, Dan's brother. That one night you talked me into seeing him was the date from hell."

Vickie threw her head back and laughed, remembering. "He grew hands that night, didn't he?"

"That's not the only thing on him that grew. I don't know how many times he told me he had a hard-on and needed my help to make it go soft. The man was as obnoxious as they come and is a perfect example that family members can be as different as day and night."

"Okay. Okay, I admit Charlie was and still is an asshole," Vickie said, grinning. "But what if Lake is what he claims to be? A man who knows what he wants. A man who's made up in his mind that what he wants is you. And before you say bullshit to that very idea, just listen to me for a minute."

"All right, I'm listening."

"Have you looked at yourself in the mirror lately? Courtney, you're beautiful and have a lot to offer a man. And it could be the reason you're still single and unattached is just like Lake Masters said. Maybe he's the one you've been waiting for."

"I doubt it."

"But are you sure?"

"No, but it stands to reason that he's wrong."

"But what if he's right and you're the one who's wrong? What if you're letting your past disappointments interfere with finding the one man any woman would want to have? What if this is the man for you? The man you deserve. The man created just for you."

A part of Courtney thought Vickie was getting just a little carried away, but her best friend had her thinking. And then there were those weird emotions she just couldn't shake. Memories of Lake Masters and just what a look from him could do to her flowed through her mind, made her insides quicken at the thought. But the image that wouldn't go away was the one when she'd first seen him. At that moment her breath had actually caught and a tingle had taken over the lower part of her body.

"So what are you going to do, Courtney?"

She knew what she wanted to do. She would just keep her guard up and not let it down.

"Courtney?"

She glanced across the table at Vickie. She sighed deeply before saying, "I think I'm going to take a chance. But in no way am I going to be taken in by this guy. I will keep my guard up and not let it down."

Vickie smiled. "I'm glad you're going to dinner with him, and I know that you'll be able to handle him," she assured her.

Courtney took another sip of her orange juice; she felt confident that she had everything under control and, just like Vickie said, she would be able to handle Lake Masters.

"Willie Baker was quite taken with you, Peggy."

Peggy glanced up from viewing all the photographs of Toni's week-old grandchild. Being the proud first-time grandparents, Toni and her husband, John, had taken over a hundred pictures.

"Peggy?"

"I heard you, but I don't know why you would think that. I'm glad his final decision went in our favor, but I merely did what you instructed me to do, which was to impress him enough to consider Orlando for the location of the amusement park."

Toni smiled over at her friend. "No, I think you did more than that. I meant it when I said I believe he was quite taken with you. And the reason I think that is because he sang your praises a number of times. More times than were needed."

Peggy took a sip of her coffee, deciding not to tell Toni that she'd been quite taken with Willie Baker, as well. He had been utterly charming in a way she wasn't used to with a man. Even with all his money, he hadn't come off as overbearing and arrogant.

"He's coming back to Orlando next week."

Peggy met Toni's gaze. She knew that look. "Okay," she said, setting her coffee cup down. "I don't know what's going through that mind of yours, but let it go."

"I can't. I know what Joe's betrayal did to you, and I don't want you to think that all men are like him."

"I don't think all men are like him, Toni. I admit that sometimes I feel I gave him some of the best years of my life, almost thirty of them, only to be kicked to the curb for a twit young enough to be his daughter, but I'm over that now. I've moved on."

"But without a man."

"I'm not looking for one."

"But what if one is interested in you?"

Peggy's stomach plummeted at the thought that Willie Baker could actually be interested in her. "Then I would tread into that territory with caution."

"But you would tread?"

"Yes."

Toni leaned back in her chair with a satisfied grin on her face. "That's good to hear, because when he said he was coming back to Orlando, I decided to have a little dinner party, and you're the person I paired him with."

"You did what!"

"You heard me." Then Toni quickly asked, "So what do you think of my precious grandchild?"

"So the reservations have been made?" Barbara asked Ron excitedly over breakfast.

He glanced over at her with a forced smile. "Yes, everything has been finalized. I've gotten someone to cover my classes for those two weeks, and we'll fly out on Thursday."

Barbara reached across the table and captured her husband's hand in hers. "Thanks, Ron, a trip away from everything is exactly what we need."

He swallowed, suddenly feeling like the asshole his sister-in-law once accused him of being. He didn't want to consider what Peggy, or anyone else for that matter, would think of him if they were to find out that the woman he was involved with would be going to Hawaii, as well—compliments of him. Most men would consider it bold. To others, it would be a stupid move, totally disrespectful of the woman he was married to. But at the moment, the only thing he could think about was the blow jobs he wouldn't have to miss getting. The freaky sex he would continue to indulge in. It was a damn risky move on his part, but worth it if he could pull it off.

A thought flashed through his mind: What if he didn't pull it off? What if he got caught? He didn't want to think what Barbara would do if she found out she'd been screwed over, made a fool of, yet again. His wife was usually mild-mannered and easygoing, but he'd seen her riled up over his women in the past, and she did say that if he ever cheated on him again, she would kill him. Of course, he didn't believe she would go that far, since she wasn't the violent kind.

"Ron, don't you agree?"

It was then that he realized he hadn't made a comment to her earlier statement. "Yes, I agree, which is the main reason I moved forward with it."

"Thanks, Ron."

"Don't thank me, baby. I'm doing it for the both of us."

He saw that look in her eye. Knew what she was about to suggest and decided he wasn't in the mood. At least not with her. "I need to take my car to get serviced this morning. Since I didn't make an appointment, it might take a while, but the Florida Mall is right next door. Would you like to go with me and while we're waiting on the car you can help me look for new golf clubs to take to Hawaii with me?" The only reason he had suggested she come along was because he knew she'd already made plans to spend a part of the morning with her sister at some spa for a day of beauty.

"I'd loved to, honey, but I'm meeting Peggy in a little while. But if you really want me to be with you, then I'll—"

"No, that's fine. After I get the car back, I plan to stop

and check in on Courtney. She's been making herself scarce lately."

"You've noticed."

He met his wife's worried gaze. "How can I not notice? I plan to have a talk with her. I think she needs to understand and accept that how we handle our personal affairs is really none of her business. She has her life to live, and we have ours. But then I also want her to know that we love her and will always be here for her."

He got up from the table and pulled Barbara into his arms and hugged her tight and kissed her lips before saying, "And that you and I will always be here for each other."

A few hours later, Ron was shrugging out of his clothes, which he proceeded to place over the back of the leather recliner in the bedroom. Ashira was already in bed, waiting on him.

"I was surprised when I got your call. It's a Saturday morning," she said, stretching her naked body atop the covers.

His gaze raked over her as a smile touched his lips. He knew what she meant. Usually his visits were in the afternoons, on his way home from work when Barbara assumed he'd gotten delayed at a staff meeting or something. But today he had been bold. Since Barbara figured that with his car in the shop being serviced he was stranded, he decided to use that time to his advantage. What she didn't know was that he had made arrangements to use one of the dealership's rentals.

He walked over to the bed. “I’m full of surprises, like this,” he said, dropping the airline ticket on her naked chest.

She scrambled up, and her eyes widened when she saw what it was. He watched her face light up with excitement. “So I am going?”

He laughed. The happiness on her face was pure delight. “Yes, you’re going. I’m flying you in a day early, so you’ll be there when I arrive.” His features then took on a serious note. “There will be rules, Ashira. Rules I expect you to follow. Under no circumstances is my wife to find out about this.”

“Hey, don’t worry, I can keep a secret and I can follow rules,” she said smiling, inching toward him and placing her arms around his neck, making the tips of her breasts, perky and firm, come to press against his hairy chest. “And I’m going to make sure you never regret taking me along.”

He liked the sound of that. “And what else will you do?”

Her smile widened. “I plan to be at your beck and call while I’m there. All you have to do is manage to get away from your wife periodically.”

He nodded, hoping that wouldn’t be a problem. But still, he wouldn’t let being with Ashira go to his head while he was there. Although his wife lacked the skills to keep him satisfied in bed, he cared for her deeply and wouldn’t want to do anything to intentionally hurt her. Then again, what she didn’t know wouldn’t hurt her.

He was glad that, although Barbara had found out

about his last affair with a woman name Melissa Langley, she hadn't known about Ashira, mainly because he was in the process of dropping Melissa for Ashira. Therefore, if Barbara and Ashira were to run into each other at the hotel in Hawaii, he didn't have to worry about them recognizing each other.

Now if he could only get Melissa to leave him alone. She had been waiting for him in the parking lot when he got off work a few weeks ago, asking if he wanted to go with her to the doctor next week. She would be having a sonogram to determine the sex of the baby. Before he could stop himself he had told her in no uncertain terms that he wouldn't go to the doctor with her and didn't give a royal shit what sex the baby was. Melissa had lied to him; had told him she was on birth control. In his book she had intentionally gotten pregnant and he didn't want to have anything to do with her or the child. He would take care of it, send her a check each month, but that was as far as his involvement would go.

Evidently Melissa hadn't understood what he'd said because she had sent a photo of the sonogram to his office yesterday, along with a note saying they were having a boy. He had called her to tell her not to send anything else to him, and he had to hang up on her when she'd proceeded to curse him out.

"So, what do you want today, Ronnie?" Ashira asked breaking into his thoughts. "Your every wish is my command," she leaned up and whispered, and then took the wet tip of her tongue and slid it down the side of his face, around his lips and ears.

His aroused body got even harder. All thoughts of Melissa's foolishness vanished. "You know what I want. I only have a couple of hours, so make it worth my while."

She grinned and leaned back. "Don't I always?"

And then she pushed him back on the bed and put her mouth to work, just the way he liked. When she took him into her mouth, he closed his eyes and lifted his hand to grab hold of her hair, to make sure her wicked mouth stayed locked in place on him. No woman could work her teeth, tongue, and gums like her. He'd thought Melissa was terrific, but she didn't come close. Ashira was causing a quiver of sensations to overtake him that went all the way down to his bones, releasing any erotic needs he had and surrendering them to her. No matter what he asked her to do, she did it without blinking an eye. It always amazed him how giving him a blow job could make her come, as well.

And what was a real turn-on was in knowing she enjoyed giving him pleasure. She would work him over with a physical intensity that could push him over the edge each and every time, but then she reveled in the sex he gave her, too. She had no complaints, so it was a win–win situation for the both of them. Besides, he was free with the money when it came to her. Already he purchased new carpeting as well as every piece furnishing this room. So far as he was concerned, this bed was his.

His entire body jerked when her mouth became more intense, and then with a concentrated effort she pulled everything out of him, and automatically his body exploded in one hell of an erotic volcanic shakedown. He heard himself utter her name over and over while he loosed his hold on her head, and knowing he'd probably at some point caused pain, he began gently massaging her scalp with his fingertips. And then she came, a climax of gigantic proportions. Her body jerked a few times while she continued to lick him clean. He stroked the side of her face while inhaling the air that was filled with a mixture of her perfume and heavy sex.

He wasn't through with her. He intended to ride her good while she was drenched in wetness from her own orgasm. He quickly changed positions and moments later he was thrusting in and out of her from behind, just like a madman. But then that was just how he felt. And when he came again, he gritted his teeth and held himself inside her, making sure she got some of him from both ends—just the way she liked.

When she screamed again, he tightened his hold on her hips and came again. And his mind filled with thoughts of having sex with her in Hawaii. It was a risk worth taking.

13

Courtney walked into the huge atrium of the Lucian restaurant. The whole interior was simply too elegant for words. The outside was modeled like a palace, and on the inside, everything—from the pure-gold-plated Swarovski crystal chandeliers to the marble three-tiered pedestal fountain—denoted wealth. In addition to the restaurant, the building housed several exquisite shops, a renowned art gallery, and a prestigious collectibles museum.

She recalled that the price of a simple entrée at the restaurant was more than a hundred dollars. And the one and only time she'd eaten there had been with her parents on high school graduation night.

Speaking of her parents . . . her father had dropped by earlier that day, concerned that she'd been avoiding them. She loved her parents and hoped their decision to stay married and work out their problems was successful. She didn't want to consider how her mother would handle it if it wasn't.

Sometimes Courtney just wanted to shake some sense into her father, but she'd long ago decided he was just one selfish bastard. His affairs had hurt her mother so deeply. Just acknowledging her husband's unfaithfulness, yet remaining by his side was a blow to any woman's pride and self-esteem. But Barbara had continued to do just that, all in the name of love. As far as Courtney was concerned, there wasn't that much love in the world.

She glanced around. Before leaving home, she had checked out her outfit more than once and knew she looked more than presentable. The moment that she'd told Vickie where she and Lake would be meeting for dinner, Vickie had insisted that this dinner date demanded a new outfit, so after her father's visit, Courtney had gone shopping.

She simply loved her new terra-cotta-colored Stenay bead jacket dress. The way the stretchy mesh hugged her figure made her feel totally feminine. And the male appreciative glances she'd received since entering Lucian made her feel doubly so.

She glanced at her watch. She was thirty minutes early, so she couldn't expect that Lake had already arrived as well. So she decided to stroll around the atrium and view all the expensive collectibles, some she understood had been imported from an actual Russian palace.

As she began her stroll, she tried to ignore the racing

of her heart. In just a few minutes, she would be seeing Lake Masters again!

When he walked out of the art gallery and his gaze lit on Courtney, he hadn't been able to take another step. Her beauty left Lake speechless, spellbound, totally in awe. The dress she was wearing fit her perfectly and draped her curves in a way that would make a dead man come alive and take notice.

She had been constantly on his mind since last night, and he had awakened this morning with an urgency to see her again. And now what he was seeing was taking his breath away. More than ever, he couldn't help wondering why someone so strikingly beautiful was not involved in a serious relationship with someone. Not that he was complaining.

He checked his watch. They were ahead of their scheduled time, so instead of making his presence known, he decided to just stay put and observe her. The area where she had strolled was a stunning reproduction of a palace, and she definitely looked the part of a queen. Emotions he had accepted last night were back, hitting him full force, making him fully aware of the reality of their connection.

He shook his head and inwardly chuckled. He'd never considered himself a romantic by any means, and even when Quinn had tried convincing him that such a thing as love at first sight existed, he had refused to believe it. Now he was a believer and had no compunction about doing whatever it took to make Courtney a believer, as well.

Checking his watch again, he inhaled deeply before moving across the floor toward her. Her back was to him, and his gaze was drawn to her perfectly shaped backside. A fiery burst of sexual need flooded his entire being. He knew, however, that to win her over, he would have to keep his physical wants and needs under wrap. He would wait with bated breath until the day came when he could set those desires free.

He stopped within five feet of her and was about to say her name, to let her know of his presence when she slowly turned around.

Courtney had heard the footsteps on the polished tile floor, and when butterflies had begun gathering in her stomach, she'd known Lake was approaching. She'd been prepared for that. But upon turning around, she hadn't been prepared for the sharp and striking handsomeness that lined his features. His perfect bearded chin, the immaculate way the dark suit he was wearing fit his body, especially in the broadness of his shoulders and the leanness of his hips. Intense male sexuality oozed from every part of him, a raw physical force that she actually felt.

She knew she was out of her element here and wondered what on earth was he thinking in wanting to pursue a relationship with her. And what had she been thinking by not taking a firm hand and discouraging him? He was a mature man, sexually and otherwise. Why on earth would he want to waste his time with her instead of seeking out a woman more his caliber? A woman who could not only match his physical desires head-on but who could also take care of them with an expertise Courtney knew she lacked. Granted, she wasn't a virgin, but she was a long way from being the experienced woman he was probably used to being involved with.

"Hello, Courtney."

His words, spoken in a deep, husky voice, flowed like warm cream over her entire body, opening a degree of sensuality she didn't know she possessed. She swallowed and somehow managed to return his greeting. "Hello, Lake."

She felt herself quiver from the look in his eyes and suddenly felt vulnerable. It had been a mistake for her to agree to meet him here. And then, as if he'd read her thoughts, he covered the remaining distance separating them, captured her hand in his, and like the night before, he lifted it to his lips and kissed it.

It took everything she possessed to keep from swooning, and she couldn't help but register the sensations that engulfed her. The dark eyes staring at her with such intensity had her so mesmerized, she couldn't have forced her gaze from his even if she wanted to.

He didn't release her hand, only lowered it. The silence between them stretched, and it seemed slow minutes dragged by when she knew in reality it was only seconds. Sensual awareness hung in the air surrounding them, and she thought her pulse couldn't possibly race any faster than it was already doing, but was proven wrong when he said in a deep seductive voice, "Our reservations are at six, and I believe they are ready for us now."

She watched his head turn, only a fraction, toward the entrance to the restaurant before his eyes reconnected to hers, and then he added, "I'm looking forward to spending time with you, Courtney."

She nodded, and although she didn't want to admit it, a part of her was looking forward to spending time with him, as well. And when he continued to hold her hand and lead her toward the restaurant, she felt a sharp stab of apprehension.

"So, tell me everything there is to know about Courtney Andrews." Lake watched her eyes lift from her wineglass to his, and his guts clenched when a smile touched the corners of her lips. Lips he'd already decided he would taste before the night was over.

"I think that will take a lot longer than our dinner date tonight, Lake," she said, breaking into his thoughts.

"No problem," he said, leaning back in his chair, relaxed. "There will be other times."

"You seem pretty sure of that."

He shrugged. "I have no reason not to be. I consider myself a pretty likable guy. What do you think?"

This time when she smiled, he saw a hidden dimple. "Yes, you're a likable guy. But . . ."

"But what?"

"I think you're expecting more out of this than you should."

If you only knew, he thought before taking a sip of his drink. "What exactly do you think I'm expecting?"

"You tell me. I'm still confused about the statement you made last night about being an intricate part of my future."

"Don't let what I said frighten you."

"It doesn't frighten me, Lake. It just confuses me."

He leaned toward her. "Don't let it confuse you either, Courtney. Like I told you last night, I'm almost forty. Too old for games, much too busy to play, nor do I want to. But what I do want is the same thing most men want."

"A woman to warm your bed."

He could only assume that the men she'd dated in the past had commitment-phobia. "Oh, she'll be doing a whole lot more than warming my bed, trust me," he stated huskily. "She will share my life, my name, have my children, and be the most cherished person on the face of the earth and the most important one in my life." He watched her take another sip of her wine and then she gave him a look like she had trouble believing him.

"If what you're saying is true, then you're most women's dream man, so why hasn't some woman found you yet?" she asked stiffly.

"Mmm, perhaps it could be that I'm a man who prefers finding the woman instead of the other way around." He had to struggle to keep from saying anything else, especially anything about how he could admit to finding just the woman he wanted, and that she was sitting directly across the table from him. Instead he said, "Enough about me for now. I want to know all about you."

For a moment she didn't say anything. "I'm an only child."

He nodded. "Are your parents still together?"

"Yes, they're still together. In fact, they celebrated their thirtieth wedding anniversary a few months ago." Then she was silent, as if giving him time to do the math, which he did. Her mother was pregnant with her at the time of the wedding.

"My mother is marketing director for Universal Studios and my father is a professor at a university here."

"How are you and Sonya related?"

"Our mothers are sisters."

Then it seemed she had a few inquiries of her own. She suddenly asked, "Are you a friend of Mike or Sonya?"

He smiled and said, "Both. However, I met Sonya before Mike."

She nodded. "Why weren't you at the wedding?"

"I left for Paris the day before. That's when I saw you walking into Devin's office. The day before I flew out for Paris. I was there for almost three weeks."

He paused, deciding it was her time to do the math. Then she would figure out that if he'd seen her the first time over three weeks ago, that meant his interest in her had lasted just that long. She didn't say anything for a while, which to him was just as well. He wanted to give her time to think through everything he said to her tonight.

After some silence, he managed to get her talking again, focusing the conversation back on her. During dinner he discovered her best friend's name was Vickie, that she and Sonya were very close, and that she considered Sonya as the older sister she never had. He also knew that she mentored a trouble teen by the name of Jetrica, and that Courtney was studying to take a test to advance in her job. Her favorite color was blue, the same as his. But unlike him, she was a die-hard Dolphins fan, and he was strongly devoted to the Patriots.

"Well, I think that's about it for me," she said, finishing off her water. He noted that she had long ago stopped the waiter from refilling her wineglass, since she would be driving home. They had established last night that she was a woman who knew her limits.

"Now I want to know everything there is about you, Lake."

He smiled smoothly. "I'm older, so telling my side of things will take longer." He checked his watch. It was after eleven already, and he knew the place would be closing in less than thirty minutes. "We won't be able to cover everything tonight."

She nodded. "Then for now, tell me something vital. Something that would clearly define you."

He wasn't sure she was ready to hear it. Besides, this wasn't the place where he wanted to tell her. "Come on, it's getting late, I'll answer your question as I walk you out."

The night's air was warm as he walked her to her car. He held her hand in his, and she seemed inclined to let him. He liked the feel of it in his and enjoyed her strolling beside him. It seemed as if that's where she belonged.

"Thanks for dinner, Lake."

They had reached her car. The parking lot was almost empty, and before she opened the car door to get in, he tightened his hold on her hand and brought her closer to him. "Now, to answer your question. The one thing that will define me is that I'm a man who works hard to get whatever it is that I want. And I've decided, Courtney Andrews, that I want you."

And before she could catch her next breath, he leaned forward, flattened his hand in the center of her back to draw her closer, and captured her lips in his.

The first thought that came to Courtney's mind while she was capable of thinking was that she had never been kissed this way before. So indecently wicked, earth-shatteringly hot, and so incredibly passionate. There were kisses—and there were kisses. He was clearly defining the difference. And the moment his tongue entered her mouth, she felt intense heat that fired through her veins. Every bone in her ached, and she actually heard herself moaning in his mouth. Slowly, methodically, thoroughly, he was making love to her mouth, using his tongue to claim every area he stroked.

She thought he had impeccable control while she was standing there losing it, burning up with a hunger she'd known nothing about until now. And just when she thought she couldn't take any more, he released her mouth and stepped back. But not before taking one last sumptuous lick of her lips.

"I'll call you."

His words, a sensuous promise, touched her in areas of her body she preferred they didn't. She was about to ask where he'd gotten her phone number when she remembered they had exchanged business cards earlier at dinner. "All right." Those were the only words she was composed enough to say.

He opened the car door for her, and she was too dazed to do anything else but slide inside while he watched her. She started the engine, and he closed the door and stepped back. And when she drove away, she glanced in her rearview mirror and saw him still standing there. She inhaled, thinking she had gotten maximum pleasure from that kiss. But then she really shouldn't be surprised. Lake Masters was one hell of a man. One who didn't do anything by half measures. One who got whatever he wanted.

And he'd said that he wanted her.

14

"Peggy, it's good seeing you again."

Peggy glanced up at the man towering over her and giving her a warm smile. "It's good seeing you again, as well, Willie."

She was trying her best to downplay the pleasure flowing through her. When Toni first told her of the dinner party, she had rebelled and had even considered not coming. But she had wanted to come, had wanted to see him.

Allowing time to get her heartbeat back on track, Peggy glanced around the spacious living room and quickly discovered Toni hadn't been quite honest with her. She had made it seem this would be a dinner party of more than just four people. It was obvious to Peggy that her friend was up to something.

"And how are things going at the office?"

Peggy looked up at him, and all the feelings she promised herself never to have toward another man were threatening to come out. If only he wasn't so good looking. There was something about him that made her feel comfortable to the point where she had a tendency to put her guard down. He'd had that sort of an effect on her from the first. "Everything is going fine," she said, taking another sip of her wine. "Have you been to McDonald's lately?"

He threw his head back and laughed. "No, unfortunately I haven't."

At that moment both Toni and John, who'd declared earlier that preparing dinner was a joint affair, came from the kitchen to announce everything was ready.

Although she felt comfortable around Willie—would even go so far as to admit to the physical attraction she was trying to downplay—she really hadn't realized just how much she liked him until dinner was over. It was easy to see that both John and Toni liked him, as well, which was a plus, since she valued their opinions. But it was Willie's personality that constantly won her over.

The man was a class act without even trying. It seemed second nature for him to be kind, caring, and compassionate. And she recalled just what a wonderful conservationist he was.

"So what about it, Peggy?"

It was then that she realized Willie had spoken to her. "I'm sorry, what was the question?" she asked, smiling, feeling foolish for having been caught inattentive.

He returned her smile. "I told John and Toni that I would love to go to Disney World on my next visit to

Orlando, and Toni suggested we go as a foursome. What about it?"

It hit Peggy that he was asking her out on a date. She didn't know whether her heart should dance in joy or cry in despair. She had married Joe right out of college, and they had been married for thirty-two years when he'd asked for a divorce. She remembered that day perfectly, since it had been on their daughter's thirtieth birthday. They had taken Sonya out to dinner to celebrate, and when they'd returned home, Joe had asked her for the divorce. It hadn't taken her long to find out the other woman was someone younger than their daughter, someone he had hired as a temporary office assistant when his regular assistant had been out for six weeks on medical leave.

"Peggy?"

She met Willie's gaze and knew that John and Toni were waiting on her response, as well. Fighting back the memories of the pain she'd endured with Joe, she smiled and said, "I think it's a wonderful idea."

She quickly looked across the table and caught Toni's eyes and saw a mixture of relief and happiness shining in their crystalline blue depths. She automatically returned Toni's smile. They both knew she had taken a huge step forward.

Although it was still fairly early, Courtney booted down her laptop, deciding to call it a night. The pharmaceutical company she worked for was launching a new drug, and there was a ton of information she had to become familiar with. In a few weeks, she would be attending a launch meeting in New York.

Earlier that day, she had dropped by her parents' home. She'd wanted to see them before they left for their two weeks in Hawaii. Her mother was simply ecstatic about the trip, and to Courtney's surprise, her father seem to be gung-ho about it, as well. This was the first time they'd planned a trip together in years. She wondered if perhaps she'd made a mistake. Maybe her parents could work out their problems and save their marriage.

She got up from her desk and headed for the kitchen. She paused at the huge vase of cut flowers she had set on the dining table yesterday when they arrived from Lake. It had been quite a surprise to receive them. She hadn't seen or heard from him since their dinner date on Saturday night. Twice she had started to call him to thank him for the flowers, but then she had remembered his promise that he would call her.

She also recalled the comment he'd made about how he preferred being the one who sought out a woman and not the other way around. In no way did she want to send him the wrong message that she was running behind him. The last thing she wanted to do was to give the man any ideas. He had enough already, thank you. If she heard from him again, that was fine, and if she didn't, that was fine, too.

Frankly, the latter wouldn't be fine, she thought as she headed toward her bathroom to take a shower. She would only be lying to herself to claim otherwise. Whether she liked it or not, Lake Masters had made an impression on her feminine senses. And every time she thought about the kiss they had shared, a sensuous heat flooded her body.

Moments later she stepped into the shower stall, hoping the warm rush of water that cascaded over her body would wash away all her thoughts of Lake. Fat chance! The only thing washing over her were more memories. She remembered how at dinner he had been so solicitous to her every need, so attentive to her every word.

Now it was her time to find out everything she could about him other than the little facts he had shared with her. She wanted to delve into his life like he'd delved into hers. When she'd gotten the flowers, she'd been tempted to call Brandy to find out what she could about him. Hadn't he basically done the same thing about her with Devin? But something had held her back. She was satisfied in thinking that she would find out what she needed to know on her own when the time came.

Less than thirty minutes later, she had toweled dry and slipped into the spandex nightshirt her aunt Peggy had given her on her last birthday. She had turned twenty-nine that day and had commented to Sonya that she'd felt her biological clock beginning to tick. Now here she was looking thirty real close in the face, and there was something else ticking inside her—overworked hormones. At the moment there was nothing to do but ignore them. But she blamed all her newfound lusty thoughts on one man.

She made her rounds, checking to make sure all the doors were locked and that the security alarm system was set when her phone rang. Thinking it was probably Vickie calling her back, she picked up and said, "Yes, and what I can do for you?"

There was a slight pause, and then a masculine voice said, "Is it possible for me to give you a list?"

Lake's deep voice sent everything woman inside Courtney into overdrive. Shivers touched her, and all she had to do was close her eyes to recall muscular arms and chest, a hard, firm abdomen, and powerful lean hips that looked good in whatever clothes he was wearing.

She paused a second to catch her breath, get a grip, and convince herself that Lake Masters was only a man. But then, what a man. Older. Mature. Sexy. She took a deep breath to calm her achy, racing heart. Exhaling, she tried saying in a teasing tone, "A list, hmm? I hope you know I'll be checking it twice."

His chuckle was rich when he said, "If you're trying to find out if I'm naughty or nice, don't bother. I'll admit to being both. I'm naughty *and* I'm nice."

Sudden images of a naughty Lake Masters torpedoed through her brain, almost causing her to moan out loud. Something within her stirred, relaxed, and then stirred again. You didn't have to be the most perceptive person in the world to figure out she was going through one hell of a hormonal meltdown. She had just finished taking a shower, was feeling cool and calm before his call. Now heat radiated off her bare skin, making her nightshirt almost sensitive against it. She'd dated a lot of men in her lifetime, some she could have written off even before her door closed behind them. But she had a feeling Lake Masters wasn't one she would forget any time soon. If ever.

"Thanks for the flowers," she decided to say, steering the conversation to safer ground.

"You're welcome. I saw them and immediately thought of you."

She glanced over at the beautiful arrangement. "In what way?"

"Colorful, vibrant, and beautiful. And like you I thought they would brighten up an entire room. Do they?"

His words touched her. "Thanks, and yes, they brighten up the room."

"I'm glad. So, when can I see you again?"

Courtney knew she was playing with fire when she asked, "And when do you want to see me?"

"As soon as I can."

It was almost on the tip of her tongue to remind him, although he might be eager to see her now, he had let four days pass without bothering to contact her.

As if he had the ability to read her thoughts, he said, "I didn't call because I wanted to give you space. Didn't want to crowd you. But I thought about you every single day, minute, hour."

That was a lot of thinking, she wanted to say. She wanted to believe a man, any man, but particularly this man, could have her on his mind that much. She wanted to believe him, wanted to be convinced he was more than a figment of her imagination and that although he seemed too good to be true, he really was true. But she'd learned to operate on the side of caution. She never took anything at face value. The first real boyfriend she'd had while in college had trampled her pride, broke her heart. It hadn't left her bitter, just wary.

"Courtney?"

She cleared her throat. "Yes?"

"I want to see you again."

The fingers holding the phone trembled. And she became starkly aware that if he was a man on the prowl, then she was a woman who wanted to get caught. But . . . within reason. She needed to get to know him. She *wanted* to get to know him. "And I want to see you again, too, Lake."

"Okay, then, how about tomorrow night?"

"Tomorrow night is fine," she said, almost stumbling over the words from the excitement flooding through her.

"Will it be okay if I come to your home and pick you up?"

"Yes, that will be okay," she said, thinking of his bigger-than-life persona and fine-as-a-dime body standing in her living room, sitting on her sofa . . . lying in her bed.

"What's the address?"

She rattled off her address, while everything feminine rattled off inside her. She swore she could smell his warm, masculine scent over the phone lines.

"Where would you like to go?"

She appreciated him asking, but she didn't have a clue. "Doesn't matter." And truly it didn't, just as long as she was with him, enjoying his company, ogling his body.

"We'll do dinner then take in a movie, perhaps."

Perhaps. She had a feeling she would enjoy any movie

with him a lot better than she had enjoyed one with Solomon Wise. "That sounds nice."

"And I'm going to make sure that it is. You'll get the nice side of me tomorrow. I'll save the naughty side until later."

She took that as a promise. "All right."

"Good night, Courtney."

"Good night, Lake."

"Pleasant dreams."

He'd said the words almost in a whisper, making the knot that had formed in her stomach tighten. She wanted to end the call, but then she didn't want to end the call. His voice alone had the ability to seduce her. She knew he wouldn't hang up until she did, so she fought back temptation to stay on the line and proceeded to slip the phone back into its cradle.

She sighed deeply while pushing her hands through her hair, frowning thoughtfully. No matter how much sex appeal Lake had, she had to keep her guard up. She couldn't let him tear it down. There was still a lot about him she didn't know, and she refused to assume anything. She knew he claimed to want to be a part of her future, but as far as she was concerned, it was just another line until she was convinced he was the real deal.

And more than anything, she hoped to God that he was.

15

"Good evening, Courtney. You look great."

Courtney could barely pay attention to Lake's compliment, too busy thinking of one she could give him. Standing in her doorway, he looked even more handsome than before, oozing sexiness from every angle. She quickly remembered how she had struggled through the evening the last time they were together, trying to keep her mind off him and all the ways he was making her feel. But just from looking at him now, she knew she would have another fight on her hands tonight. Her gaze immediately latched on to his mouth and saw the fullness of his lips curve into a smile. It was a smile that was already doing things to her. A smile that had her pulse jumping erratically.

She drew in a deep breath and forced herself to say,

"Thank you, and you look nice, too." And that, she thought, was putting it mildly. "Would you like to come in and have a drink before we leave?"

"Yes, thanks."

She stepped back as Lake moved forward. When he reached the middle of the room, he stopped and glanced around, and she couldn't help wondering what he was thinking.

The thought that was running through Lake's mind at that moment was that instead of them going out, he would much prefer if they stayed in and got to know each other up close and as personal as a couple can get. He wished he would have suggested that but knew it would not have been a good idea for a second date. He had to work his way up to reaching that goal, only after proving his worthiness. And he would.

"Like you, your home is beautiful," he said, meaning every word. He once described her as colorful, vibrant, and beautiful, and he felt the same would extend to everything she owned. This particular room was no exception. He had been in advertising long enough to know top quality when he saw it. And it was here, surrounding him, in the richness of her mahogany furniture. Her taste, it appeared, leaned more on the modern and traditional, with a couple of Queen Anne pieces thrown into the mix to provide a different style. One of grace and elegance.

"Thanks for the compliment. What would you like to drink?" she asked, coming to stand in front of him.

"A glass of wine would be nice," he said, as his gaze drifted over her black printed skirt, off-white colored blouse, and sandals. She looked hot. Sexy. Today her hair was up, away from her face, which only gave him more of her beautiful features to look at.

"Then a glass of wine is what you'll get," she said, smiling. "Excuse me for a moment. Feel free to take a tour if you'd like. This place is small but is perfect for my needs."

And then she walked off and he watched, feeling a fiery tingle stirring in his gut with every step she took. Her back view was astounding. The shape of her rear end almost had his hands getting clammy. And then there were those long shapely legs, her small waist, and those nice sensuous curves.

Damn. The explosive chemistry between them was back. In truth, it had never left. He was getting aroused and thought the best thing to do was to move. She had invited him to take a tour of her home, and now was the time to do it. He needed something other than taking Courtney to bed to weigh on his mind.

He moved around her condo, going from room to room, and the more he saw, the more he liked. He could tell that she wasn't a person who liked clutter. Neither was he. He liked order. Even in his life. Especially in his life. He didn't like chaos. Detested drama and preferred staying away from it.

He headed back toward her living room, thinking that his hardest moment had been when he'd walked into her bedroom, seen her huge bed, and pictured her sleeping in it alone. And then he had imagined her sleeping in it with him. His body had ignited, as if lit by a torch, at the mere thought of tangling with her between the sheets, making love to her in a way a man made love to the woman who he considered his soul mate. The flowers he'd sent were in her bedroom on a table not far from her bed. She had mentioned earlier that she had moved them from the dining room to take full advantage of the sun coming through a bedroom window. Did she think of him whenever she saw them? He hoped so.

He had made it back to the living room when she reappeared carrying two glasses of wine. "Sorry I got detained. My mom called on my cell phone to let me know she and my father had made it to California."

He accepted the glass she handed him. "They went out of town on a trip?"

She smiled. "Yes. They're spending two weeks on vacation in Hawaii."

"Nice."

"I know, and I'm hoping that they enjoy themselves."

"In Hawaii? I'm sure they will. There's a lot to see and do."

She nodded, taking a sip, too. "I take it that you've been there."

A smile touched his lips. "Yes, several times. I have a couple of clients there."

"Umm, tell me about the advertising business. Tell me about you," she said, moving toward the sofa.

He wondered if that was her cue to let him know she wanted to find out more about him before dinner and not during. That was fine with him. He much preferred being here alone with her than in a public place surrounded by others.

He decided to take a seat in one of her Queen Anne chairs and not give in to temptation and sit beside her on the sofa. If he were to pull such a move, they would never get any talking done. Already he was champing at the bit to taste her mouth again. The need to kiss her was overwhelming. But then there was a deep need for her to get to know him as the man who would be a part of her life.

So, while the two of them sipped their wine, they talked, mainly about him. He told her everything she needed to know and then some. He mentioned his family and how close he was to them, especially to his siblings. He even told her that he would be a new uncle soon, when his older brother Shane and his wife, Faith, had their first baby.

Then they talked about the advertising business. He had good people working for him. Employees he knew he could count on to make things happen, but in some ways he was still a hands-on guy.

A painting on her wall caught his eye. It had from the first moment he'd walked into the room. It was beautiful, and he doubted he'd seen anything like it before. Like her, it was colorful, and it was filled with eye-catching abstract shapes. It had been hand-painted on canvas and would be the centerpiece of whatever room it was in. Courtney had chosen this room for it, smartly so. It blended well.

"That's a beautiful painting," he said, trying to make

out the signature on it from where he sat. "I'm familiar with a number of artists, but not that one."

She glanced over her shoulder at the painting. "Isn't it gorgeous? Jetrica gave that to me as a gift."

He racked his brain, trying to remember the name. Apparently the person was someone she had mentioned to him previously. He then remembered. "Jetrica? Is that the teenage girl you mentioned that you mentor? The one whose mother is serving time. She's being raised by her twenty-year-old sister?"

Courtney nodded. "Yes, that's the one."

"She has an extraordinary degree of talent."

"I've tried telling her that. Others have, too. But I think she actually thinks we're full of it. She sees her work as something she engages in when she wants to get out of doing real work, mainly her schoolwork. And she's an excellent student once she applies herself. I think her problem is that she sees herself as a burden on her sister. Her sister gave up a chance to go off to college on a scholarship to stay back and raise Jetrica so she wouldn't be put into the system, and possibly have to go to a foster home."

Then Courtney's house phone rang and she stood. "Excuse me for a moment. Few people have my home number, so it's probably Vickie."

He watched her cross the room and decided to take that time to get a closer view of the painting. It was hard to believe it had been done by a fourteen-year-old. This Jetrica was definitely way advanced for her age.

"Excuse me, something has come up, Lake, and I have to go."

He spun around and saw the worried look on her face. "What's wrong?" he asked, as if it was his right to know.

"That was Bethany, Jetrica's sister. The two of them had an argument earlier, a pretty bad one, and Jetrica left. Bethany is worried."

Lake frowned, wondering what this Bethany thought Courtney could do about it.

As if reading his thoughts, she said, "I've got to find her. Usually I'm the only one who can talk some sense into her when she gets like this."

He nodded. "So in other words, your relationship with her goes beyond just mentoring."

"Yes, I'm also her friend, or at least I try to be. Jetrica has a way of putting her guard up at times, like she's afraid to let anyone get too close. She's afraid to get too attached."

He picked up on Courtney's frustration when she said, "I'm sorry our evening has to end like this, and I was looking forward to it. We haven't even made it to dinner yet."

"And we will. I was looking forward to dinner, too."

"I would invite you to stay here until I get back, but I don't know when that will be. I have to try and help find Jetrica."

He crossed the room to her. Took her hand in his. They were trembling, which meant she was worried. "Thanks for the invite, but how about if I go with you? Let's go find her together."

She looked up at him with grateful eyes. "Are you sure?"

"Positive. And we can take my car so I can drive."

"Thanks. Just let me grab my purse." And then he watched her take off toward her bedroom. He shook his head. Hadn't he just moments earlier inwardly proclaimed that he preferred not to indulge in drama of any kind?

Courtney tried to think of things other than what she wanted to do to Jetrica once she found her. Wringing her little neck wasn't legal, neither was slapping some sense into her, but she was tempted. Bethany was worried that Jetrica had gone off to meet some boy. For some reason Courtney didn't think that was the case, but Bethany was seriously worried that Jetrica might do something stupid just for spite.

She glanced over at Lake and saw how he was calmly and expertly maneuvering his SUV in traffic, which was another reason to wring Jetrica's neck. Courtney hated traffic, and Orlando was full of it. She studied Lake's profile. He was quiet and had been since she'd given him directions to where they were going. It was a section of Orlando people tended to forget and definitely tried to avoid. You say *Orlando,* and people everywhere immediately thought of Disney World. But every city had its less-than-desirable section, and that's where they were headed.

"Do you meet with her here often?"

She glanced up at Lake's face. Traffic was at a standstill. She knew why he was asking. The area where they were headed wasn't one a person should go too often alone. Bethany was working to change that. She had put in for a new apartment through the city's housing department. But things were going slow. "No, usually we meet at her high school, but I've met with her here before."

Traffic was moving again, and his attention was back on his driving. This afforded her the opportunity to study him some more. While at her place, she had deliberately jumped from topic to topic to make sure he didn't feel like he was under interrogation. It worked. He had revealed a lot of personal information about himself. It wasn't hard to conclude that he was a confident man. He loved family. He loved his job and was very successful.

And he was getting to her like nobody's business.

In a way, she should be grateful to Jetrica for causing this stir. At least it had gotten her and Lake out of the house. Had they stayed, they would have sipped more wine, started feeling a little loose, probably too comfy, and ended up doing something they might later have regretted. Umm, then maybe not. She certainly wouldn't feel apologetic if she'd suddenly found herself in his arms with his lips devouring hers again. And then there were his hands, especially those sexy fingers. She could just imagine them touching her all over, especially her breasts. She had a weakness when it came to her breasts. A tongue on them could drive her over the edge in a flash. The problem she'd encountered was that most men didn't enjoy foreplay. They much preferred to cut to the chase, go right between the legs. Another problem was that she was selective with the men she slept with. Usually it was a right they had to earn, work hard to get. Some cut the mustard. Some didn't. She wasn't about to lower her standards by any means, but Lake was a temptation she wasn't sure she could resist for much longer. Just sharing car space with him was causing an ache that was only intensifying with every mile they drove. They were sexually attracted to each other. That was a gimme. And if they continued to see each other, they would share a bed. That was a gimme, as well. What she wasn't clear on was when they would do so. If the throbbing between her legs kept up or got any more intense, it would be sooner than later. That thought didn't bother her. In fact, it sort of calmed her.

"How long have you been Jetrica's mentor?"

Lake's question had cut into her thoughts. Just as well, she decided. She needed to stay focused, and later tonight, if he was willing, they could do something to take off the edge she felt. They had gotten off Interstate 4 and were now headed toward the apartments where Jetrica and her sister lived. "For almost a year," she finally answered. "My best friend Vickie was one of her teachers and saw something in Jetrica. I do, too. She's not really a bad kid. Just one who needs direction and doesn't want to take it from her older sister."

"Like I told you earlier back at your place," Lake said, "I think the kid is mega-talented. If she concentrates on her studies and her art, she'll be able to capitalize on both."

Courtney was glad Lake thought that. "I agree one hundred percent. And as her mentor, I try to get her to see that."

It was dark, and they were headed deeper and deeper into an area most referred to as the projects. She glanced out the window and saw something, someone she immediately recognized. "Wait! Stop! That's her walking over there."

Lake stopped the car and leaned forward to look out the windshield. "Doesn't she know walking alone in the dark is dangerous, especially in this area?"

Courtney heard what he said but was already out of the car. "Jetrica!" she yelled out and sighed in relief when the girl turned around and began walking toward them.

"Ms. Andrews? What are you doing here?"

"Don't ask any questions, Jetrica, just get in the car."

It was easy to tell that Jetrica didn't like her tone. She placed her hands on her hips, pouted her lips, glared, and said, "And if I don't?"

"Don't push your luck with me tonight, kid. Get in!"

Evidently there was something in Courtney's voice that made Jetrica think twice about not following that order. She grudgingly opened the door and climbed in the backseat of Lake's SUV. She saw him and glared at him, as well. Then within seconds, she cocked her head and smiled at him. When Courtney got back in the truck and snapped on her seat belt, Jetrica commented from the backseat. "Hey Ms. A, your boyfriend is kind of cute."

Courtney glanced over at Lake. At the moment she didn't want to imagine what he was thinking. So much for a second date. This would probably be their last. Instead of dwelling on that, she responded to Jetrica's comment, deciding not to correct her thinking that Lake was her boyfriend. "Thanks. Yes, he is cute and is probably pissed that because of you we're missing dinner."

"Nobody tell you to come looking for me. I can take care of myself."

"Walking alone in this area, Jetrica, is a rape just waiting to happen. Use your common sense, will you? What are you trying to prove?" Courtney turned around in her seat to ask.

Jetrica didn't say anything for a moment, but even with the brevity of the light coming into the truck, Courtney could see the hurt and anguish on the young girl's face. "I'm trying to prove that I can take care of myself," she said in a low and broken tone. "Bethany is talking about not going back to school in the fall because of me. Money's tight so she can't register for the college classes she needs, and it's all my fault. I offered to get a job, but she won't let me."

Courtney frowned. "Get a job? Doing what? You're only fourteen."

"Yes, but there has to be something I can do."

Yes, there was plenty she could do, and none of it legal, Courtney thought. Jetrica was a pretty girl. She could just imagine some hard-up-ass man convincing her to make money doing something really stupid like selling her body. Unfortunately, teens who were hard up for money were easily pulled into that sort of lifestyle. "Look, let's get together on Friday and talk about this. Maybe I can talk to my aunt Peggy to see if there's something you can do at the place where she works. Although a lot of the jobs the teens do there is strictly voluntary, they might be able to swing something for you to—"

"I don't want charity!"

Courtney inhaled, downplaying the temptation to wring the girl's neck after all. "Look, Jetrica, don't push it, and don't push me. We meet Friday at school, and you better show up. Understood?"

Jetrica glared at her. "Yeah, whatever." She then eased back onto the soft leather cushions of the backseat. She shot Lake a glance and said, "Hey, mister, your girlfriend can be a real bitch at times." A smile touched Jetrica's face when she added, "But I like her."

16

"Thanks for everything tonight, Lake."

A hour later, and they were back at her home. After returning Jetrica to the apartment she shared with her sister, and after giving her another tongue-lashing for good measure, Courtney had suggested to Lake that they grab some take-out and then go back to her place to eat it. He had agreed.

He also hadn't said much, she noted. She knew that someone like Jetrica was probably a lot to get used to, but he really wouldn't have to get used to her. Courtney had a feeling that after tonight, any thoughts of an involvement with her was long gone from Lake Masters's mind. What woman in her right mind would use her date's time and money—since the cost of gas wasn't cheap these days—to go chasing after some smart-mouth kid? Not many with good common sense. Men were scarce, and those worth keeping were extremely rare. For whatever reason, such a man had been blown her way, and just her luck she had blown him toward someone else.

She took a deep breath and pushed her food container aside. Last week he had fed her from one of the most expensive restaurants in Orlando. Tonight, she had fed him Chinese food from the Fire Dragon. A vast difference. And he had refused to let her pay for it, although she had offered.

"We'll do the movie another time."

She blinked, not sure she'd heard him correctly. He couldn't possibly be telling her he wanted to see her again. "Excuse me?"

He smiled. "Since we didn't make it to the movies tonight, we'll do that the next time."

She was still having a problem keeping up with him, and at the risk of sounding dense she asked, "The next time?"

"Yes, the next time. What are you doing this weekend?"

She shrugged. "Nothing really. I haven't made any plans."

"Then how about Saturday night?"

"Saturday night?"

"Yes." He pushed his own take-out box aside and leaned over the table and stared at her. "Are you all right?"

"Not sure. You want to take me out again?"

He lifted a brow. "Yes, you sound surprised."

"I am. What about tonight?"

He reached across the table, took her hand in his, and lifted it up to his lips and kissed it before saying, "As far as I'm concerned, it's not over yet. There are still a number of possibilities."

"I'm talking about earlier tonight. You had plans to take me out and enjoy a meal and a movie. Not to encounter unnecessary drama."

"You're right there, but it's okay. We did enjoy a meal together, and we're doing the movie on Saturday." The smile on his lips stretched into a sensuous grin. "I told you that I was nice. Now you see that I'm also flexible."

He was definitely that, she immediately thought. But in just the little time she'd gotten to know him, she'd determined that he was kind and understanding, and she appreciated that.

"Before we left to find Jetrica, you and I were in the getting-to-know-each-other-better stage. Is there anything else you want to know about me?" he asked.

Courtney stared at him. The look she saw in his eyes had made her pulse flutter and had her stomach twisting in knots. There was fire in their dark depths, enough to ignite more than a spark within her. The throb between her legs returned with a vengeance.

"Yes, there's something that I would like to know," she said softly, trying to ignore the sensations assailing her.

He nodded. "Go ahead and ask."

"Why aren't you with someone already? I know what you said the other night at dinner about preferring to seek out your own woman. But still."

The smile on his lips curved to intensify all those

sensations she was feeling. "Mainly interest. You're the first woman I've been interested in in a long time."

Her stomach tightened at his words. "And just how interested are you?"

"As interested as a man can get in a woman, Courtney."

She wasn't ready to let it go yet. "That sounds deep and scary."

He lifted a brow. "Why scary?"

"I don't know of any man who's been that interested in me. Ever."

"You're going to discover that I'm different from most men."

She'd already discovered that fact.

"Especially any other man in your past," he continued saying. "I'm in it for the long haul. I've told you that before, and you didn't believe me."

She still didn't and couldn't understand how he could make such a statement. They'd known each other for only a couple of weeks. And although she knew more about him now than she did before, a part of her still felt things were moving too fast. But then another part, the one that controlled that intense throbbing between her legs, was convinced that things weren't moving fast enough.

"What are your plans for us?" she asked curiously. For some reason, she felt he had some. There was no doubt in her mind that Lake Masters was a man with an agenda, and maybe it was time she found out what it was.

He tilted his head as if to study her before saying, "Sorry if I haven't made my plans clear. I thought that first night when I told you that I would be an integral part of your future, and on our first date when I told you I wanted more in my life than a woman to warm my bed, that you understood my intentions. My plans for us are simple. At some point in time, I want marriage. So in other words, Courtney, my plans are to marry you."

Courtney stared at him. *Marry me? Is he joking?* But his expression told her he wasn't. The very idea that this man had thoughts of marrying her sent her pulse skittering.

"I know what you're probably thinking," he said in a husky tone.

"Do you?"

"Yes. You're probably thinking that it won't happen. But only because you haven't been fully convinced that it will."

"Yes, that's about it," she agreed.

"But it will, Courtney, and do you know why?"

She shook her head. "No, I don't have a clue. Why?"

"Because I want you."

He said it as if that settled it. "And what if I don't want you?" She couldn't help asking.

"Then I think I better get busy and change your mind about that. Starting now."

Courtney watched as Lake stood from his seat and came around the table. Dark eyes were latched on to her with heated, blatant intent. She felt herself getting weak in the knees even while sitting down. Physical desire, swamped her already aroused body. There was a deep churning in her stomach, and her nipples, pressed against her blouse, were aching.

When he came to a stop before her and gave her his hand, she didn't hesitate to place hers in his. The moment their hands touched, he went still. She, however, stood up on shaky legs. She swallowed deeply, thinking she needed a drink. But quickly concluded that no, she didn't need a drink. What she needed was Lake.

She wondered if he knew what she wanted, and if so, would he take the initiative to make it happen? She didn't want him to be noble, at least not tonight. He'd said he intended to change her mind about a few things, starting tonight. Why was he hesitating?

As if he read the questions in her eyes, he said in a low tone, "I want you to know what you're getting into, Courtney. Once I make love to you, I'll consider you mine." At the widening of her eyes, he added, "No, and I'm not some sort of obsessive control freak. I'm a man who wants you so much, the intensity of the desire is about to kill me. A man who wants to marry you one day, build a future with you. I know you don't see it now, but you will."

He was right. She didn't see it. Nor did she understand it. How was it possible to spend a third of your life dreaming, looking, and praying for that perfect man, and when she was about to give up hope that such a man truly existed for her, to have him show up in her life—when she wasn't looking—with the belief that he had every right to be there. Usually it took a man a long time to figure out what he needed and wanted in life, and most men put a lasting relationship with a woman at the bottom of the list.

But not Lake Masters.

And she had a feeling from this night forward her life would never be the same.

Lake sensed her acceptance of what was between them, although he was certain she didn't fully understand it. It took him a while to understand it himself. But like he'd told her. In time she would. She still had her doubts, which was understandable. He'd hit her with some heavy stuff. And was about to hit her with more.

She took a breath when he stepped closer to her, and immediately his front connected to hers. There was no way she could not feel his aroused body pressing against her. He'd told her that he wanted her. Now she knew to what extent.

He lifted his hand and released one of her hairpins and then watched her hair drop in soft waves around her shoulders. She didn't say anything, just continued to stare at him. And then he was lowering his head, determined to taste her like she'd probably never been tasted before. Their last kiss wouldn't even come close.

When he got close to her mouth, he angled his head in a way that he knew would give him deeper penetration, a lot more depth. And then without missing a beat, or taking a breath, he sank his mouth onto hers, latched on to it with a greediness that immediately had her moaning in response.

His tongue had never failed him when it came to kissing a woman, and he didn't intend for it to fail him now. It had whip-snapping speed when needed and could be methodically slow at other times. He was using both, rotating, mating, devouring, and igniting sensations of pleasures that passed from her mouth to his.

He deepened the kiss further, at the same time that he drew her closer into his arms, letting the palms of his hand come to rest firmly on that backside that he enjoyed looking at so much. Of her own accord, she tilted her head back, took her tongue, and begin playing cat-and-mouse with his, knowing what would happen if it got caught. He could tell from the last time that she wasn't used to getting such detailed and energetic kisses. But he was glad she was a quick study. She was not only following his lead but was also trying to create a few moves of her own. He would definitely give her an A for effort.

Moments later he drew back. It was either that or he would have gone up in smoke. He breathed in deeply, watched her watch him, saw the unevenness of her breathing, studied her lips and saw they were still moist from their kiss.

Deciding he hadn't gotten enough and wanted another go at it, he held her gaze as he leaned in closer. He took the tip of his tongue and traced it from corner to corner and when her lips parted in a sigh, it was on again. She offered no resistance. In fact, she seemed ready for his intrusion and sank into his embrace like she was made for it. She positioned her head in a way that left him no choice but to deepen the kiss, which he did.

A while later she was the one who pulled back, needing air. But that didn't stop him. His tongue continued to torment her, shifting from her lips to the hollow of her throat, then sideways beneath her ears. She was responsive to his touch, and when she began quivering in his arms, he tightened his hold on her. He inhaled deeply, drawing air into his lungs, and with it came her womanly scent. From that heated aroma, he knew just how aroused she was.

Lake knew if he was going to leave that now was the time to do it. Otherwise, he would have her spread out on the table in no time. He wanted to stay. He wanted to make love to her tonight. But it would have to be her decision. Still keeping a hold on her, he eased back. Their gazes held, and he whispered in a strained voice, "It's getting late. Time for me to go."

At first he wasn't sure if she was going to say anything, or merely show him to the door. But she continued to hold his gaze, and then in a move that almost brought everything male in him to the forefront—if it wasn't there already—she took a step to lean fully against him, fitting their bodies together in a way that made it seem as if the hardness of him was the one thing she sought. Then she lifted her arms and wrapped them around his neck, and in a voice whose subtle warmth was a direct hit on his lips, she whispered, "I want you to stay, Lake."

17

Technically, I've invited him to spend the night, Courtney thought. A first for her. But she'd had no qualms in issuing an invitation to Lake. And from the dark look in his eyes, he intended to accept it.

How could she explain to him that sleeping with a guy she'd met barely two weeks ago wasn't the norm for her? Usually she would slow things down before they got a chance to move too fast. But with Lake, she hadn't been given the chance. She couldn't claim that he had taken her by surprise, not when she'd seen it coming. Her only excuse was that she had been too far gone to deal with him on that level. However, now after a little bit of small talk and a rather laid-back getting-to-know-you session, she felt they were more than ready to get it on.

Before she could think anything further, she was

suddenly scooped up into massive strong arms, and a hungry mouth clamped down on hers. Then the only thoughts that flashed in her mind were that she could get pushed over the edge just by kissing him. He had the ability to awaken every sense she possessed and send enough heat storming through her body to melt her bones.

And then he was lifting his mouth off hers, gazing down at her with an expression that looked as if he was trying to regain his control. She knew the feeling. "Are you sure this is what you want?" he asked in a deep, husky voice that seemed to trace along her nerve endings, causing even more pulsating desire to overtake her.

She knew what he was asking and why. He wanted her to be absolutely sure before they went any further. "Yes. I want you, so that means this *is* what I want." Then she put it back on him when she asked, "Are you sure this is what *you* want?"

"I know it is," he quickly said. And then as if following her lead he said, "I want you, so that means this is what I want." And then he was kissing her all over again, sending her mind and body into a tailspin of desire. She once again became lost in their kiss and responded in ways that only he had the ability to make her do.

This time when he lifted his head, he studied her for a moment before taking his finger and gently tipping her chin up. "Fair warning," he whispered throatily. "I want you *bad*."

She looked at him quizzically, knowing he was trying to tell her something. "Which means?" she asked.

"It won't be over any time soon."

She stared at him, understanding completely. "Will I be able to go to work tomorrow?"

"Probably not."

She drew in a startled breath. "Oh."

"What do you have to say to that, Courtney?"

She couldn't quite bring herself to say anything, but since she knew he was waiting for some sort of response from her, she said, "Thanks for the warning."

With Courtney cradled in his arms, Lake headed for the bedroom. Never had making love to a woman meant so much to him, mainly because he had determined from that first night that she wasn't just any woman. She was his woman, his soul mate, and she had been signed, sealed, and delivered to him in a way he couldn't deny. And now he would connect their lives together in a way neither of them would forget.

When he entered her bedroom, he crossed the room to the bed and lowered her to the mattress and then he took a step back. "The first thing I plan on doing is undressing you," he said in a voice so low, he barely recognized it as his own. She was sitting on her haunches in the middle of the bed, looking as sexy as any woman had a right to look.

"Now it's my time to give *you* fair warning," she said.

He zeroed in on her gaze. "About what?"

"About the fact that when it comes to my breasts, I'm overly sensitive there. If you touch them too much, I'm liable to . . ."

He lifted a dark brow. "To what?"

"Come."

Damn, he wished she hadn't told him that. Didn't she know that sharing information like that with a man was paramount to sealing her fate? If what she'd said was true, then she would be coming a lot, because he definitely planned to touch them. In fact, he planned on doing more than just touch them.

Returning to the bed, he reached out his hand and she took it, and he slowly drew her closer to him. First her blouse and bra had to go, he thought, anxious to get a taste of her bare breasts, as well as to see if her warning was true. Once her breasts were exposed, he leaned over and latched on to a nipple and began sucking on it, liking the taste, the way it fit in his mouth. He could feel her nipple getting firmer in his mouth, and his tongue enjoyed the feel of it doing so. In no time at all, just as she had warned, an explosion hit her and he could feel her intense shivers in the depth of his mouth. But that didn't stop him as he continued to make love to her breasts, sucking on them like a newborn baby.

Afterward, he pulled her trembling body into his arms, propped his chin on the top of her head, thinking what just happened was special. He whispered, "Baby, you can come for me anytime."

He heard her soft chuckle before she said, "I don't have a choice, Lake. It happens."

And he wanted it to happen again, but later. There were other parts of her he wanted to explore and taste. Gripping the soft material of her skirt, he slowly eased it down her legs. Then her sandals went, leaving her clad in only a pair of black panties. He reached out and touched them at the center between her legs. They were drenched with her wetness. That knowledge had a direct hit on his erection. He felt it get even more hard.

Lake held her gaze as he slipped her panties down her legs, inhaling her feminine scent. As soon as she was naked in front of him, his focus and attention went directly to her womanly core, and he thought it had to be the most beautiful site on her body. His erection throbbed at the thought of claiming it. Making love to it. But not before he got a chance to taste it.

He made a guttural sound all the way in the back of his throat when he gently eased her back on the bed and began kissing her mouth. Moments later, he was kissing her all over as he made his way down south. She had closed her eyes, and when she felt the warmth of his breath against her thigh, she opened them back up and gazed down at him.

He felt her body immediately tense, and could tell from her reaction that no man had gone down on her before. That was fine with him. He would enjoy introducing her to this special form of lovemaking. He placed a wet kiss on her stomach, right below her navel, before moving lower. And then he gripped her hips before nudging her thighs apart with his nose.

She whispered his name just seconds before his tongue entered her, and then it began to move with sure, powerful strokes. The more he tasted, the more he wanted and the deeper he delved to be satisfied. He gripped her hips tighter when she began thrashing about in the bed. And nothing, not even the loud scream she suddenly made when her body was hit with another orgasm, was enough to pull him away. It did just the opposite. It urged him on, and he could feel her inner muscles contracting around his tongue. Her hand reached down and clutched at his head, at first in an attempt to pull him away, but then to hold him there.

When the last tremor had passed through her body, he eased off the bed to remove his clothes. It was time to acquaint her body with the only man it would need to know from this day forward.

He wasted no time removing his clothes, knowing her eyes were on him the entire while. Even when he pulled a condom from his wallet and slipped it on, she stared. Especially at that area of his body that showed just how much he wanted her. Seeing was believing.

Naked, he crossed the room back to her, eased onto the bed, and immediately placed his body in position over hers. He met her gaze. Words he'd never said to another woman were there on the tip of his tongue—right along with the taste of her. He wanted to tell her how he was dealing with emotions he'd never dealt with before, but he knew she wouldn't believe him if he did. She was a skeptic, but it was his intent to eventually make a believer out of her.

He reached his hand down and gently stroked the area between her legs. "I'm about to get naughty," he whispered, and before she could make any reply to that, he entered her in a thrust that was so deep, she bucked her body in response.

And then they mated.

She lifted her body to meet his every thrust and he gave it to her, over and over again. He closed his eyes as a raw, urgent need consumed him, and he blotted out everything, except for how she was making him feel. When he was inside her, he felt he was there at the base of her womb, and that's when her muscles would contract and tighten around him to hold him inside her. He would manage to pull out only to thrust back in again.

He set the pace; she followed. Her nails dug deep into his back, but he couldn't think about pain, only pleasure. Tonight he was testing his strength, his endurance. He had no power to fight the next climax that hit them, nor did he want to. And when he felt her legs tighten around his waist, he threw his head back and gave in to a fierce release that shook his insides. A guttural sound escaped from between his clenched teeth, and he knew one thing was definitely for certain. Courtney Andrews was everything he could possibly want in a woman.

Courtney could feel Lake stir beside her while he slept, and she glanced over at him, thinking the man was simply amazing. Even now her body was poised and ready for him to wake up so they could do it all over again. Not that they hadn't done it enough already.

All through the night, he had made love to her. The only time they had taken breaks was when he had gotten up to go into the bathroom to dispense of his condom and put on another one. And then there was that time after their last mating session when he had gone into the bathroom to retrieve a warm washcloth and a bottle of body oil.

In a move she felt was intimate as well as caring, he gently wiped her body down and then applied the oil in certain areas. They were areas he felt he might have scratched with his beard. After giving her such personal care, he had pulled her into his arms while they had both drifted off to sleep.

Now she was awake, and her body was throbbing again for his touch. She shifted in bed and immediately felt the soreness between her legs. No wonder he said she wouldn't be going into work today.

She gazed up at his face. He looked peaceful while he slept. Even relaxed. Definitely sexy. She like the way his beard was neatly trimmed around his mouth, giving him a somewhat roguish appeal.

Her glance went to the window. It was daylight. And she believed it would be a beautiful day. As beautiful as the way Lake had made her feel last night.

"You're awake."

She shifted and tilted her head toward the sound of the voice. She met his gaze and smiled. "Yes, I'm awake."

Concern then appeared in his features. "Are you okay?" He asked the question at the same time she could feel his hand drift over her body, moving lower to the area between her legs. He gently touched her there. She wasn't used to a man touching her so freely but liked the feel of his fingers.

"Yes, I'm okay."

"Good."

And then he leaned over and kissed her, and the moment their lips fused, she felt sensations overtake her. His tongue scorched every part of her mouth it touched, stroked, sucked, and when he shifted, placing one of his thighs over hers, she felt the hardness of his erection pressed against her.

He wanted her again like she wanted him. And this time when he eased his body over hers and entered her, pushed all the way inside, she wrapped her legs around him, needing and wanting everything he was giving. He broke the kiss and glanced down at her and smiled. "I'm about to show you just how naughty I can get."

He withdrew a little and then thrust back in. Over and over again. She whimpered in the back of her throat, an instinctive reaction to what he was doing. "I thought you had shown me. Last night," she managed to say.

"I'm not through yet."

And went on to prove that he wasn't.

He made love to her slow and easy, then fast and hard. Then slow and deep all over again, sending waves and waves of pleasure rushing through her. He seemed to know just what spots to hit, what moves to make, what liberties to take. And she moaned out loud in response. By the time an explosion hit the two of them, she was convinced that a naughty Lake was worth knowing.

Lake stood in Courtney's living room before the painting that Jetrica had done. He was still simply amazed that the smart-mouth kid he'd met last night was capable of creating something like this.

"I don't care how much you like it, you're not getting it."

He turned to the sound of Courtney's voice when she same out of the kitchen and smiled. After making love that morning, they had showered together. Afterward, he had gotten dressed to leave. If he stayed any longer, she would never get the rest she had been deprived of the night before.

She came to stand beside him wearing a robe. His gaze drifted down her body. It didn't help matters knowing she was naked underneath. His groin ached for more of her, and he suddenly felt like one greedy bastard where she was concerned.

He turned and pulled her into his arms, sliding his hands around her waist and leaning down and slowly kissing the corners of her lips. "And there's nothing I can do to convince you otherwise?" he murmured hotly against her lips.

"Umm, you can try."

He chuckled as he took a step back. If he didn't leave now, he would be tempted to do just that. Desire already had him in a tight squeeze, and it wouldn't take much to scoop her up into his arms, carry her in that bedroom, and get downright naughty with her all over again. Then she would have reason to take another day off work.

He glanced at the painting again. He remembered the teen's conversation that night with Courtney as she explained why she had argued with her sister. He turned to Courtney again. "Jetrica wants a job. I might have one for her."

Courtney lifted a brow. "Doing what?"

"This," he said, pointing at the painting. "It would be on a part-time basis, but I think I have a client who'd be willing to commission her to do this. She loves this sort of art. That would help make Jetrica a contributor to the household, and she wouldn't have to miss school. She'll be doing something she enjoys while getting paid for it. And we're talking about good money."

He could tell Courtney's interest was piqued. "How good are we talking?"

Lake shrugged. "Hard to say, but at least five thousand dollars a painting. Possibly more."

"Wow! That could help toward her college fund as well as assist her sister with household expenses. Her major problem is that she thinks she's a burden on Bethany."

"I'll check on it today and try to get things rolling. She's a minor, so there are child-labor laws we have to take into consideration, and of course my client would want to see Jetrica's other work."

Courtney nodded excitedly. "That can be arranged. I'll even consider doing a private showing for Jetrica here if that will help."

"How soon could that be arranged?" Lake asked.

"Just say when." Courtney smiled, then on tiptoe she leaned up and placed a kiss on Lake's lips. "Thanks for being such a nice guy and coming up with such a wonderful idea to help Jetrica. You're simply amazing."

He pulled her closer into his arms and whispered against her lips, "I'm glad you think so. And now for my good-bye kiss." He proceeded to claim her mouth with a greediness that astounded even him.

18

Peggy tugged off her earring before picking up the phone. "Yes, Sharon?"

"You have a call on line three."

"Thanks." Peggy then clicked on the other line. "Yes, this is Peggy Morrison."

"Peg, this is Joe. I need to meet with you today for lunch."

Peggy went still at the sound of her ex-husband's voice. Although they would run into each other on occasion, the last time being at their daughter's wedding almost a month ago, he hadn't called her in over two years, and she couldn't help wondering why he was calling her now. And why did he want to meet with her for lunch?

She regained her composure and decided to ask, "What's this about, Joe?"

"There's something I want to talk to you about."

She lifted a brow. She couldn't imagine what. He now had a life with his child bride and she had hers. As far as she was concerned, they had nothing to discuss. Unless . . .

"Is it about Sonya?"

"No."

"Then what is it?"

"I'd rather we didn't discuss it over the phone."

She sighed deeply. No matter what it was, she rather they didn't discuss it at all. "Look, Joe, I'm extremely busy and—"

"I understand, Peg, but I really do need to talk to you."

"Why?"

"Like I said, I'd rather tell you in person. What I have to tell you is important. I wouldn't have called otherwise."

She could believe that. Now he had her curious. "All right, lunch today will be fine. Where would you like to meet?"

A few moments later, she was hanging up the phone. She considered Joe's request for them to meet for lunch strange and wondered what the meeting would be about. She glanced at the clock on her desk. In three hours, she would find out.

Ron eased out of bed beside his wife. Although the clock on the nightstand indicated it was only five in the morning, he was still operating on Orlando's time. Besides, knowing Ashira was somewhere in the hotel wasn't helping matters. He'd hoped he would have time to check her out last night, but Barbara had been clingy and had wanted his attention since they'd arrived in Hawaii.

He'd almost made it to the bathroom when the sound of his wife's voice stopped him dead in his tracks. "Ron, where are you going this early?"

He pasted a smile on his face and turned around. "Good morning, sweetheart. I'm still operating on Orlando time and can't sleep any longer. I thought I'd get up and go work out. I understand they have a real nice spa and fitness center here."

"All right." Her eyes were heavy-lidded from sleep, but she managed to smile over at him. "Well, after last night, I don't need another workout, so I think I'll sleep in awhile."

He nodded, understanding why. He had satisfied her needs by making love to her last night. "Okay, sweetheart. Do you want me to wake you later, or do you prefer sleeping through breakfast?"

"If you don't mind, I think I'll sleep through breakfast. Then we can go on that island tour the man at the concierge's desk told us about."

"Sounds good."

He smiled, pleased that she was sleeping in this morning. He also had plans to sleep in, but in someone else's bed. He was convinced more than ever that he'd made the right decision in bringing Ashira along.

Half an hour later with a hard-on out of this world, he was standing by the bank of phones near the hotel's business center. The operator was ringing Ashira's room.

"Yes?"

He smiled. She had a sleepy voice, like she had just been awakened. "This is Ron. Where are you?"

"Third floor of the west tower, room 1215."

Good. His and Barbara's hotel room was in the east tower. "Get those legs open. I'll be there in around ten minutes after I grab a cup of coffee from the café."

He hung up the phone thinking that besides the oral sex, another thing he liked was talking dirty to her. He wouldn't dare say some of the things he said to Ashira to Barbara.

He headed in the direction of the café, thinking his wife had generously given him at least two hours with his other woman.

Ashira quickly hung up the phone. Her legs were open and had been all night. She turned to the man in the bed beside her. They had met a couple of days ago when she arrived at the hotel. When he had brought up her luggage to her room, she had homed in on his interest and she had reciprocated with hers. They had been doing the nasty practically ever since.

He got out of bed and quickly slipped on his pants. "That was your sugar daddy?"

She smiled. "Yes, and you need to haul ass. He doesn't like sharing."

The man grinned. For the life of her, she couldn't rightly recall his name. It was either Dean or David, she wasn't sure. The only thing she was sure of was that he knew how to use his pecker and his mouth.

"But you don't have a problem with sharing?" he ask smartly, breaking into her thoughts.

She watched him slip into his shirt, thinking he had nice muscles in his biceps and a tight abdomen. He said he worked out regularly, and she believed him. "No, I don't have a problem with it. His wife's money is what's paying my bills and providing some extra amenities on the side. He can keep her. She's no threat. In fact, I see her as a benefit."

"So you don't want to marry the guy?"

"Hell no!" she said, easing out of bed to take a quick shower. "What's to keep him from screwing around on me like he's screwing around on her? I don't mind being the other woman."

"And what if he decides to dump you for someone else?"

Ashira frowned. She'd never thought of him getting rid of her. Ever. She knew he'd had other women in the past, but she intended to be the final act and had said as much to him more than once. She would fry his ass if he tried dumping her. "He won't," she said with confidence. "I make things too good for him. I deliver whatever he wants and he gives me what I want."

"Hey, sounds like you got a good deal going."

"And I intend to keep it that way. Now leave."

He gave her a smooth smile as he headed for the door. "You haven't seen the last of me, baby."

Ashira laughed when the door closed behind him. She hoped not.

Peggy walked into the Cheesecake Factory and glanced around. Joe had already gotten a table in the back and was waving to get her attention. As she got closer to the table, she saw how hot, tired, and drained he looked. She inwardly smiled. Looked like trying to keep up with Suzette was taking a toll. Served him right.

"Joe," she said when she reached the table and slid into her seat.

"Peggy," he acknowledged. "You look nice."

"Thanks." She could take his compliment with ease because she felt that she really did look nice. There were a few more areas of her body she wanted to firm up, and if she had the money to splurge, she would definitely get a tummy tuck, but considering everything, she thought she looked pretty good. Those routines she and Toni had picked up in their Jazzercise classes were working, and she had changed her eating habits, not that she'd ever been a big eater.

"So what's this about, Joe? Why did you want to meet with me?"

He opened his mouth to say something, and then a waiter appeared to take their order. She didn't want to share a meal with him, so she just ordered coffee. So did he.

When the waiter walked off, Peggy focused her attention back on Joe. "You were saying?"

He sighed deeply and reclined back in his chair. He met her gaze and said, "Suzette's pregnant, and I wanted you to hear it from me."

At first Peggy sat stunned. Then she had to force herself not to grate her teeth. She had to remember that Joe meant nothing to her anymore. Whatever they had shared was in the past. The only thing they shared now was Sonya, and later if Sonya had kids, they would share grandkids. He had destroyed all her dreams; he had broken all the vows he'd made on their wedding day. But she was over that now. It was water under the bridge where she was concerned. She had finally moved on with her life and was glad he and Suzette seemed to be moving on with theirs.

She inhaled deeply. He was nervously watching her, waiting for her reaction to his news. She wouldn't give him the satisfaction of thinking that his starting fatherhood all over again mattered to her.

Although she had to force the words from her mouth, she said them nonetheless. "Congratulations, Joe, that's wonderful. I'm sure Suzette is excited. Have you told Sonya that she should be expecting a brother or sister soon?"

He nervously picked up his eating utensils as if checking the shine. He couldn't look at her, she noticed. "No, I haven't talked to her since she returned from her honeymoon. Suzette said Sonya gave a party the other weekend but we weren't invited."

Peggy rolled her eyes. *And no doubt Suzette made a big friggin' dramatic production out of it.* "Sonya didn't give the party, Joe. Carla did to welcome Sonya and Mike back from their honeymoon. Considering Suzette's behavior whenever she is invited to functions, I guess the decision was made to leave the two of you off the guest list."

He shrugged his shoulders. "She's young."

Peggy chuckled. "I'm the last person you have to remind of your child bride."

He seemed grateful when the waiter returned with their coffee. She watched over her cup as he took his own sip. He then put the cup down and looked over at her. He inhaled and then said, "There's something else I need to discuss with you."

"What?"

"Your alimony payments."

She frowned. "What about them?"

"I just thought you should know that I'll be seeing my attorney about getting them stopped. It's not like you need the money. And you are working now."

Peggy leaned back in her chair when she felt dangerously close to reaching out and slapping him. What he wasn't saying was that he could no longer afford to pay her alimony payments and take care of his expensive wife. No doubt Suzette had convinced him that with the baby on the way, they needed all the money they could get. And what was so sad was that the business Joe owned was successful and was bringing in good money, but Suzette was spending it as fast as he made it. As far as she was concerned, that was his problem and not hers.

"Regardless of whether I need the money or not, I deserve it. Need I remind you whose money it was that got you started in your business and who helped bring you in the customers? Then there's that point about us being married for over thirty years and during that time you never wanted me to work or have my own career."

She leaned in closer. "Don't waste your money on an attorney, Joe. Start buying diapers instead. Go back and tell your wife that you asked and I said no, I won't give up my alimony. In fact," she said, deciding to be a real bitch about it, "if you get an attorney, I'll do the same and take you back to court for an increase."

She got supreme satisfaction with the anger she saw in his face. She stood, deciding it was time for her to leave since they had nothing else to say to each other. "And I prefer that you not call me. You've made your bed, so wallow in it."

She then turned and walked out. It was only when she got to her car that she realized she hadn't paid her check. She shrugged, so what if Joe got stiffed with a couple of dollars for her coffee. She really didn't give a shit.

"May I help you?"

Barbara smiled at the salesclerk. "No, I think I'll just browse a bit."

"All right. If I can be of any assistance, just let me know."

"Okay."

Barbara took a deep breath as she moved around in the hotel gift shop. This one was a specialty store that mainly sold lingerie of the risqué kind. She almost blushed while checking out a few pieces. All were perfect for a night of seduction.

They had been in Hawaii a week already and she still hadn't made any new moves on Ron because when she thought of doing so she got cold feet. Would he really want her to behave in such a manner in the bedroom?

"Now that, in my opinion, is one red-hot piece."

Barbara turned to find a woman standing beside her, looking at the same outfit that she'd been looking at. The woman was a few years older than Barbara—possibly as many as five or six—but judging from the outfit the woman was wearing, a short clingy dress, Barbara quickly saw that she kept herself in great shape. Barbara thought the woman was rather attractive, with her curly red hair and green eyes.

Barbara looked from the woman back to the outfit. "Yes, but I can't imagine wearing it."

"I can. James would love it on me. We've been married forty years. The kids are all grown so it's just the two of us, and we've reverted back to the days before kids, when we spent most of our time in the bedroom."

Barbara couldn't believe the woman was sharing such information with a total stranger. But then she decided to say, "My husband and I have been married thirty years and we have a daughter. Ron and I are here for a second honeymoon. One that's long overdue."

The woman nodded as if she understood. She then leaned over and whispered, "Take it from me. When it comes to your man, you have to work hard and play harder. But if he's a good man then it's all worth it. Romance is the key to a successful marriage." She laughed. "Before making love on any given day or night, I ask

James who he wants—his wife or his girlfriend because I can be both. I *am* both."

Barbara laughed. She liked that, and more than anything she admired the woman's confident attitude. It was apparent she had recognized long ago how to keep her man happy and satisfied and had no qualms about doing whatever it took.

Less than thirty minutes later, Barbara left the shop with an outfit she'd first thought was too daring, but now she knew it would be perfect. She would time things just so and would know when the time was right to spring it on Ron.

She smiled. She couldn't wait.

19

"So, what's going on with you?"

Courtney met Sonya's gaze over her glass. Her cousin had surprised her and shown up on her doorstep around lunchtime. The two of them were sitting in the kitchen sharing the sandwiches and lemonade she had made. "Umm, nothing's going on. Why do you ask?"

"I ran into Devin at the mall earlier, and he said you had an appointment with him this morning about some new drug but had contacted his office manager to reschedule. He thought you were under the weather or something."

Courtney shrugged. "You know how it is sometimes. I needed a day to unwind, relax." *Work the soreness out of my body*. "So, how's married life?" she decided to ask, not sure she was ready to share with Sonya how she had met a guy a couple of weeks ago and had slept with him already. Not that Sonya would think it was a big deal, since she'd admitted to engaging in a few one-night stands in her days before Mike.

A huge smile lit up Sonya's face when she said, "Married life is wonderful. Mike is wonderful. Sex continues to be great. I'm truly a happy woman."

Courtney could tell. It was all over her. She wore exuberance well.

"We didn't get a chance to chat long at the party the other night, so I thought I'd drop by, especially when Devin said he thought you were sick," Sonya continued. "How are things going with the little black book I gave you? Have you contacted anyone in it yet?"

Courtney shrugged her shoulders again. "Umm, yes, a few."

Sonya's eyes perked up. "And are you having fun?"

"Not exactly since I decided they weren't my type," she said, deciding not to go into any details about her date with the three.

A surprised look appeared on Sonya's face. "Really? What about—?"

At that moment the phone rang, and hoping it was Lake, Courtney quickly got up from her chair. "Excuse me, I'm expecting a call." Instead of picking up the phone extension in the kitchen, she walked into the living room.

"Yes?"

"I was thinking about you."

Her stomach spiked at the sound of the sexy voice in her ear, and as if on cue, the area between her legs—still slightly sore—began throbbing. “I was thinking about you, too.”

In truth, he had been in her thoughts constantly since the time he had walked out the door. Instead of leaving when he’d planned, after pulling her into his arms to kiss her good-bye, they had ended up going back into the bedroom and making love again.

“How do you feel?”

She smiled, knowing why he was asking. Having nonstop sex could take a toll on your body. “I’ll survive.”

“I’m going to make sure that you do. What are your plans for later?”

She inhaled. Now was the time to tell him that she thought they were moving too fast. She needed to pull back while she was capable of thinking with a clear head. He was convinced that he was her soul mate, but she wasn’t convinced of anything yet—other than his skill in bedroom. The man had moves that should be patented. Besides, it was important to her that they continue to get to know each other. There was still a lot about him she didn’t know.

“Courtney?”

“I don’t have any plans. What about you?”

“Umm, I thought maybe you’d like to do the movie we missed last night.”

“I’d better not, since I skipped work and didn’t see a couple of doctors today. I need to stay in and get caught up on a few things.”

“Would you like company later?”

She wondered if he was hinting at another sleepover. “Sure.”

"All right. I'll call you before I come to make sure nothing has changed."

She lifted a brow. "Nothing like what?"

"You might have changed your mind about wanting company later."

If he was the company, she doubted it. But instead she said, "Okay."

She hung up the phone, sighed deeply, and went back to the kitchen. Sonya turned when she entered and gave her a funny look. "What?" Courtney asked.

Sonya stood to cross the room and put her plate and glass in the sink. "You tell me, girlfriend. You could have easily answered the phone in here, so what's going on? You have a secret lover or something?"

Courtney couldn't help but chuckle. Leave it to Sonya to be perceptive where her love life was concerned. "Not really, but I have met someone. In fact, we met at your party, the one Carla gave you a few weeks ago."

Sonya turned and lifted an arched brow. "Umm, then he should be someone I know."

"He is."

Sonya crossed her arms over her chest and tilted her head expectantly. "Well, who is he?"

Courtney sighed and decided to spit it out. Sonya would bug her to death until she did anyway. "Lake Masters."

The look on Sonya's face, Courtney thought, was priceless. "You're seeing Lake Masters?" Sonya asked, almost in disbelief.

Now it was Courtney who raised an arched brow. "Yes. Is that good or bad?"

Sonya threw her head back and laughed. "Definitely good, since he's a prime catch. And the two of you met at my party?"

"Yes."

"I think that's awesome."

Courtney smiled. "Evidently you also think he's a nice guy."

"Gosh, yes. All the Masters men are nice. You know Grey, and I think you've met Quinn, the one who's married to Alexia Bennett-Masters. Then there's Shane, who you haven't met. He the oldest and recently got married last year to a woman named Faith. I hear it's an understanding in the Masters family that Lake is the lone wolf. When it comes to women, he prefers doing his own hunting."

Courtney nodded. Although Lake had said it differently, basically it had equated to the same thing.

"Do you know what this means?" Sonya asked her.

Other than the fact I think he's great in bed? Courtney thought to herself. "No, what does it mean?" she asked, opening the refrigerator to take out a bottle of water.

"It means that you're it."

She slid a sideways glance over at Sonya. "What do you mean that I'm it?"

"If Lake checked you out at the party, and the two of you have been an item since, then that means he's really serious about you."

He had said as much, but Courtney still had to be convinced. "We'll see."

Sonya's lips quirked in a grin. "No, I won't see, but trust me, you will."

"Meaning?"

"Lake is also known as someone who gets whatever he wants."

Courtney nodded. She could believe that, since he certainly got her last night, in every position she could think of. And there was no doubt in her mind that he had wanted her. The size of his erection every time they made love could attest to that. However, the big question was whether his belief that they had a future was the real deal. Would he continue to want her, or would he eventually lose interest and become a rolling stone like her dad?

"Like I said, Sonya, we will see."

Sonya grinned. "And like I said, Courtney. I won't, but you will."

Peggy watched an angry Toni pace around her office and tried to recall the last time she'd seen her friend so upset. Then she remembered. It was the time back in high school when another student had called Peggy an Oreo for being Toni's friend and hanging out with her. Toni hadn't taken that remark too kindly then, and she wasn't taking what Peggy had shared regarding her lunch date with Joe too kindly now.

Toni finally stopped pacing and sharply turned around, sending a mass of blond hair swirling around her face and shoulders. "You know I liked Joe in the beginning. He was real nice at your wedding, and the four of us—me, you, Joe, and John—all became close buddies and did a lot of weekend stuff together. I thought he'd lost his mind when he left you for another woman but chalked it up to a case of testosterone gone berserk. But for him to suggest that you stop receiving alimony payments has made me thoroughly convinced the man is nothing but an educated, hen-pecked asshole of the third degree."

Peggy wanted to burst out and laugh but didn't think Toni would appreciate her amusement in her present mood. "Hey, don't worry about it, because I'm not," she said to calm Toni down.

Toni studied her for a moment. "Not even the baby thing."

Peggy shrugged. "Suzette has to hold on to Joe's money some way. Even if they decided to split up later, he'll have a kid to take care of for eighteen years. I definitely don't see retirement in his future any time soon. He'll still be working when he's past eighty."

"Serves him right. Does Sonya know?"

Peggy shook her head. "Not yet. I left it up to him to tell her. She would have called if he had."

Toni crossed the room to sit on the edge of Peggy's desk. Her frown was then replaced with a smile. "Look, the reason I came in was to tell you that I got a call from Willie Baker."

At the mention of the man's name, Peggy felt her stomach beginning to do somersaults. "And?"

"And he's coming back to Orlando next weekend and wants to see if we're free to do the Disney World thing then."

Peggy tried downplaying her delight at the thought of

seeing him again. She simply smiled at Toni and said calmly, "Okay."

Toni glared at her. "Will you get down from jumping all over the desk?"

Peggy rolled her eyes. "What do you want from me?"

"A little excitement wouldn't hurt. The man has the hots for you."

Peggy threw her head back and laughed. "Toni, take a look. I'm a fifty-seven-year-old woman. I figure Willie Baker is fifty-nine. We're both too old to have the hots for anything."

"Wanna bet. John still gets the hots for me. The man has the hots for you, just like I know you have the hots for him, although you're trying not to let it show. But I'm not stupid."

Peggy sighed. No,Toni wasn't stupid. And Toni was also right in thinking that she had the hots for Willie. "So, what if I do have the hots for him? What do you suggest I do?"

She could see the twinkle that came in Toni's gaze. "Let's go shopping this weekend, and I'll tell you just what you need to do."

Peggy shook her head. That's what she was afraid of.

Suzette was pitching a fit. "What do you mean she didn't agree to stop her alimony payments!"

"I did as you suggested and told her I would be seeing an attorney but that didn't move her one bit," Joe said, grabbing the remote off the table. "In fact," he added, "I think it pissed her off."

"Who cares?" Suzette all but yelled. "We need more money. I want my baby to have the best of everything. Peggy has no right to expect you to continue to pay her money every month just because she was your wife for all those years."

This was when Joe knew to tune Suzette out. She didn't like his ex-wife or his daughter. Evidently, she thought they were a threat to her, which he constantly tried assuring her they weren't. Occasionally she would get on a roll, and he refused to listen. For once he would like to come home from the office and get some peace and quiet instead of a lot of bitching.

"Joe? Are you listening?"

He glanced over at her. "Yes, I'm listening," he lied.

"Then do something."

He rolled his eyes. "Suzette, we better leave well enough alone. No judge in this state is going to let me drop Peggy's alimony payments, and if we piss her off, she might take me back to court for an increase. She even hinted at such."

Anger flared in Suzette's face even more. "She can't do that!"

"Evidently, you don't know the law, because she can, so let it go."

"What about all that baby furniture I ordered yesterday?"

That got Joe's attention. "I thought I asked you not to buy anything else without my approval. Are you trying to put us in the poorhouse?"

She glared at him. "Of course not. You said for me not

to buy anything. I assumed you meant for myself. The furniture I bought is for the baby."

He shook his head. She had found out about her pregnancy just a week ago and was buying baby furniture already? Angrily, he stood. "You knew what I meant and deliberately did what I asked you not to do," he said, raising his voice.

"Joe, I'm getting upset, and you know what the doctor said about me getting upset."

He placed his hands on his hips. "No, I know what you *claimed* the doctor said about you getting upset."

"Are you saying you don't believe me?"

Joe suddenly decided he wanted to be any place other than here. "Look, I'm going out."

"Where?"

"Out." And he kept walking, even though she was engaging in one hell of a hissy fit behind him.

20

Courtney stared at her laptop, trying to think, but it was difficult given that Lake was on his way over. He had called earlier to verify that she still wouldn't mind him dropping by, and she'd told him she was fine with it. Bottom line, she had missed him today and wanted to see him. She sighed, knowing such a thing made her seem like a needy child. But that wasn't it. There was nothing about her need for Lake Masters that was childlike. She was definitely feeling the emotions—sexual and otherwise—of a grown woman.

She stood and glanced down at herself. The moment he had called, she showered and changed into a sundress. She figured the outfit she had on earlier hadn't been sexy enough, and whenever Lake saw her, she wanted him to think sexy. What Sonya had said earlier that day was true. He was a prime catch, and for some reason he was convinced—as Sonya also stated—that she was the one.

She nibbled nervously on her bottom lip when she heard the sound of his truck outside. Was she really the one, or did he just think so for the time being? She truly wished these insecurities would go away. But then, what did she expect when constantly dating men who were losers? And when she finally met one who was everything in a man she'd ever dreamed about, it was hard to accept. She knew it simply wasn't rational to feel the way she did. Where most women would count such a man coming into their lives as a blessing and move on with it, she couldn't. She had to get over this ingrained fear that all men were like her father and her uncle Joe. Doing so was hard because those were the men she'd been around the most while growing up, and both had greatly disappointed her.

Her pulse jumped at the sound of the doorbell, and she took a deep breath to calm her jittery nerves. What do you say to a man whom you had spent a night making love with nonstop? How did you react? Was she supposed to invite him to stay again or chalk it up as a one-time deal? Dang, where was Sonya when she needed her? Knowing Sonya, she was probably somewhere making out with Mike.

"Who is it?" she asked when she reached the door.

"Lake."

Taking one last huge gulp of breath, she slowly opened the door. When she saw him, she opened her mouth to say something and then said nothing. No words seemed capable of forming in her mouth. The light from the streetlamp outlined his features. They were features she'd seen before, up-close and personal, but there was something about him standing there on her doorstep, looking as sexy-as-he-wanna-be that started her blood stirring in a way that couldn't be normal. The raw physical force of him was impacting her senses. The one word that seemed to readily come to mind whenever she saw him was *sexy*.

Since it seemed she couldn't say anything, he did. "Hello, Courtney."

The deep voice stirred sensations within her some more, and then there was the way he was looking at her, like he could eat her alive. Hell, when she thought of all the oral sex he'd introduced her to last night, he'd almost done that very thing.

Knowing he couldn't stand outside on her doorstep forever while she pulled herself together, she forced herself to respond to his greeting. "Hello, Lake. Won't you come in?"

What she wanted to ask was, *Won't you come in and make love to me again with the same intensity that you did last night? Who cares if I probably won't be able to walk in the morning and will have to take another day off work?*

But she didn't ask. She merely took a couple of steps back when he came in taking a couple steps forward, which put them standing directly in front of each other, face to face, body to body, heat to heat.

Trying to ignore the breathless fluttering taking place inside her stomach, she studied his features, mainly his lips. They were perfectly shaped and extraordinary skilled.

"You're still working," he said in a throaty voice when he glanced across the room and saw her laptop on the sofa.

"Yes, but I'm almost finished. Would you like anything while you wait?" It was only after she said the words that it occurred to her that she didn't particularly like the way they sounded. What was he supposed to be waiting on? It was as if he was only there for one thing. Was he?

"No, I'm fine. Besides, I brought my own work with me," he said, pulling a BlackBerry out of his pocket. "No rush."

"All right, make yourself at home, and if you change your mind and do decide you want something, my refrigerator is stocked and I also have beer, wine, sodas, water—"

"I'm fine, honestly."

He didn't have to convince her of that. All she had to do was look at his body, remember that same body on top of her, inside her, sleeping beside her . . .

"Okay." She then made a move to take a step back, but he caught her wrist. She glanced up at him and he smiled. That smile sent a quiver rushing through her.

"At least I'll be fine once I do this," he said in a husky voice.

And then he was pulling her closer to his hard, masculine chest to kiss her in a way she was convinced that only he knew how to do. Tongues mated, dueled, tangled. Slow—methodically slow. Deep—unerringly deep. Thorough—imploringly so. And as absolute as you could get. She experienced it all. Then there was his taste that she was getting used to. A taste she was beginning to crave.

He pulled back and sucked in a deep breath. She did

the same. She watched as he licked his lips as if he hadn't gotten enough of her mouth. And then he said, "I think you need to get back to work. Just pretend I'm not here."

Fat chance! That wasn't possible when his very presence at any given time demanded attention. "I'll try," she said, smiling up at him before turning and walking on wobbly knees across the room back to the sofa to her laptop.

Out of the corner of her eye, she saw him move toward the breakfast bar that separated the kitchen from her dining room. She tried not to watch as he eased onto a barstool how his firm thighs in a pair of jeans literally stretched the leather cushion.

She breathed in deeply, struggled to cope, fought to resist temptation as she turned her attention back to her laptop. The first three months after a new drug hit the market were crucial, and she needed to know everything there was about it to educate her doctors. With that thought in mind, she tried concentrating on the information on the computer screen.

Unfortunately, she found the task wasn't easy.

Lake clicked off his BlackBerry. It always amazed him how much business he could take care of on the wireless instrument. He had discovered it had the ability to maximize his time and maintained relationships that were vital to his business.

He then thought of something—more specifically, someone—that he considered vital to his piece of mind.

That flash of insight made him look across the room at Courtney. She was busy studying whatever was on her laptop screen and had been doing so for the past hour. As he'd told her when he had arrived, he didn't want to take her away from her work. He would just wait.

Even if the wait was killing him.

Suddenly he felt guilty when he thought of how much lovemaking they had done the night before. He could just imagine how her body must have felt this morning. The soreness had to have been almost unbearable. In a way, he'd known it would be, which was the reason he had suggested she take the day off work. He, of all people, was aware of the intensity of his lovemaking and had figured with her it would be doubly so. She was his, and he had wanted to stamp his brand all over her. And he had. He doubted there was a spot on Courtney Andrews's body that he hadn't touched or tasted. The memory made him hard, and he shifted in his seat. The sound caught her attention, and she glanced over at him. And stared.

Something in the air surrounding them changed. There was this crackle of sexual awareness, a charge of heated desire that encased them. She tilted her head, as if trying to make sense of it, and it was on the tip of his tongue to tell her not to waste her time. Nothing made sense other than the fact they wanted each other. As far as he was concerned, there was nothing more certain than that.

He knew that even after last night she was still having a hard time accepting it, was putting roadblocks in the way, figured things were moving too fast for her. He understood. He even sympathized with her to a degree. But he refused to let up. Courtney wouldn't know what hit her until it was too late. He was a man with a plan, and his plan was to marry her before the end of the year.

As they continued to watch each other, she slowly closed her laptop and placed it aside. Then she eased off the sofa and stretched, and he felt a deep, intense stirring in his body. The woman had luscious curves, nice breasts, and legs that could wrap around him and hold him tight inside her body.

He forced down the urge to cross the room and take her then and there. The guilt set back in, and he knew he couldn't make her any more sore than she already was. Her body needed a night of reprieve. So what he intended to do was kiss the soreness away. He practically licked his lips at the very thought.

He blinked when he saw her move, and then she was crossing the room to him. He met her halfway. They stopped right in front of each other, and she leaned into him, twined her arms around his neck, stretched up against him, and then whispered against his lips, "Sorry to have kept you waiting."

And then she was giving him a kiss, taking her tongue and tracing the lines of his lips. On his sharp intake of breath, she eased her tongue inside his mouth, caught hold of his, and began sucking on it in such a decadent manner, it nearly brought him to his knees. But he fought to be in charge, and when he couldn't take any more, he took control of the kiss. And the night. Tonight belonged to her. His pleasure would come in pleasuring her.

Besides, last night she had given him enough enjoyment and satisfaction to last a lifetime.

He pulled back slightly from her mouth and whispered against moist lips. "You're still sore?"

The look in her eyes told him she wasn't comfortable discussing such a personal thing to him. But he figured that soon enough she would discover they had no secrets and could talk about anything. Intimate or otherwise. When she didn't immediately respond, he asked her again, "Are you still sore?"

Seeing he wouldn't let up until he got an answer, she said, "A little." She then arched her body against him, as if trying to take his mind off the physical state of her body. "No big deal."

That's where she was wrong. To him it was a big deal. "I'm going to take the soreness away, sweetheart," he bent his head to whisper in her ear.

She leaned back and looked at him. "How?"

"By kissing it away."

Her eyes widened slightly when it became apparent just what he meant. "You're . . ."

She couldn't complete what she was about to say, apparently not sure she could say it. He decided to finish it for her. "I am going to . . ." And he leaned even closer to her and whispered in a low voice, but clear enough to be heard, "Yes, I am going to make love to you with my mouth, Courtney."

Courtney stared at Lake. Not knowing just what to say. He had made love to her with his mouth last night, while alternating with his manhood for deep penetration. So did that mean he wouldn't be going inside her, at least not with his aroused body part? And it was aroused—she could feel the hardness pressed against her.

He evidently suspected her concern and said, "You don't need that tonight."

A frown touched the corners of her lips. Who was he to say what she needed?

It was obvious that he detected her rebellion. He asked, "Do you want to have to take another day off work?"

Her frown deepened. "No. Are you trying to tell me that each and every time, after a night of lovemaking with you, that I won't be able to go to work the next day?"

"Possibly. Depending how intense it is, and right now I can't see it being anything other than that. I want you with a passion, but I plan to control it tonight because I know your body doesn't need it again so soon."

She glared at him. "And what if I don't agree."

"Doesn't matter."

She didn't like the sound of that. But she refused to stand there and argue with him. She would let him think he was in complete control, but before the night was over, she would show him that she had a problem when it came to being stubborn. It was a flaw he would have to get used to if he decided to stick around.

She took a step closer to him, felt his hardness, and knew before the night was over she would have it. "I'm not going to argue with you, Lake."

"Then don't. Let's do this instead."

And then he was kissing her with an intensity that

robbed her every thought. She felt his hands all over her as he tried relieving her of her sundress. He broke the kiss momentarily to ease the garment over her head, leaving her clad in nothing but her panties, since she hadn't been wearing a bra. She saw where his gaze immediately went, saw the way he licked his lips, and decided she should remind him again. "You know what's going to happen if you go there."

She watched the smile that spread across his lips. "Yes, I know." And then before she could catch her next breath, he bent his head and went there, taking one hardened nipple into his mouth. She squeezed her eyes shut as sensations speared through her, straight to the area between her legs. Her body tightened in sensuous need as he tightened his mouth on her breast and began sucking, while using the tip of his tongue to massage. If that wasn't bad enough, she suddenly felt him easing his fingers inside her panties and going straight to her womanly core. She was already wet, and her thighs immediately parted with his touch. And then, while his mouth moved to latch on to her other breast, his fingers went to work, penetrating deeper, as they made their way inside her.

Her climax came easy. It was so mind-twistingly complete, she could have died right there. She couldn't stop the whimpers of pleasure that seemed to flow nonstop from her mouth, and it was taking all she had to catch her breath. Then she felt herself being lifted in strong arms and placed on the barstool. He raised her hips just enough to remove her panties, and then he knelt down in front of her and widened her legs open. Before she could regain her senses, he leaned forward at the same time he gripped her hips to bring her to the warmth of his waiting mouth.

She let out a scream of pleasure the moment his tongue touched her. His tongue was urgent, demanding, and greedy, and she couldn't do anything but press her back against the soft leather cushion of the stool while he blew her mind.

Last night he had introduced her to oral sex, but if he kept this up, she would become addicted. She felt her body shattering into a million pieces when she exploded in an orgasm of gigantic proportions, flying her to the stars. She began whimpering again, calling his name, but he continued to hold her to his mouth, refusing to let go, tightening his grip on her hips even more.

It was only after the last tremor left her body, that he finally released her. He leaned over and kissed her, and she tasted herself on his lips. And she knew that if she didn't do something, he would leave her alone tonight without getting his own pleasure.

So she decided to take matters into her own hands. Literally.

While she had him so wrapped up in their kiss, she extended her hand toward the zipper of his jeans and slowly slid it down. He wasn't aware of what she was doing until her hand had made its way inside his boxers and had clamped hold of him. He immediately broke off the kiss and tried pulling away, but she held tight.

"No, Lake, it's my turn. Please. Let me taste you the way you've tasted me."

Her request seemed to overwhelm him. She watched his expression. He was trying to refocus, regain control, but no doubt it was hard with the firm grip she had on his erection. Then she took the tip of her finger and began lightly tracing across the softer skin, and in a voice lower still, she said, "Please. I want to do this."

Their gazes locked. She knew the exact moment he made up his mind to relent, surrender, and admit defeat. He took a step back, and she eased to her feet to stand in front of him. He began undoing his belt, but she reached out and stopped him, placing her hand over his. "No, I want to do it all, Lake."

He studied her gaze before letting his arms go limp at his sides. She decided she wanted to taste him all over, which meant removing all his clothes and not just his jeans, so she proceeded to do so. This was her first time undressing a man, and she was enjoying it immensely—especially when it was a body whose very exposure sent wantonness all through her.

She eased his shirt from him and then took off his socks, shoes, pants, and boxers with his help. When he stood before her completely nude, she felt a sensual longing that tried taking over the very essence of her being. And then she began taking care of business. Starting with the corner of his lips, she took the tip of her tongue and grazed a heated trail across his chin, down the hollow of his neck, then lower to concentrate on the two buds on his chest. She heard the sound of his breathing and the sharp intake of his breath, as her mouth began moving even lower, easing down on her knees to do so.

She discovered she really liked his navel and placed plenty of kisses there. And his hipbone, as well. And when she came face-to-face with his erection, stared straight at it, saw it hard, solid as a rock, bigger than life, she gripped it in her hand and brought it to her mouth, slowly licking it all over before inserting it into her mouth like a lollipop she had to have. And she discovered she was enjoying it just as much.

She felt his fingers when they reached down and took hold of her hair, at first she thought to pull her away, and then she knew it was to keep her there. But he didn't have to worry; she wasn't going anywhere. She knew the moment he was about to come and prepared herself for it, but he had other ideas.

"No more," he said throatily before reaching down and hauling her to her feet.

She let her thighs brush his and brought her naked body against him, pressing her womanly core against his still-hard erection. While she knew he was fighting for control, denying himself the one thing she wanted to give him, she leaned over and whispered, "Put it inside of me, Lake. I need it."

He met her gaze. Stared at her as if he wasn't sure to believe her. But evidently something in her eyes convinced him. However, deciding that he wasn't responding quickly enough to suit her, she shifted their bodies to literally push him back onto the barstool, and then she proceeded to straddle him. She lowered her body downward onto his erection, and since there was no other way for it to go other than up, she basically forced him to enter her.

He went completely still. Held his body immobile. But she kept going, pushing further downward while at the same time wrapping her legs around him to keep him deeply embedded within her. She liked the feel of his throbbing erection inside her body. It was an erection that she had gotten primed and ready with her mouth.

Feeling smug and victorious, she tilted her head back and looked at him, daring him to ask her to get off him. He still hadn't moved, although she felt his hands go to the back of her spread thighs to give more support. He met her haughty gaze and said in a low but clear voice, "Forgot something, didn't you?"

She immediately racked her brain, trying to figure out what. And when she felt him growing even bigger inside her, she remembered. A condom.

Ooops. She closed her eyes. If he were to pull out of her now, she would die. For a moment she thought that she did feel him easing out, but then as if he'd made his mind up about something, he clutched her thighs tighter and pushed back in, going even deeper, all the way to the hilt.

She opened her eyes to find him staring intently at her. Then he said, "You know what could happen, don't you?"

Unable to speak, she nodded.

"I'm safe. I get a physical every year," he then offered.

She nodded again, and then somehow managed to say, "So do I."

It was his time to nod. "The only other thing we need to worry about is a baby," he said huskily. "I never got around to asking if you wanted children."

"Yes." She raised a brow. "Do you?"

His lips curved into a smile. "Yes. Ours."

There was no doubt in her mind that he felt the tremor that touched her body with his words. What he'd done was reiterated what he'd been trying to get her to accept all along. And by consenting to take the risk of becoming the father of her child, he was acknowledging what he'd said the first night they had met—that he was an intricate part of her future.

Courtney became overwhelmed at the possibility that Sonya was right. The hunter had captured the prey he wanted. Just knowing she was the one pushed her entire body into a state of arousal. Instead of saying anything, she leaned over and captured his lips, letting her actions express what she couldn't for the moment say in words.

He began moving inside her the moment her tongue began dueling with his. Their lovemaking tonight was different. No restrictions were in place. They were accepting any risks.

She broke off the kiss and threw her head back when he began thrusting inside her with whipcord speed, relentless perseverance, and enduring passion. The sensation of being skin to skin, flesh to flesh with him made her crave his aroused flesh even more.

And then she felt him buck beneath her, felt the firm grip of his hands on her thighs tighten even more, and then he spread her legs wider as he thrust upward one last time before she felt him exploding inside her, shooting his release.

The sensations ignited her own sensuous eruption, and

she tightened her legs around him and held on. Never had she felt such an urgent need for what a man had to give her. Never had she wanted it so badly. She felt cherished when he wrapped her into his arms, pulled her closer, kept their bodies locked together until completion.

But he still didn't release her. Nor did she release him. She needed this time. This period of understanding and realization to think. And when he leaned up and captured her lips with his, she ceased thinking at all.

21

It was daybreak when Courtney awakened to find Lake was no longer in bed with her. But he had left a note on the pillow beside her. She shifted positions to sit up to read what he had written.

> *Sweetheart,*
>
> *I don't know your schedule today, but if possible I'd like to have lunch with you. Call me and let me know if that's a possibility.*
>
> *Lake*

She smiled and held the note close to her heart. He had referred to her as *sweetheart*. Closing her eyes, she lay back in the bed as memories of last night ran through her mind. After making love on the barstool of all places, he had gathered her into his arms, and they had gotten into her bed, where he had held her the entire night. At some point, she had awakened and had tried to persuade him to make love to her again, but he had refused, reminding her that he wouldn't have done so earlier if she hadn't forced the issue.

She grinned proudly. That would teach him to think twice about holding out on her. He wasn't the only one who could go after what he wanted.

Courtney opened her eyes and glanced over at the clock. It was time to get ready for work. She had a full day of appointments with her doctors, but would definitely make time to join Lake for lunch. Deciding she needed to get moving, she slid out of bed and went into the bathroom.

An hour later, she was fully dressed and ready to grab her briefcase to head out the door when the phone rang. Thinking it could be Lake, she quickly picked it up. "Yes?"

"Courtney? I just wanted to check to see how you're doing."

She smiled as she dropped down on the sofa. "Mom? I'm doing fine. How's Hawaii?"

"Wonderful. Your father and I are having a fantastic time. He's still operating on Orlando time, so he gets up every morning at the crack of dawn and goes to the hotel's fitness center. Then he joins a couple of guys he's met here for breakfast and to play a few hours of golf. I prefer sleeping in until noon, then just lounging around, taking it easy. But it's nice having the time away and for us to spend together. It's like having a second honeymoon."

Courtney heard the excitement in her mother's voice. "I'm glad, Mom. Sounds like things are working out the way you want them to."

"They are, sweetie. Your dad has been just wonderful. No matter what I want to do, he does it. We've taken several tours around the island together."

Courtney smiled. "Sounds like fun. So when are the two of you coming home?"

"We have another week, and then we'll be back. Your dad has already suggested that I look into us going somewhere else together next summer. Possibly a weeklong cruise to Alaska."

"Sounds nice."

"It will be. I know it's time for you to head out for work, but I wanted to check on you to make sure everything is okay. I talked to Peggy last night, and she said she'd seen you Sunday at the mall . . ."

Courtney and her mom chatted for a few more minutes before ending the call. As she locked up, she felt her chest swell with pride at her parents' attempt to work out their problems and save their marriage. She had been a major naysayer only because she didn't want her mom risking her heart yet again to the whims of her father. But now it seemed that Ron Andrews was truly trying to do the right thing and build a relationship with his wife. Courtney couldn't help but give her father an A for effort, and would tell him just how proud she was of him when her parents returned to town.

Ignoring the fact that Ashira had just climaxed for the third time beneath him, Ron kept on riding her, not close to getting enough. Luckily for him, a doctor friend had given him a prescription for Viagra before he left Orlando. Normally, he stayed away from the stuff, never needed medication to keep him hard. But he knew satisfying two women on this trip was going to be a challenge. Barbara would expect him to do his duty by her, and he couldn't risk raising her suspicions about anything if he wasn't in the mood. Viagra always kept him in the mood. Barbara was getting it whenever she wanted, and Ashira was giving it whenever he wanted it. Lucky for him, Barbara's demands weren't often, and their lovemaking sessions always ended quickly. The time he spent with Ashira was another story. The more he got from her, the more he wanted. His lust was insatiable.

"Are you sure you're not on anything?" Ashira asked when he thrust into her yet again. "You've been acting like a sex maniac since you arrived on this island."

He laughed as he spread her legs farther apart for deeper penetration. "No, I'm not taking anything," he said, lying easily to her. "Must be the environment," he said, still going strong, ramming in and out of her.

"What about your old lady? Aren't you getting any from her this trip?"

"That's none of your damn business as long as I'm getting it from you." He preferred not to talk, and she was asking too many questions to suit him. It's not like he was poking into her twenty-four hours a day. Just the morning hours while Barbara was still sleeping, so why was Ashira complaining? "If you're starting to have problems handling me, then let me know," he said angrily. "I can get someone else."

"I'm not having problems—it's just you want it every day."

He frowned. "And what's the hell wrong with that? That's why I brought you along, so stop whining. You're my morning delight. Barbara thinks I work out every morning and then meet up with some guys and play golf." He chuckled. "At least she got part of it right. I am working out." He glared down at her. "Now shut the hell up—I'm still hard."

She got quiet, which was fine with him. But after so many more thrusts, she began making sounds to let him know she was coming again. Boy, she was wet, and the wetter she got, the harder he got. Her stuff was ripe. He liked it like that.

He glanced over at the clock. He had another hour to go. It didn't take Ashira long to come again, and he smiled. Not bad for a relatively older man. He bet a young punk couldn't do what he was doing. She'd had five orgasms in less than two hours. Yes, he was counting. Damn, but he enjoyed hearing her every gasp, whimper, and moan when she came. Barbara would bury her face in the pillow or bedspread to deaden the sound, and that would piss him off. What a waste of good physical exertion.

He felt sensations running through his body and knew

he was beginning to explode again, but that wouldn't make him go soft. And he intended to keep at it with her until he did . . . or until he ran out of time.

He threw his head back, and his body began rocking when an explosion hit. A smile spread across his face. He was a man with the best of both worlds.

Peggy frowned over at Toni. "What do you mean you and John can't go to Disney World with me and Willie this weekend?"

Toni smiled. "John was supposed to come home Friday night and can't make it back. He called this morning and suggested that I fly out and join him in Atlanta. Then we can rent a car and drive over to Knoxville to see our grandbaby," she said excitedly.

"Umm, why do I feel like I'm being set up?"

Toni gave her an innocent look. "Come on, Peg. Would I do something like that?"

"Yes. Don't think I haven't caught on to what you're doing. Like the dinner party the other night. I guess you're going to try and convince me that all those other guests you claimed were coming canceled out at the last minute."

"Well . . ."

"Don't try it, Toni. I know you."

Toni smiled and leaned over the table. "Then you know how much I love you and want you to be happy."

Peggy shook her head. "I think you're all wrong about Willie Baker's attraction to me. He's just being nice."

Toni rolled her eyes. "He's a man interested in a

woman. John and I both saw the way he kept looking at you the other night. You've just been out of the dating scene for so long that you can't recognize the signs."

Peggy took a sip of her drink, wondering if what Toni said was true. Was she not able to read the signs? "Now you have me worried."

"Why? You've spent time with him by yourself before. And thanks to our shopping spree today, you have several nice outfits to choose from. You'll be fine."

Peggy sighed deeply. She hoped so.

Courtney walked into the restaurant and glanced around before giving the head waiter her name. He led her to the table where Lake was already seated. He stood and kissed her on the lips, just as if they were a couple.

"Hi," he said, releasing her hand, but not before lifting it to his lips for another kiss.

"Hi, yourself. Thanks for inviting me to lunch."

"You're welcome." He returned to his seat and looked over at her. "And you're smiling," he observed. "Not that I'm not accustomed to your smiles, but you seem in a particularly good mood today."

"I am."

"And the reason?"

She glanced around before leaning over the table and whispering. "Well, I have two reasons for my good mood and smile. I've slept with a wonderful man for the last two nights, and I heard from my mom this morning. She and my dad are having a wonderful time together in Hawaii."

He lifted a brow, latching on to the latter part of what she had said. "You didn't think they would have a good time together?"

She sighed deeply and sat back. "Honestly, no. The trip was my mother's idea. Dad went along with it just to make her happy."

Seeing the confused look on his face, she said, "Over the years, my parents have had problems with their marriage. Major problems. My father has a problem with being faithful."

Lake waited until the waiter delivered their menus before asking her, "What do you mean he has a problem being faithful to your mother?"

She shrugged as she reached over and grabbed a breadstick out of the basket. "He's had several affairs over the years, Lake. Two of them resulted in children, so I guess I was wrong in saying I was an only child."

"Your mother know about these affairs?" he asked in a quiet tone of voice.

"Yes, eventually she always finds out. Once, maybe twice, she's left him. One time I remember when I was in my early teens coming home to find all his clothes thrown over the lawn. That was a waste of Mom's time and energy, because in six months she had let him move back. Things are good between them until he screws up again, which he always does."

"And why do you think she stays with him?"

Courtney smiled. She could hear the bafflement in his voice. She understood. "Because she loves him. He screwed up just last year with a student of his. Not for the first time,

I might add. Don't know why the university keeps him on when he enjoys mixing business with pleasure. Anyway, Mom found out and they split for a few months. I really thought that was the end of it and thought it was about time. I was sure she'd had enough and was ready to tell him where he could shove that thing that he likes using on other women. Then I get a call where they invite me to dinner, and instead of telling me they've finally decided to get a divorce, they told me they were going to try to work things out again. I truly don't understand why she continues to trust him."

Lake reached over and took her hand. "The reason is what you said earlier, Courtney. She loves him, and I know firsthand that in some cases, love can be blind."

She opened her mouth to ask what situation was that but was interrupted when the waiter came to their table to take their order.

Lake didn't say anything for a long moment, thinking about what Courtney had told him. Talk about major drama. It seemed her parents had it. It explained a lot. Especially why she was so cautious in accepting that they had a future together. Did a part of her think all men were like her father?

"No, I don't think that."

He glanced up. "What?"

She shrugged. "I know what you're probably thinking. You're wondering if I have a problem with men because of my father . . . and my uncle."

He lifted a brow. "Your uncle?"

"Yes, Sonya's father. Uncle Joe screwed around on Aunt Peggy, too. He got involved with a young girl. Aunt Peggy found out when he asked her for a divorce to marry his child bride. At the time, he was fifty-six, and she was twenty-three."

Courtney took a sip of her drink. "I'd be the first to admit that because of my father and uncle I don't have a healthy view of relationships. Over the years, I tried seeing my family as the exception and not the norm, but found it hard at times. I do have friends whose parents have long-standing, loving relationships, so I believe it can happen . . . for the right people."

He nodded and smiled over at her. "Then I have to convince you that we are the right people."

She inhaled deeply. "I want to believe that, but I think we're moving too fast."

He heard a little distress in her voice. "Okay. Tell me what you need from me."

She didn't say anything for a moment, and then, "To slow down. I need time and space. You overwhelmed me from the first. You're still overwhelming me. And last night, I took risks with you that I've never taken before. Even now I can't believe that I did it, and what's so strange is that I don't have any regrets."

Lake wondered if she knew why she'd done it, why she didn't have any regrets. Did she have any clue why the thought of him fathering her child didn't bother her, like the thought of her mothering his child didn't bother him? Last night while he'd held her in his arms as she slept, he had thought about everything they had shared, every single thing they had done. There had been a reason for such madness, and he was more than convinced that it hadn't entirely been due to lust. But she would have to figure those things out on her own.

"We started out as lovers before becoming friends," he heard her say, breaking into his thoughts. "Mainly because you're convinced that in the end you'll get the same result—a marriage between us. What I need is for us to be friends," she said in a low voice.

He frowned. "I thought that we were."

She chuckled. "We're lovers. We're good in bed together, but when push comes to shove, we're miles apart because you see a future for us and I'm just getting used to what's happening now. Today. I can't think that far ahead yet."

He nodded, trying to keep up with her. Trying to get a grasp on what she was saying, although he had a fairly good idea. And he didn't like what he was hearing. "So you don't want us to see each other anymore, is that it?" he asked.

"No, that's not it, Lake. I just think we need to slow the pace down a bit. We've known each other for three weeks and have spent two nights together, and if I let it happen, we will be spending a third and a fourth. We're not building a relationship; we're having an affair."

"No," he said tensely. "I want more."

"I want to believe that."

And even after the two nights they had spent together, he was amazed that she still didn't. He leaned closer to her over the table and asked, "And if last night left you pregnant?"

She shook her head. "That's not a possibility, since I'm on the pill."

He smiled. "There are always possibilities. Nothing is one hundred percent sure."

"I know, but I honestly don't think we'll have that to worry about," she whispered.

Lake figured that now was not the time to tell her that if she was pregnant, he would want the baby as much as he wanted her. But then he'd made that clear last night. "Okay," he said. He would give her space while he worked on another strategy. "Starting now, there will only be friendship between us. Until you say otherwise."

Courtney gave him what he perceived as a relieved smile. "Thanks. I appreciate that."

Be careful what you ask for.

Two days later, and Courtney was questioning her decision regarding Lake. When she had confided in Sonya and told her what she'd done, her cousin had gone ballistic. Men were extinct, Sonya had exclaimed. Good ones were rare, hard to find. When you found one, you didn't do something real stupid like throw him back out there. You did that to the rejects. The ones who weren't worthy of your time, attention, or body. Sonya had gotten vocal. She had gotten loud. She'd truly been pissed. Letting Lake go had been plain stupid, she had said over and over. Then after Sonya had finally calmed down, she had explained that she nearly lost Mike by not accepting what he was trying to get her to see. They had a future together. And she didn't want Courtney to make the same mistake.

Okay, Courtney admitted, there was a possibility she had screwed up, big-time. Maybe she should have handled things differently. But still, it was important to her that she and Lake build a relationship outside of sex. He had called yesterday to give her a status on the client who was interested in purchasing some of Jetrica's work. The call had been short. He'd been very cordial. Nice. A part of her, the part that would throb in the wee hours of the night, missed spending time with the naughty Lake.

So here it was a Friday night and things were just like before. She had no date. No man to call her own. Okay, it was her fault, she would admit that much. But it wasn't like she had actually sent him away. She'd only asked that they be friends first. Friends did go out on occasion, so why hadn't he called to invite her to go somewhere? Friends just didn't have sex every single night. Could it be that's all he had wanted from her all along?

She picked up the TV schedule to see what was coming on the tube tonight, and then the phone rang. She reached over and picked it up. "Yes?"

"Hello, friend."

Flutters went off in her stomach at the sound of the voice. He had called. She dropped down on the sofa. She doubted her legs could hold her up. "Hi, Lake, how are you?"

"Fine. I was sitting around not doing anything and wondered if you would like to go out with me? Nowhere fancy. Just somewhere to grab a burger and fries. Maybe go to a movie as friends."

She threw her head back and laughed. This was what she wanted. "Yes. I'd love going out with you."

"Good. I'll be by in an hour."

22

"I had a nice time this afternoon with you, Peggy," Willie said when they reached her front door.

She turned and smiled up at him. "And I had a nice time with you, as well. I can't remember the last time I spent an entire day at Disney World." She chuckled. "I think Sonya had to have been around ten. Needless to say, when we left the park that day, I swore when she went back she would be old enough to take herself. She wanted to ride on just about everything that was there."

He grinned down at her. "Oh, like you did today?"

Peggy couldn't help but laugh. She would admit that she had persuaded him to join her on a lot of the rides. For the first time in years, she had felt young and full of life. And each time she had caught him looking at her the way a man looked at a woman he was interested in, she had felt attractive. Toni had been right. Although she couldn't understand why, Willie was interested in her. There had to be a number of other women who would love the attention . . . not that she didn't. She just didn't feel worthy. It's not like she was a knockout or anything like that. She would think he'd want a much younger woman. Maybe not so young as Joe's child bride, but definitely a woman in her forties or early fifties.

"Okay, what's going on in that beautiful head of yours?"

She smiled up at him. Another thing she liked about him was that he was free with compliments. "I was thinking that it's still relatively early," she said, glancing at her watch. "It's a little before seven. Would you like to come in and visit for a while?"

He held her gaze. "Are you sure that won't be putting you out? You have spent the majority of the day with me."

"Yes, and I loved every minute," she said, smiling.

He gave her a dazzling smile, and she felt a stirring in her stomach. "Then I would love to visit with you some more."

Courtney's chest tightened at the sound of the doorbell announcing Lake's arrival. How did you backpedal and become friends with a man who just a few nights ago had been your lover in the most intimate way possible?

That's for you to figure out since this entire "just friends" thing was your idea, she muttered to herself as she headed for the door. But no matter what one part of her mind was thinking—as well as the dress-down she'd gotten from Sonya—she wanted to believe she was doing the right thing. Her parents' marriage initially had been based on lust and not love, and her unexpected conception didn't help matters. Over the years, she doubted they had ever truly been friends, and she prayed it wasn't too late. She hoped their trip to Hawaii was just the beginning.

She opened the door to find a handsome Lake Masters standing there smiling at her. She returned his smile and fought back the urge to reach out and wrap her arms around his neck and devour his lips. No, she couldn't do that, since they were just friends.

"Lake," she greeted. "Won't you come in."

"Sure."

She stepped aside for him to enter, taking in his arousing male scent. "I just need to grab my purse off the table." She quickly crossed the room.

"You look nice."

She got her purse and turned around. "Thanks. You look good, too."

He chuckled. "Appreciate the compliment."

She could give him others, she thought, when she walked back across the room to him. She could tell him how good he smelled and how nice he was built. She could also mention how good it felt when his bare flesh touched hers or how butterflies went off in her stomach just from the sound of his voice.

"I'm ready," she said, thinking her voice sounded rather breathy and deep.

"All right."

For a split second, she thought his gaze turned hot and intimate. She blinked and the look was gone. Had she imagined it, or did he have that sort of control of his emotions?

"I thought that we would go see a movie, as well. Is that all right with you?"

"Yes, that's fine."

"Good."

He then led the way to the front door, and the one thing she noticed was that he hadn't taken hold of her hand as he usually did. She missed the contact.

"I think I'm going to get up early tomorrow and join you in the fitness room."

"Huh." Ron, who was lounging on the sofa in his hotel suite flipping channels with the remote control, glanced over at his wife. He hoped he had heard her wrong.

"I said that I'm going to the fitness room with you tomorrow. I need to start doing something. I've been eating a lot this week. Maybe the treadmill will do me some good."

He sat up. "Yes, but are you sure you want to work out that early? I'm there before seven."

She gave a half laugh. "Yes, I'm sure. In fact, I plan to spend the entire day with you tomorrow and for the rest of the trip. We only have a few days left before we fly home."

"Sweetheart, you don't have to do that," he said, his mind thinking about those few days he had left without getting a blow job. He was a true addict.

"I know I don't have to, but I want to. And to make

sure, I plan on going to bed early tonight. That way I can get up when you do in the morning. But now I plan on visiting the salon downstairs. I want to get my nails done."

He got up off the sofa and crossed the room to her. He took her hands in his and looked at her nails. "There's nothing wrong with your nails; they look fine."

She smiled. "I want to change the color of the polish."

He cleared his throat. "Will you be gone long?"

"Not too long. Why do you ask? Do you have something you want us to do later?"

"Nah, I was just asking. Take your time. While you're gone, I might go play a game of golf or something," he said.

His pecker was throbbing, since it knew just what that *something* was. If he couldn't get satisfied in the morning, then he would contact Ashira now. He just hoped she was in her room. Her afternoons were usually free, since that's the time he spent with Barbara. Damn it to hell, his wife had messed up his pleasure schedule.

Ashira felt herself coming apart under David's mouth when his tongue continued to lick her inside out. If they were giving a prize to the woman who'd come the most in a given week, she bet that she would win hands down. This had been some vacation, and she appreciated Ronnie for bringing her. As long as she could put up with his grueling sex in the morning, her afternoons belonged to her . . . and David. Oh, and she couldn't forget Evan, another guy she had met a few days ago. But unlike David, she hadn't invited Evan up to her room. They had done the thing in his room on a day his wife had taken a trip to one of the other islands to go sightseeing.

She heard the phone, wondering who would be calling and figured it could be only one person. "Don't stop," she all but screamed at David when he pulled his mouth away. "Ignore it."

He smiled up at her before leaning back down and settling his mouth back on her. She sighed in contentment when his frisky tongue went to work on her again.

Anger flared in Ron's eyes. Where the hell was Ashira? Granted, he had never tried contacting her in the afternoons before, but hell, she should be at his beck and call no matter what time it was. That suite he was paying for her to stay in wasn't cheap.

He dropped back on the sofa, thinking she was probably out shopping, spending more of his money. She had a lot to make up to him, whether it was here or when they got back to Orlando. There would be payday. He grabbed the remote off the table. His pecker was still throbbing. He needed to do something. It would be taking a huge risk, especially if Barbara was around and wanted to be clingy, but he needed to get a quick fix from Ashira and bad.

Since she had arrived on the island a few days before they had, she would be leaving the island before they did. He wanted some time with her before she left. But at the moment, thanks to Barbara, he couldn't figure out just how he was going to fit it into his schedule.

He jumped off the sofa when he heard the sound of his cell phone ringing and raced across the room to get it, hoping it was Ashira calling him back. He frowned when he recognized the caller ID. It wasn't Ashira. It was Melissa. Why the hell was she calling him?

Angry beyond belief, he didn't give her a chance to say anything and blared into the phone. "Listen, bitch, stop calling me. I don't want you anymore. Get it? And if you call me again I'm going to file harassment charges and you'll be locked up."

He clicked off the phone and hoped like hell that he'd heard the last of her.

"So tell me about Peggy Morrison."

Peggy glanced over at Willie. They were sitting on her back patio that overlooked a huge lake. Some of her neighbors had taken their boats out, and they watched as they made their way through the still waters. "I'm divorced and have been for almost four years now."

"Are you and your husband still friends?"

Not hardly. She shook her head. Deciding to provide him with an honest answer, she said, "No, we are far from being, friends especially since our marriage ended because he was unfaithful."

He held her gaze. "I'm sorry."

"Thanks, but I'm over it now. It took me a while, though. We had been married for over thirty years. He met a woman and decided he wanted her more than me. So he asked me for a divorce to marry her."

Willie didn't say anything for a moment, and then he said, "I can't imagine a man leaving you for another woman."

She appreciated his comment. "Well, he did. But then what I failed to tell you about the woman was that she was younger than our daughter. So I guess in his book, he felt he was getting a good deal."

"Well, the clock is ticking for the both of them," Willie said quietly. "Your husband is aging, and so is she. Right before each other's eyes. You have to have more in a marriage than looks and lust. There has to be love."

She agreed. "I truly thought we had that. I also thought we were the perfect family. He showed me just how wrong I was."

"No, it sounds like he was the one who was wrong. I loved, honored, and cherished my wife until the day she died. I never put another woman before her, was never tempted to. When we said 'till death do us part,' I meant it."

Peggy thought Joe should have meant it as well, but he hadn't.

"I understand you recently were the mother of the bride."

Willie words cut into her thoughts. "Yes," she said, smiling proudly. "Sonya got married a last month. It was a beautiful wedding."

"And I'm sure you were a radiant mother of the bride."

"Thank you," she said, holding his gaze. She wanted to think he wasn't saying the words merely to be kind. That he really meant them.

She watched him glance at his watch, and then he

looked back at her and said, "How would you like to take in a movie tonight?"

She lifted her brow. "A movie?" She said the words as if she'd never heard them before.

He chuckled. "Yes, a movie. It's still fairly early—at least too early for the teenagers. Believe it or not, they start to arrive at midnight. I noticed more and more kids don't have curfews. Kelly did when she was growing up. I didn't allow her to be out past eleven."

She and Joe had had a similar curfew time for Sonya, Peggy thought.

"If we go to the movies, I prefer not being there with a bunch of teens. Some of them have no respect," Willie said.

She had to agree. It had been ages since she'd gone to the movies, and then one night Barbara had talked her into going and they ended up leaving the theater before the movie had ended. There had been more action going on around them than on the big screen.

"Do you want to go?"

"Yes." She pushed herself to her feet and smiled over at him. "I'd love to go."

He stood up, as well, close beside her. "And I'd love to take you."

At that moment, Peggy became aware of just how close they were standing, and then as if her lips were finally getting something they had wanted all day, he lowered his head and she leaned up and met him halfway.

Surprise and excitement rammed through her body the moment their lips touched, and it seemed that his fitted perfectly against the fullness of hers. Then he began kissing her in a way that she had never been kissed before. She felt her heart racing and heat flaming through her body, and then when she thought she was about to go up in smoke, he slowly released her mouth.

He then took the tip of his finger and traced it along her cheekbone as he stared deep into her eyes. He smiled. "I like kissing you, Peggy Morrison," he said huskily against her moist lips.

"And I like being kissed by you," she said honestly. "Please do it again."

And he did.

"Have you told Sonya about the baby yet?"

Joe glanced over at Suzette. God, he hoped it wasn't going to be one of those days. He was getting too old for this. "No, I haven't told her."

"Why?"

He rolled his eyes. "Mainly because I haven't spoken with her since she's been back from her honeymoon. She's a married woman now with a husband to take care of."

Suzette snorted. "But that didn't keep her from having a party, a party we didn't get invited to."

He wished for once he could come home to relax and not to his wife's bitching. "According to Peggy, Sonya didn't give the party. Carla did."

"I don't care who gave it," she snapped. "We weren't invited. If you ask me, we barely got invited to the wedding."

He sighed, wondering why she was bringing all that back up again. She had beat it to death last month. "I don't want to talk about it, Suzette. You've made it known to all who want to hear, just how you feel."

"Well, that's not good enough. I want to have a party. Here."

"And who will you invite?" He didn't want to have to remind her that she had few friends. She'd even lost those she had before marrying him after rubbing in their faces the things she had and they didn't.

"I'll think of somebody," she said, smiling excitedly.

"We don't have money for a party, Suzette," he said firmly.

"Sure we do. You work every day."

And he knew he would be working for a long while to come if he continued to let her spend all their money. He had put her on a budget, but that hadn't worked. "We don't have money for a party, Suzette," he repeated.

He figured she finally heard him loud and clear, because after muttering a few choice words, she turned and stormed out of the room.

He pulled himself up off the sofa, deciding to call Sonya. He'd rather tell her in person, but Suzette had taken that opportunity away from him. Out of spite, Suzette wouldn't hesitate to call Sonya herself and tell her. It was best that his daughter hear it from him. Taking his cell phone, he headed out to the garage, where he could make a call in private.

"Barbara, I think I'll go out for a walk. Do you want to join me?" Ron asked, knowing that she wouldn't want to.

While at the salon, she had gotten her toes done, too, and he doubted she wanted to mess anything up with a pair of walking shoes.

"Yes, I'll join you."

He swirled around, surprised she had accepted his invitation.

She raised a brow. "What's wrong?"

He shrugged and tried not to show his disappointment. "Nothing. I'm just surprised you'd want to go. You're going to mess up your toenails when you put on your walking shoes."

She looked down at her feet. "No, I won't, since I'm wearing my open-toe sandals. And they are so comfortable. I'll be fine," she said, crossing the room and taking his hand in hers.

He wanted to snatch his hand back but didn't. She was screwing up his plans for the afternoon.

"So where are we walking?" she asked.

"Nowhere in particular. I thought we'd take a leisurely stroll."

"All right."

On their way out the door, she leaned over and whispered, "And I have a surprise for you tonight, Ron." By the tone of her voice, he knew whatever surprise she had would be sexual in nature. She probably had purchased a sexy nightgown or something.

"A surprise?" He gave her a forced smile. "I like surprises."

She chuckled as he ushered her out the door and said, "I know you do."

Mike glanced up when Sonya walked into the room. He immediately stood up from his desk when he saw a strange look on her face. "What is it, honey?"

He held out his arms, and she walked straight into them, not even wondering how he knew she needed a hug. She looked at him, into his gorgeous blue eyes that were tinged with concern. "That was Dad. He had something to tell me."

"What?"

"He and Suzette are having a baby."

Mike didn't say anything for a moment, and then he said, "And?"

She pulled back and glanced up at him with a puzzled look on her face. "And what?"

"And what else is there?"

She frowned. "What makes you think there's more?"

"Because you're upset."

"Yes, I'm upset. Don't you think that's enough to get me upset?" she snapped.

"No, honestly I don't. Your father and Suzette are married. She's young and although he's older, evidently he can still produce babies. What's the big deal?"

Sonya pulled out of his arms and glared at him. The issue of her parents was one they could never agree on. "The big deal, Mike, is that my father is too old to have a baby."

"If he isn't too old to make one, then he's not too old to have one."

Sonya ignored him and kept talking. "When that child is graduating from high school, Dad will probably be in a nursing home."

"You don't know that, Sonya."

"Maybe not for certain, but chances are that he will be."

"Okay, so what's your point?"

She placed her hand on her hips. "My point is, and I repeat, my father is too old to have a baby. Suzette got pregnant on purpose to tie him to her."

Mike laughed. "Sweetheart, do you honestly think Suzette forced your father to perform in bed with her?"

"Mike, this isn't funny."

"You're right. It isn't." He reached out, and although she tried to resist him, he pulled her back into his arms. "You want to know what I think?"

"No."

He smiled when he placed her head beneath his chin. "I'm going to tell you anyway. I think you're jealous."

She jerked back, bumping his chin in the process. "I am not jealous."

"Aren't you? For years you never shared your father. Then you had to share him with Suzette and now a new baby. Yes, you're jealous."

"You don't know that, Mike."

"No, but I know you. Get over it. Get over Suzette. Get over them."

Sonya shook her head. "I can't. They hurt Mom. I'm the one who went through hell when she couldn't handle her husband of thirty years leaving her for a younger woman."

"Yes, they did hurt your mom. They also hurt you. But life goes on, Sonya. Your mom is doing fine now, and so are you. And as for your father and Suzette, be happy for them. They deserve each other. Think positive. You're getting a baby sister or brother."

"Mike, I—"

He didn't let her finish. He pulled her into his arms and kissed her. The touch of his lips on hers immediately silenced her. They also inflamed her senses and made her think of one thing—one person. Mike.

She felt herself being pulled down with him to the sofa. She didn't protest. Nor did she resist. When her back touched the leather cushions, she gazed up at him and said, "You know we haven't finished talking about that, don't you."

He stood back and began removing his shirt. He smiled down at her with sparkling blue eyes. "Yes, we have."

Ron eased out of bed and glanced at the bathroom door. Barbara was taking a mighty long time coming out of it, he thought, annoyed. She had gone into the bathroom a few moments ago and had been locked in there ever since. So she had bought a new nightgown, big deal. How many new ones had he seen so far on this trip? At least five. And all of them had been cute and typical Barbara. Nothing to make him go hard or would make him want to rip the material off her body.

His mind then shifted to Ashira. He had tried reaching

her again and hadn't made a connection. Where the hell was she? He had tried sneaking away, but Barbara hadn't allowed him any free time. And she still insisted that she would be going to the fitness center with him in the morning.

"Ron?"

His brow creased when he glanced at the bathroom door. It was cracked a little. "What?"

"Are you ready?"

As ready as I'm going to ever be, he thought. But to her he said. "Yes, I'm ready." *Not hard but ready,* he didn't tack on.

"Okay, I'm coming out."

Whatever. He watched the bathroom door open just a little wider and then a little more. He was sitting there getting bored to tears when suddenly it was flung wide open. He sat straight up. "Holy shit!"

The words escaped his lips before he could call them back. The woman standing in the doorway was wearing a black barely-there something. And it looked damn good on her. Barbara always had a nice shape, and tonight she was working it in that skimpy material.

"Wh-what are you doing?" His tongue felt thick in his mouth.

She smiled at him in a way he'd never seen her smile before. She then began walking toward him, and his eyes almost popped out of his head. When she walked, he could clearly see the dark triangle between her thighs.

"Come here, Ron."

She wasn't asking him. She was telling him. She'd never been bossy in the bedroom. He liked it. His body suddenly began to ache. He immediately felt hard. Fire was raging through his loins. Barbara had never been able to get this sort of a reaction out of him. And just from seeing her in a gown that showed more of her nakedness than he was used to being displayed. And to top it off, she was wearing stiletto heels. He'd totally forgotten what nice legs she had.

"Ron?"

He slowly pulled himself from the chair and began walking over toward her. The hardness of his prick made it seem like he was carrying an extra load. The look in her eyes promised that she would lighten it. Blood began gushing through his veins.

He came to a stop in front of her. "Take off your pajamas and lie on the bed, Ron."

He did as she ordered. He stretched out, wondering what she planned to do. It didn't take long for her to show him. She eased on the bed with him and started kissing him on his mouth. Then moved lower. He closed his eyes, not believing this. Wondering if she was really going to do what he hoped to God she was.

The instant her lips touched his prick, he almost bucked off the bed. Desire, as raw as it could get, cut through him. He could feel his testicles throbbing, his member hardening. And when she sucked him into her mouth, he released one hell of a loud moan. He couldn't believe it. This was his wife, and she was going down on him, and she seemed to be enjoying it.

Then he felt himself about to come and knew exactly where he wanted to be when he did. Opening his eyes, he moved quickly, flipped her on her back, pushed her gown out of his way, and entered her in one powerful thrust. She felt, hot, tight, and he knew it had been a long time since he'd gone inside her so deep. It felt good.

He continued to ride her, and she began making sounds. Real noise that she wasn't trying to smother. The louder she got, the harder he rode. And then he couldn't hold back any longer, which was just as well, because as soon as an explosion hit her, it hit him, as well. He slammed his mouth on hers, claiming it in one hell of a long kiss. He couldn't seem to let up. Didn't want to let up.

And then he was coming again, and all he could think about was that the woman beneath him was his wife. Nobody else's wife. His.

Ron couldn't move. His body felt like it had just been through a time warp. He and Barbara had been married for thirty years, and he couldn't ever remember experiencing anything so hot with her. It's a wonder the sheets hadn't gotten scorched. She owed him some answers. He refused to believe she'd been holding back on him all these years.

He forced his head to move, to gaze her at her. Like him, she was lying flat on her back and barely breathing. Her eyes were closed. The lower part of her body was still quivering. Beads of perspiration had settled between her breasts. They were breasts, he would have to admit, that still looked good for a woman her age. He'd always appreciated the fact that they didn't sag.

He sat up and bent over her. "You have some explaining to do," he whispered.

Without opening her eyes, she smiled. Then asked, "Did you like it?"

He chuckled. Now was not the time to tell her he had a weakness for blow jobs. She'd been pretty damned terrific. He frowned. Too terrific for a beginner. "Who taught you how to do that?" he asked, suddenly needing to know.

She opened her eyes and met his. Her smile brightened to one full of pride. "I took classes."

"What!"

She laughed. He didn't see a damn thing funny. "What do you mean you took classes?"

Despite his anger, she continued to laugh. The more she laughed, the angrier he got. When he made a move to get out of bed, she grabbed hold of his thigh. "Calm down, Ron. I don't mean that kind of class."

"Then tell me what you do mean, Barbara."

"Okay," she said, easing up in a sitting position. "I was looking through a magazine and saw this ad in the back. It was supposed to teach you how to do certain things to keep your man satisfied. So I sent off for the video."

"Video."

"It was a self-taught video." She chuckled softly. "You won't believe how many Popsicles it took."

He raised a brow. "Popsicles?"

"Yes. For practice I used Popsicles to get the sucking motion right. I wanted to learn everything there was to know, since from what you revealed to the therapist, that was one area of our marriage where I was lacking."

Suddenly he couldn't meet her eyes. He shifted his attention across the room to a picture on the wall. "I never said you were lacking."

"You didn't have to, Ron," she said softly. "Your affairs with all those women said it enough."

He looked back at her then. Saw the pain he heard in her words reflected in her eyes. Seeing it hit him below the gut. "Barbara, I—"

"No, I don't want to talk about the past, Ron. I know what you've done before, and I agreed to put it behind us and move on. But still, I knew I had to do something or you would stray again. I had to become your every woman."

My every woman. He studied her features, felt a momentary rush of joy that she loved him that much. Then he felt like a total asshole because he knew he wasn't deserving of her love. Never had been, even from the first. But she meant something to him. Always had. She had always been there for him, and he'd taken her for granted. Treated her like crap. He'd let other women disrespect her, and she still hung on to a man who wasn't worthy of her. Not even now. If she ever found out just what he'd pulled with Ashira, how he'd brought his other woman on a trip meant to rebuild their marriage, he knew he would literally kiss her good-bye. That was one time she would never forgive him. Even now, he couldn't forgive himself.

"Am I, Ron?"

Her question cut into his thoughts. "Are you what, Barbara?"

"Your every woman?"

He stared at her. Remembered the first time he'd seen her that day on campus. She'd been attending Spellman, and had come on the Morehouse campus with a group of friends. He thought her classy then and thought her classy now. And she was loyal to a fault. She had screwed up when she had married him. He was a man with a deep problem, an addiction he couldn't seem to kick. At one time, he had felt a desire to get help but had failed to do so. Now he knew he had no choice. Every time he messed with other women, he was destroying the only person who ever truly loved him. He had to find a way to recover from his compulsive sexual behavior. It was Ashira now, but he knew eventually it would be another woman later. He couldn't go on hurting his wife this way. He had hurt her enough.

"Ron?"

He leaned down and kissed her softly and then said, "Yes, Barbara, you're my every woman." And then he kissed her again.

"Thanks for taking me to the movies. I enjoyed it."

Lake smiled. "So did I."

Courtney felt her lips tingle. She wanted him to kiss her but knew friends didn't kiss. At least they didn't engage in the type of kiss she wanted. Lake had walked her to the front door. She wouldn't invite him in. It would be plain suicide to do so. She knew her limits. She also knew her weaknesses.

"Well, I better go on in. It's getting late," she said, missing him already.

"All right. And I'll be leaving on Tuesday, going out of town for a few days. I'll be back on Thursday."

"Oh. Well, have a nice trip."

"I will." And then he leaned down and kissed her on the cheek. "Good night."

"Good night." And then he stood there until she had opened the door and slipped inside, closing it behind her.

Courtney quickly moved to the window and glanced out. She watched Lake's tall form get inside his truck and stood at the window until he drove off. She had wanted him to kiss her. But he hadn't, only because of what she had asked of him.

Okay, so she really shouldn't be disappointed that he hadn't done so anyway. After all, she had asked for his friendship. She had told him she didn't want him for a lover, just a friend. She should be excited about the relationship they were now building. She should be grateful they were now taking things slow. Instead, she wanted to call Sonya to come over and give her one good hard kick.

Her phone rang, and she immediately glanced at the clock. It was after eleven. Who would be calling her at this hour? Thinking it could possibly be Lake contacting her on his cell phone, she quickly crossed the room. What if he asked to come back? What if he told her he didn't like the friendship thing and wanted to be her lover again? She reached for the phone, wishing she had added caller ID to her phone plan. "Yes?"

"Where have you been?"

She raised a brow. "Sonya?"

"What?"

"What's wrong?" Something wasn't right. She could hear it in her cousin's voice. What was she doing calling her and not somewhere in bed with her husband? She thought newlyweds had sex all the time, or at least every chance they got. Did she and Mike have a fight?

"Sonya, where's Mike?"

"He's in bed asleep. I think I wore him out."

Courtney smiled. Apparently they didn't have a fight, and if they did have one, they had made up. So, if it wasn't Mike, then what was wrong? "I went to the movies with Lake," she said, deciding to answer Sonya's earlier question.

"And he's gone? You didn't invite him to spend the night?"

"No. We only went out as friends."

She heard her cousin's deep sigh and then, "Courtney. Courtney. Courtney. When will you learn?"

"Definitely not tonight, so what's up? What got you calling this late?" she asked.

"Dad."

"Excuse me?" Courtney said, not sure she'd heard Sonya right.

“I said Dad.”

Courtney raised a brow. “Uncle Joe?”

“Yes.”

“What about him?”

“He’s going to be a father. Suzette is friggin’ pregnant.”

23

Jetrica grabbed Courtney's hand and shook it. "Ms. A, are you listening?"

Courtney raised her head and glanced over at Jetrica, whose eyes were bright and serious. No, she hadn't been listening. Her mind was somewhere else, which wasn't fair to Jetrica. This was their time. And if she remembered correctly, Jetrica was sharing some good news with her.

"Sorry, my mind was elsewhere, Jetrica, and I apologize for—"

"You were thinking about your boyfriend, weren't you?" Jetrica interrupted.

The question surprised Courtney. "What makes you think that?"

Jetrica rolled her eyes. "I figured as much. He's a looker. I'd think about him all the time, too."

"Well, I don't." Courtney leaned back in her seat, wondering how to get the conversation back on track. Jetrica had been telling her about the money she had made selling one of her paintings.

"I saw him, you know."

Courtney raised a brow. "You saw who?"

"Your boyfriend, Mr. Masters. Me and Bethany met with him and that old lady who bought my painting on Monday. He looks pretty good to be an older guy. And he's a sharp dresser with a nice office. Bethany thinks he's good-looking too." And then she added, "He has a picture of you on his desk."

Courtney thought she heard Jetrica wrong. "Excuse me?"

"I said he has a picture of you on his desk. It's a picture the two of you took together."

Courtney began racking her brain, trying to remember when she and Lake posed for a picture together, and then she did remember. That night he had taken her to the movies. While waiting for the beginning of the next show, they had walked the mall. A street vendor had been snapping pictures of anyone who walked by. She and Lake had paused long enough for him to get a shot of them. But she didn't recall Lake making arrangements to buy the picture. He must have contacted the photographer later.

"The two of you look good as a couple, like you belong together."

Butterflies went off in Courtney's stomach. She considered Jetrica's statement as too much insight to be coming from a teenage girl, especially one who'd had such hardships in her life. She would never have thought Jetrica had a romantic bone in her body.

Like you belong together.

Sonya thought the same thing, that she and Lake belonged together. Vickie, who'd heard all about Lake from her, thought so, as well. Why could they see the very thing she couldn't? Why was it so hard to accept the fact that maybe, just maybe, there was a man capable of being both her friend as well as her lover, no matter what order they came in? A man who wouldn't be unfaithful like her father and uncle. A man who was what dreams were made of. A man who represented the male species in such a way that couldn't get any better.

Deciding to steer the conversation off Lake, Courtney said, "Now that you are Madam Artist, how would you like to have a private showing of all of your work in my home?"

She saw Jetrica's gaze light up. "Wow! That would be neat. I'd like that."

Courtney smiled. "Okay, let's get together next week and plan one for the summer. Now what were you saying before my mind started drifting?"

Jetrica leaned in closer with excitement in her eyes. "I said with the money I'm making off that painting, Bethany and I will use it to move into a bigger apartment on the other side of town, one in a safer neighborhood. And after putting money into an account for my college, there will be enough left over for Bethany to start taking classes again at the university. Isn't all that neat?"

At that moment, Courtney felt a lot of gratitude in her heart for Lake and what he'd done to bring that sparkle to Jetrica's eyes. "Yes," she said, smiling. "All that is really neat."

"Are you going to invite Courtney to Mom's birthday party?"

Lake glanced across the table at Grey. Their mother would be turning sixty-five next month, and all the Masterses would be headed to Savannah for the celebration. He knew why Grey was asking. It would be the perfect time to introduce Courtney to the family as the woman he intended to marry.

"At the moment no. I was moving too fast, and she asked that I slow it down."

Grey chuckled. "You were getting too overwhelming, uhh?"

"I suppose."

"Masterses have a tendency to do that at times."

Lake took a sip of his drink and then asked, "Were you?"

Grey smiled. "I probably was, but then my focus was on trying to keep Brandy alive."

Lake nodded. Brandy's cousins had hired Grey as Brandy's bodyguard when she began receiving threats against her life.

"So how slow are you moving things now?" Grey asked.

Lake couldn't help but think about the last time he'd seen her, a week ago today. He had taken her to a movie and had returned her home and left her there . . . without kissing her good-bye. At least not what he considered as a real kiss. That had been hard. It had been even harder not picking up the phone to call her whenever he thought about her. She wanted space, and he was giving it to her. But he didn't like it. He especially didn't like the ache he felt every time he thought about her or the nights he had lain in bed missing her.

"Too slow. I think it's time for me to start speeding things up a little."

Grey laughed. "Now why doesn't that surprise me?"

Ron knew he had decisions to make, and the first one would be regarding Ashira. He and Barbara had arrived back in Orlando a few days ago, and he knew what he had to do. First he would break off with Ashira, and then he would tell Barbara the truth. Chances were he would lose her, but he couldn't continue deceiving her, living a lie.

And then he planned on getting help. Already he had gone on the Internet and researched his problem and had gathered quite a bit of information on sexual addiction. He had discovered that it was among the least talked about and least understood addictions, but it was a reality that affected thousands of people.

The good thing was that there was help to those who wanted it. He had an appointment with a psychotherapist next week and actually looked forward to the visit. Knowing there was a chance of recovery gave him hope.

He rubbed his hand down his face. He hadn't seen or talked to Ashira since Hawaii. He never gave a thought to visiting her hotel room after that special night with Barbara. The only woman he had wanted to be with had been his wife, but he was afraid that desire would soon wear off if he didn't get the help he needed.

Later that evening after staying after hours for a staff meeting, Ron was making his way across the parking lot to his car. It was Friday and just beginning to get dark. Most of the students had already left campus to start their weekend, so the parking lot was basically deserted. He thought about the stop he had to make before he got home. He had called Ashira and told her to expect his visit. He could tell from the tone of her voice that she was annoyed that he hadn't called sooner or that he hadn't tried contacting her any more while they were in Hawaii. He offered no excuses and gave no apologies, which he knew probably angered her even more.

Ron knew Ashira would make ending things with her difficult. She had enjoyed being the center of his attention, had liked getting all the things he bought for her, liked thinking she controlled him with the kind of kinky sex he liked. But all that would have to end. And then later tonight when he got home, he would tell Barbara everything, especially the fact that he had acknowledged his problem and was seeking professional help. He hoped. He prayed that she would forgive him and give him another chance to be the husband to her that he believed that he could be.

He was about to open his car door when he heard someone call his name. The voice was hard to discern, and he turned around. He looked at the person standing almost five feet away from him, saw the gun flash, and heard a loud popping sound at the same time he felt a sudden pain slice through his body. The last thing he remembered was losing his grip on reality and succumbing to icy darkness.

Knowing when to admit you were wrong was everything, Courtney thought as she stood in front of Lake's door. Doubt had messed with her mind, had convinced her that there was no possible way a man could see her one day and decide without exchanging one word with her, that she was the woman for him. Typically, relationships between men and women didn't develop that way, but she now accepted that with some people, anything was possible.

Lake Masters, she believed, was one of those people. He saw what he wanted. He went after it. And he didn't give up until he got it. His strategy had been so smooth, as suave as anything could be and as persuasive as it could get. She had put up a shield to protect her heart, but he'd found an opening and had wiggled his way inside anyway. The man worked fast. He was definitely thorough. He was capable of stripping you of your defenses. And she had come to a decision that she wanted to be both his friend and lover, and it no longer mattered to her in what order they came. She would eventually become both. She knew that she loved him.

Taking a deep breath, she rang his doorbell. He wasn't expecting her. Would probably be surprised to see her.

She hoped he would welcome her inside and hear what she had to say.

The door opened and he stood there, as sexy as any man could be. He was casually dressed in a pair of jeans and a pullover shirt. And as she scanned lower, she saw he was in his bare feet. He looked at home. He looked mouthwateringly good. He looked like the man she wanted.

"Courtney?"

Just from the sound of her name off his lips, she felt a tightening in her stomach, a sudden throb between her legs. Boy, she had it bad. She moved her gaze back up to his face to stare at him, and he stared straight back at her. She drew in a deep breath, cleared her throat. "Hi, Lake," she finally said. "May I come in?"

"Sure."

He moved aside, and when she passed him, she caught his scent. Ultra male. Sexy as hell. She turned to face him when he closed the door behind her. "I hope I'm not catching her at a bad time. Maybe I should have called first."

"No, you're not catching me at a bad time, and as far as calling first, you don't have to do that. You'll always be welcome to my home at any time, Courtney."

"Thanks."

"You're welcome."

She thought their words sounded too formal, almost stilted. And she knew why. She had requested friendship, and he was giving her just what she wanted, just what she had asked for.

"Would you like something to drink?"

She shook her head. "No thanks." And then glanced around. "You have a nice place."

"Thanks."

"You're welcome."

She saw his lips lift and knew what he thought was funny. "We're a bunch of nice people today, aren't we?" she said, chuckling. "All nice and polite."

"How would you prefer I be?"

She met his gaze. Understood what he was asking her. His voice had changed when he'd asked the question. It had lowered. It had a seductive tone and was sending shivers all through her body.

"Courtney?"

She inhaled deeply as she crossed the room, pressed as closed to him as her body could, and then wrapped her arms around his neck. "Naughty. I prefer for you to be as naughty as you can get."

She saw the flicker of a yearning in his eyes. "What about your friendship thing?"

Arching against him, she felt his hardness. It was thick, engorged. She reached her hand down and cupped him. Heard his sharp intake of breath when she did so. Then she began fondling him through his jeans. "I want to be both your friend and your lover, Lake. Tonight I need to be your lover. Please let me."

The yearning in his eyes turned to heated desire and then a scorching promise. "Do you know what you're asking for?"

"Yes," she said, stretching up against him. "But tomorrow is Saturday, so I don't have to worry about being physically able to go to work. So don't hold anything back."

He bent his head, came close to her lips, and whispered, "I won't."

And then he was scooping her into his arms while kissing her, taking her straight into what she figured was his bedroom. It wasn't. It was a game room. She noticed that fact the moment he pressed her back against an air hockey table. She took only a minute to glance around to see all the other equipment in the room, and she knew that before the night was over, he would take her on every single piece. Tonight he intended to be extremely naughty.

He didn't waste time removing her clothes, tossing them out of his way. Then he removed his and did likewise. She held his gaze when he stood between her open legs. "We're about ready to play?" she asked.

He gave her a smile that intensified the throbbing in her womanly core. "Yeah, we're about ready to play. You know the rules?"

She shook her head. "No."

His smile widened. "The object of the game is for me to shoot the puck into your goal. We're going to keep this simple. This is going to be the puck," he said, easing one of her hands down to touch his manhood. "And this," he said, reaching out and teasing her hot, wet womanhood with the tips of his fingers, "is the goal."

She held his heated gaze. Barely got the words out when she asked, "Is it?"

"You betcha. It is definitely *my* goal."

She swallowed deeply. "So let the games begin."

His manhood was erect, pointed, ready at the entrance of her core. A shiver touched her when she felt the head of it right there, primed, hot and ready. And then he thrust into her in a way that totally stole her breath. She had to inhale deep to catch it again. And then he was playing his game, one he was evidently good at. His puck continuously, nonstop, over and over again, hit his goal.

He held on to her hips to make sure she stayed immobile on the table and she couldn't do anything but lie there and let him hit his mark time and time again, reveling in his skill. But she decided to show him she was a worthy opponent. She managed to lift her face up, and she stuck out her tongue and caught his lips.

He opened his mouth on a breathless sigh and she went in, determined to seduce him with her tongue, make him feel as powerless as he'd made her feel earlier. She greedily lapped him up, drank him in, tasted him like he was the best dessert she'd ever eaten. And when he broke free of her lips, threw his head back, and yelled, she knew what was coming. They both were. She felt his hot liquid shoot deep inside her, meeting his goal, and she couldn't do anything but allow a similar shudder to take over her body, surrender to him and to the passion he had created for them.

It seemed everything around them shook. She actually felt like the sky was falling. And sensations tore through her in a way that had her body bursting into flames. He leaned down and captured her mouth again, kissing her hungrily, and she returned his hunger in kind.

He pulled away from her mouth, and when he was

able to catch his breath, he whispered hotly against her moist lips, "Now we try the billiards table."

The ringing of the phone awakened Lake. Courtney stirred in his arms when he reached to answer it. He glanced at the clock on the nightstand next to the bed. It wasn't even ten o' clock yet. He smiled, remembering all the games they had played. He and Courtney had had reason to make it an early night. "Yes?"

"Lake, sorry to bother you. This is Sonya. I got your phone number from Brandy and Grey."

"That's fine," he said in a low voice as he pulled himself up slightly, careful not to wake Courtney. "What can I do for you?"

"I'm trying to find Courtney, and her cell phone is off. I was wondering if perhaps you knew where she was?"

Lake smiled. Yes, he knew where she was. "Courtney is here with me," he said, liking the way it sounded.

"Thank God. I need to speak with her, please. It's a family emergency."

It was then that he heard the frantic sound of Sonya's voice. Something was wrong. "Sure. Hold on."

He gave Courtney a few shakes before her eyes opened. She looked at him and smiled, was about to wrap her arms around his neck when he said, "Sonya is on the phone. She wants to talk to you. Said it's a family emergency."

Courtney pulled herself up in bed and quickly took the phone he handed her. "Sonya? What's wrong?"

Lake didn't know what Sonya was saying, but he saw the widening of Courtney's eyes, the tears that suddenly appeared in them, and how the hand holding the phone began trembling. Courtney then threw the phone down in the bed, covered her face with her hand, and burst into tears.

Lake pulled her into his arms as he quickly picked up the phone. "Sonya? What the hell is going on? What did you tell her?"

He heard Sonya's own broken voice. "It's her father, Lake. Uncle Ron has been shot. He's been taken to surgery, and it doesn't look good."

24

Detective Rick Blair found an unobtrusive spot in the hospital to glance down at his pad and study his notes. A college professor had been shot on campus while getting into his car. Blair had dismissed the possibility of a robbery when he arrived at the scene. The man was still wearing his Rolex watch, and he'd had a wallet full of cash that was still intact. Yes, Blair was convinced robbery had not been the motive. It was clear to see that the professor had been on someone's shit list and that someone wanted him dead. Who? An angry student, perhaps? A betrayed wife? A disgruntled lover? The husband or boyfriend of a lover? Or possibly someone to whom the professor owed money? He shook his head. The possibilities were unlimited.

He glanced up when his partner, Theo Hollis, appeared. Theo, a young upstart, had been asking questions and taking statements. Another teacher, the one who'd found Professor Andrews slumped over his car in the parking lot, said he'd heard shots just moments before seeing a light-colored car racing away from the crime scene. It had been too dark to identify the make and model of the vehicle. But he did say the driver appeared to be a woman. That was all the information the man could provide. Too sketchy to base anything definitively.

"Aren't you glad this is your last month on the force?" Hollis said, grinning. "Everybody isn't blessed to be able to retire twice."

Blair knew what Hollis was referring to. Blair had retired after twenty-five years as head of the FBI's investigative services. He and his wife had relocated from Denver to Orlando for warmer weather and a chance to live out the rest of their lives enjoying the good life. Less than a month after the move, his wife of twenty years was killed in a senseless car-jacking. When the local police could not come up with any leads, Blair had joined the force with one goal—to bring the men responsible for his wife's death to justice. In less than two weeks, he had done that very thing and had been asked by the police chief to remain to head up the Detective Division. That was ten years ago, and now he was ready to retire again. In a way, he couldn't wait to leave, especially when they dumped eager beavers like Hollis in his lap to train. The man was a hothead who relied only on what he saw as the facts and didn't waste time adding gut instinct into the mix.

Instead of responding to Hollis's comment, he asked, "Okay, what you got?"

Hollis grinned. "This one is a piece of cake. I just finished interviewing Andrews's girlfriend, and—"

"Girlfriend?" At Hollis's nod, Blair then asked, "How did you find out about her?"

"Andrews's cell phone. That was the last number he called, so I checked things out. And according to Ashira Wilson, Andrews had planned on asking his wife for a divorce to marry her."

"Do we have proof of that?" Blair asked.

"No, but I do have proof that Andrews recently took both his wife and girlfriend on a two-week trip to Hawaii. They just returned a few days ago. Shit, how he could afford to do that, I don't know. I can't take my old lady on a trip out of Florida, and he was able to foot the bill for two women. Anyway, Wilson has airline and hotel receipts to prove it."

A smile curved Hollis's lips when he added, "Seems like he was bedding both of them on the trip. The girlfriend in the morning and the wife in the afternoon. Wilson figured the wife must have found out about it, as well as the fact he was about to ask her for a divorce, and shot him. You know how it is, Blair. Hell knows no fury like a woman scorned."

Blair shook his head, thinking that if the man had really done what Hollis claimed, then he was really a low-down dirty prick to disrespect his wife in such a manner. "Before we fly off the handle and accuse the wife of anything, let's talk to her and see what she has to say."

A few moments later, they entered the waiting room. Blair immediately focused on the occupants. His trained eye latched on to who he believed was Mrs. Ronald Andrews. Even in her seemingly distraught state, he thought she was a very beautiful woman. Dignified looking. Refined.

Then there was a woman by her side, a younger version, whom he immediately figured was the daughter. Another older woman was standing close by who bore a resemblance to the older Mrs. Andrews, so Blair knew he could count on her being a sister or a close family member. He also noted a man in his late thirties or early forties standing by the window whose sharp gaze had the younger Ms. Andrews within its scope. Blair quickly assumed he was the younger woman's husband or lover.

By the look of things, now was not a good time to ask questions; the family was clearly upset. He would even go so far as to say they were still in shock. However, a man was in surgery fighting for his life, and it was Blair's and Hollis's job to piece together what had happened and to make sure the person responsible was brought to justice.

Before Blair could open his mouth to announce their presence, Hollis, in his unsympathetic way, walked into the center of the room and said, "I am Detective Hollis, and this is my partner, Detective Blair. Whoever is Barbara Andrews, we need to ask you some questions."

Everyone glanced over at Hollis, and Blair could just imagine what was going through their minds. They were probably thinking the same thing he had a few times over the past month: that Hollis needed to improve on his people skills and grab a bunch of manners while he was at it. Blair decided to hang back and be an observer, when everyone gave him only a cursory once-over before returning their gaze to Hollis, evidently erroneously assuming Hollis was the man in charge. Blair wasn't surprised when the woman he figured to be Ronald Andrews's wife slowly stood and asked, "I'm Barbara Andrews—what questions do you have to ask me?"

Hollis forced a smile. "Several. But the main one is what reason did you have for shooting your husband?"

Blair flinched. He could tell Hollis's accusation was like a slap to the woman's face. He watched her blanch before grabbing a nearby chair for support. Before she could bother responding—although Blair doubted that she would have been capable of doing so anyway—the younger woman, flanked by the other older woman, came to stand beside Barbara Andrews. Even the man who'd been standing by the window had moved beside the three women. It was the younger woman who spoke, getting right in Hollis's face while doing so.

"How dare you accuse my mother of something like that! What gives you the right to—?"

"Facts that I've gathered, ma'am. That's what gives me the right. Apparently it's a fact that the two of them were having martial problems. And just who might you be?"

"Courtney Andrews. And that man who is in surgery fighting for his life is my father, and I won't allow you to throw your accusations at my mother instead of going out and doing your job and getting the person who is really responsible. And as far as my parents having marital problems, what married couple don't have problems at one time or another. But wherever you got your information, they evidently forgot to mention that my parents were working out their problems and had just returned from spending two wonderful weeks together in Hawaii on what they considered a second honeymoon."

"Now isn't that sweet," Hollis sneered. "Or another way to look at it is that it's really sick, since according to what we've learned, your father also paid the way for someone else to be with him while on this trip."

"What are you talking about, Detective?" the man asked.

Hollis raised a dark brow and met Lake's eyes. "And who are you?"

"I'm a close friend of Courtney's. Lake Masters. Now please tell us what you're talking about."

Instead of answering Lake, Hollis turned his attention back to Barbara Andrews. "Do you know an Ashira Wilson?"

Blair watched the woman's brow crease in deep concentration as she tried to remember someone with that name. He suddenly felt a sense of uneasiness as he watched her. If the information Ashira Wilson had given Hollis earlier was true, then something wasn't right.

"No, I don't know Ashira Wilson," she finally said.

Hollis smiled. "Ms. Wilson claims that you do know her. She also claims that the reason you shot your husband is because you found out that he had been having an affair with her and that he had the gall to also take her along to Hawaii with the two of you, and that he had put her in a suite on the other side of the same hotel. She alleges that you found out he was bedding the both of you—"

Blair straightened from leaning on the wall when his gut instinct kicked in. All four persons had stunned looks on their faces, but the one who appeared to be more shocked than anyone was Barbara Andrews. Blair knew at that moment there was no way she had known what her husband had done. The look on her face was proof enough. She wasn't that good an actress. Suddenly his heart went out to her, a woman who was finding out from Hollis in the most uncouth manner just what an asshole her husband really was. She had been disrespected as a wife in the worst way possible. Blair inhaled in deep anger. Ronald Andrews had a lot of balls. As far as he was concerned, the person who'd shot him should have gone for the lower part of his body, right below the belt, instead of the man's chest.

Refusing to let Hollis continue his brutish way of handling things, Blair quickly stepped forward. "That's enough, Hollis. Dammit, she didn't know. Just look at her. Dammit, it's evident that she didn't know."

Hollis shut his mouth while Barbara Andrews dropped to her knees and started crying out like a puppy who'd gotten kicked.

Less than an hour later, Blair sat at a table in the hospital cafeteria, downing a cup of coffee. To get her to calm down, the doctors had to sedate Barbara Andrews. Being told that the man who claimed to love her had taken another woman on a trip meant to rebuild their marriage was a low blow to everyone who'd heard what Hollis had said. She hadn't known about Ashira Wilson being in Hawaii. And if he were to believe that, he also believed she knew nothing about Ronald Andrews's plans to ask for a divorce to marry the young woman. If what Wilson claimed about the divorce bit was true.

To get rid of Hollis for a while, Blair had sent him back to the university to follow up a new lead. The university had called. One of the students had come forward to say a woman driving a light-colored car had stopped him when he was leaving the campus earlier that day, to ask where the college professors normally parked. She had also asked if he knew whether Professor Andrews was teaching classes that day. The student would be taken downtown to headquarters to work with the police artist. Hopefully they would be able to come up with a composite sketch of the woman. The one thing Blair had found interesting was that according to the student, the woman was young, possibly in her middle twenties, which definitely wasn't Barbara Andrews. Blair wondered if perhaps Ashira Wilson had pointed the finger at someone else to hide her own involvement.

"Detective Blair?"

He glanced up from sipping his coffee and looked into the face of Courtney Andrews, a younger version of her mother. Barbara was a very beautiful woman who hadn't deserved what her husband had done, and Courtney didn't deserve it either.

He got to his feet. “Ms. Andrews, how’s your mother?” he asked, genuinely concerned.

“She’s resting. Thanks for putting a stop to Detective Hollis’s heartless badgering,” she said, taking the chair across from him. “My mother honestly didn’t know what my father had done. She really thought their trip to Hawaii had been productive.”

Blair nodded as he sat back down. For Ronald Andrews, it had been. He’d had two women at his beck and call. “It would really help if I got answers to a couple questions. And I prefer asking them than letting Hollis do it.”

She nodded. “And I prefer that you do the asking, too.”

“All right.” He pulled a pad out his jacket pocket. “I’m convinced your mother didn’t know about the affair in Hawaii. Were there others?”

Courtney nodded sadly. “Yes, my father has a history of being unfaithful.”

“Okay. Who was the most recent woman, other than Ashira Wilson, that your father was involved with?”

“A woman by the name of Melissa Langley.”

“Your mother knew about her?”

“Not until Melissa decided to go public with their affair by calling my mother and informing her about it. Melissa also sent photos of them together in compromising positions just in case my mother didn’t believe her.”

“Did your parents split because of it?”

Courtney shook her head. “Yes, for a couple of months, but Mom took him back.”

Blair continued to write on the pad, thinking a woman like Barbara Andrews should have been loved and pampered instead of being made a fool of. Andrews had taken advantage of his wife's forgiving nature. "What else can you tell me about Melissa Langley?"

"I can tell you that she claimed she was pregnant, but for a while Dad was saying the baby wasn't his."

"Has the baby been born yet?" Blair asked.

Courtney shrugged. "I'm not sure. She was due to deliver in a few months."

Blair lifted a brow. "Didn't your father keep up with that sort of thing?"

"No. For him it was out of sight, out of mind. Another child-care payment to work into his budget. I tried keeping in touch with the other two women who gave birth to my father's children, but they moved away from Orlando and wouldn't respond to my calls. It was evident they wanted no contact, just the monthly payments they were receiving."

Blair jotted down the information on the pad. He then asked a few more questions. The more he learned about Ronald Andrews, the more he disliked the man . . . and the more he admired Barbara Andrews. There were some who would call her a fool for sticking by her husband after so many episodes of infidelity, but to Blair, her actions were that of a woman who loved her man—for better or for worse.

Blair leaned back in his chair. "Can you think of anything else I need to know?"

He watched her inhale deeply. "Yes, after what my father did to my mom," she said softly, with tears fanning her eyes, "I don't think I'll ever be able to forgive him."

A few hours later, Lake glanced across the kitchen table at Courtney. Somehow he had convinced her to let him take her home so she could rest. They had been at the hospital over eight hours. Ron Andrews had made it through surgery, but his condition was still critical.

Everyone had convinced Courtney's mom to go home for a while. She had been through enough. She had agreed to do so only when Courtney promised to remain at the hospital until she returned. Peggy had been there to drive Barbara home and had brought her back a few hours later. That had been when Lake convinced Courtney to go home for a while, as well. Neither woman would be doing Ron Andrews any good if they were to fall ill themselves.

Lake could just imagine what emotions Courtney was feeling toward her father right now. Hell, he could just imagine what Barbara's feelings were, as well. But it seemed both had put their hurt and pain aside to be by the side of a man who truly didn't deserve their loyalty. He found such a thing admirable, especially coming from Barbara. What Ron Andrews had pulled in Hawaii, the disrespect he'd done to his wife, was incomprehensible to Lake.

And it hadn't helped matters when Ashira Wilson

had shown up at the hospital, causing a scene. The young woman had hurled her accusations at Courtney after finding out Barbara had left to go home. In a way, it had been a blessing that Barbara hadn't been there. Talk about drama. The woman, as far as Lake was concerned—in hoochie-mama style—had painted a vivid picture of just what her relationship with Ron Andrews entailed. And she was determined to make sure Barbara rotted in hell for taking her lover away.

"Do you want any more coffee?" he asked Courtney. She had been quiet since he'd brought her home. She had taken a shower and changed clothes, but refused to lie down as he'd suggested. It was morning, a new day, and he knew she would be spending most of it at the hospital like her mother.

She tried assuring him with a smile. "No, I'm fine."

He knew she wasn't fine. She was hurting, and he wanted to make her feel better. He stood and walked around the table, and before she could say anything, he swooped her up into his arms and carried her into the bedroom. He placed her on the bed and then joined her there, just to hold her. She didn't need anything else from him right now. The only thing she needed was to know he was there with her, he was holding her in his arms, protecting her as best he could, and loving her with all his heart.

All his heart.

He inhaled sharply. Grey had been right. Everyone comes with drama, but how much you were willing to tolerate depended on how much that person meant to you. He knew at that moment that Courtney was his everything. He wanted to marry her, give her his babies, treat her a hell of a lot better than her father had treated her mother.

The one thing Courtney had shared with him on the drive from the hospital was that her mother would remain with her father until it was known his condition was out of danger; then she could see Barbara finally breaking ties and getting a divorce. Courtney strongly believed whatever love Barbara Andrews had had for her husband was destroyed the moment Detective Hollis revealed just what he'd done.

"I love you, Lake." This was the first time she'd said the words to him, although she had felt it in her heart.

He stared down at Courtney. "And I love you, too, sweetheart," he whispered, saying them for the first time, as well. "I'm sorry about what you and your mother are going through."

"Yes," she said softly. "I'm sorry, too. Especially for Mom. She loved him so much. But no woman deserves to be treated like he has treated her, and what he pulled in Hawaii, taking that woman with them, exposing my mother to heaven knows what each time he slept with her, was thoughtless, heartless, inconsiderate, and unforgivable. I truly don't think Mom will forgive him this time."

Lake pulled her closer to his arms and then leaned down and kissed her. When he released her lips, he said softly, "You're tired. Go ahead and take a nap, and when you wake up, we'll go back to the hospital."

Courtney nodded and cuddled closer to Lake. And he knew that he would love and protect her for the rest of his life.

25

A Week Later

Although Ron Andrews hadn't regained consciousness, the doctors felt his condition was improving every day. After glancing across the room at her husband, who was sleeping soundly in the hospital bed, Barbara stood to stretch her legs. Courtney and Sonya had left to go bring her something for lunch.

She walked over to the window and glanced out. Ron would be getting better, and she was glad of that. However, as she had told Courtney that morning, she did not intend to wait until he fully recovered. She had already met with an attorney to end their marriage. She was here now out of loyalty he truly didn't deserve, and she wouldn't waste another day of her life loving a man who had done nothing during the last thirty years but treat her like crap. He had continued to do so because she had let him, but all that would be coming to an end. Courtney had agreed with her decision.

"Mrs. Andrews?"

She turned to find Detective Blair standing in the doorway. She smiled over at him. The man had been kind. Every day he had dropped by to see how she was doing and to let her know how the investigation was going. She knew she owed him a bit of gratitude. He had believed her when she'd said that she had not been the one to shoot Ron. His partner, Detective Hollis, would have had her locked up in jail by now, since he'd been fully convinced that she had.

She crossed the room to him. "Detective Blair. How are you?"

"Fine. Is there somewhere we can talk privately?"

She nodded. "How about the coffee shop? I was about to leave and go downstairs and get a cup."

"I feel the need for a cup myself."

Together they began walking toward the bank of elevators. "I understand your husband's condition is improving," he said, glancing over at her.

Without looking at him, she said, "Yes. As you saw, he's still hooked up to various machines, but the doctors are confident that he's doing better each day. He's a very lucky man."

"In more ways than one, Mrs. Andrews. There are probably a lot of women who went through what you have, discovering what you did, who would not have come back, regardless of how severe their husband's condition. You are a remarkably loyal woman."

She stopped walking when they reached the elevators. She looked at him then. "I used to be," she said in a low voice. "But every one has a tolerance level, and mine has reached its limit. It had to be my decision to make. My daughter or sister couldn't make it for me. And I've made that decision. Several of them, in fact."

Blair didn't have to wonder what those decisions were, and he couldn't blame her too much. Ronald Andrews would be losing his wife at a time when he would need her the most.

Moments later, they were sitting across from each other in the coffee shop. And not for the first time, he thought she was a beautiful woman. Sophisticated. Graceful. Classy and stylish. He had met Ashira Wilson, as well as Melissa Langley. Neither had a classy or stylish bone in their bodies. Both were young, immature, and foolish and thought the best way to get the things they wanted in life was with the use of their bodies. Personally, if he'd been given a choice, he would have chosen Barbara Andrews over them, hands down. Andrews hadn't realized what a jewel he had, he hadn't appreciated it. It would definitely be his loss.

"You said you had something to talk to me about, Detective."

"Yes," he said, looking at her, almost falling victim to the darkness of her eyes. Eyes he thought were simply beautiful. Hell, he even thought she had beautiful hands. His gaze moved to the one holding the coffee cup up to her lips. Mmm, beautiful lips, too. At that moment he decided she was someone he would like to know further. Later, when all this was over, he would contact her again, and it wouldn't be a business call.

He shifted in his seat and cleared his throat. "I wanted to be the one to tell you that we have arrested the person responsible for shooting your husband."

He watched her beautiful eyes widen. He watched as her beautiful hands placed the coffee cup aside. He then watched those beautiful lips move. "Who?" she asked in an almost whisper.

"Melissa Langley. She had lost their baby and tried calling Mr. Andrews to let him know, and he went off on her before she had a chance to tell him. Got ugly with her. Said some mean things. She felt distraught, bitter, and hateful. The reason she had exposed their affair to you was because he was dropping her for Ashira Wilson. Instead of you reacting like she had expected you to do, you did just the opposite and remained married. And then, somehow she found out that Andrews was also seeing Ashira, her replacement. That only made matters worse, and losing the baby was the icing on the cake."

He paused for a moment and said, "Just so you know, her attorney is trying to work on an insanity plea, and in this case, she just might get it."

Barbara really didn't surprise him when she smiled and said, "And I hope in this case she does."

Sonya smiled over at Courtney as they headed back toward the hospital. Traffic wasn't so bad, which she appreciated.

She hated being stalled in traffic. "So, I see that you and Lake are truly together now."

Courtney glanced over at her and returned her smile. "Yes, and I know what he feels toward me is the real thing. He's been just wonderful these past couple of weeks, especially with what's happening with Dad. He's truly special."

Sonya grinned. "Yes, and I knew it the moment we met. That's why I added him to my little black book."

Courtney blinked. "Excuse me?"

Sonya laughed. "You didn't even know it. It was priceless. I will never forget that day you told me none of the guys from the black book met your approval and then you told me about meeting Lake. I knew then that you hadn't realized his name was in the book."

Courtney opened her mouth, then snapped it shut. She then opened it again, needing to know something. "You were once interested in Lake?"

Sonya gave her a sly smile. "No, I thought he was special when we first met at a party that Carla gave, and that's why his name went into the book. I considered him a future prospect, but that was when I was trying to fight my attraction to Mike. I really wasn't focused on other guys as I wanted to be then."

Courtney smiled. "But in the end, everything worked out for you."

"And everything worked out for you, as well. I think you and Lake make a beautiful couple. I've seen how much attention he gives you. How he sees to your every need when the two of you are together. The man simply adores you."

Courtney was pleased that Sonya thought so. "He's asked me to go to Savannah in a couple of weeks to meet his family. It's his mother's sixty-fifth birthday."

"Are you going to go?"

"Yes. As long as Dad's condition continues to improve, I plan to go."

Sonya nodded as she pulled into the hospital's parking garage. "Has your mom made any decisions about Uncle Ron?"

"Yes, she plans to divorce him," Courtney said without any regret in her voice. "And I support her decision. It's about time she moves on with her life and finds her someone who appreciates the woman she is."

Then deciding to switch subjects, she asked, "Have you come to terms with Suzette's pregnancy, Sonya?"

"Not completely, but I'm getting there. Dad's another one who's made some stupid mistakes in his lifetime, but he's my dad and I love him." She then smiled brightly. "Mom's doing great. She's dating this man named Willie Baker. He lives in Texas, and they go out together whenever he comes to town. She claims they are just friends, but I can see it growing into something more. She likes him, and it's obvious that he likes her."

"And I'm happy for her," Courtney said. "It's my prayer that Mom will eventually find someone, as well. Life is too short not to live it happily." Joy spread through her entire being. She still had the issue of her father to deal with, and every day she was praying that God gave her the strength to forgive him for the pain he had caused her mother. He was her father, and she loved him—that would never change—but she no longer respected him, and it would be a long time before she would feel differently.

3 Days Later

Barbara walked into Ron's hospital room to find that the nurses had raised him up in bed. He had begun regaining consciousness a day or so before and had spoken briefly with Detective Blair, confirming that Melissa had been the person who'd pulled the trigger. He had yet to be told that everyone knew about his Hawaii tryst with Ashira. The woman had come to the hospital a few times, demanding to see him, but Barbara had requested that hospital security keep her from doing so . . . for the time being.

She saw how Ron tried to smile when he saw her. Any other time, his smile would have been all she'd needed, but not anymore. Those days were over. "I was wondering when you were coming," he said in a slurred voice. There was a tube that went through his nose that still made talking difficult for him.

"I told you last night I would be back in this morning." She had stopped staying all night. She refused to sleep uncomfortable any longer in the cot the nurses would bring in. He didn't deserve that of her. "Ron, we need to talk," she said, deciding this would be the day she made him aware of what she knew.

"Yes," he agreed. "There's a lot I need to tell you, Barbara. Things I want you to know."

She wondered if it was true-confession time for him. If coming so close to death had made him a "changed" man. If so, he could continue to go through his transformation without her. She would no longer be a part of his life. "There's no need, Ron. If you want to tell me about Ashira Wilson, don't bother. She's told me everything. I know you paid for her to go to Hawaii with us."

"Barbara, I—"

"No. Please don't," she said, holding up her hand. "Please don't make matters any worse by apologizing. You did what you did because it was what you wanted to do, without any care or concern about me. Over the years, I've put up with your affairs, but no longer. What you did in Hawaii was unforgivable. You put me at risk. You—"

"No, Barbara. I never had sex with any of the others without using a condom. I would never do that to you," he said in a whispered tone.

"But there should not have been a need for a condom, Ron. I was your wife. The only woman you should have been sleeping with. But—"

"I'm sick, Barbara. I have this sexual addiction, and I plan to get help."

She nodded, believing him. But for her, it didn't matter. It didn't make a difference. "I'm glad, Ron, and I hope the next woman you marry reaps the full benefits of your recovery."

"I don't understand what you mean."

She inhaled deeply. "I've filed for a divorce. According to what Ashira Wilson is saying, you were going to divorce me anyway to marry her."

“She’s lying.”

“It doesn’t matter. She’s told so many truths about certain things that her lies don’t make a difference now. According to the doctor, if you continue to improve, you’ll be able to go home in a week or so. I won’t be coming back to see you. I had a moving company take your belongings to an apartment I’ve gotten for you. It’s close to your job and should be convenient. Things between us end here, Ron. I wish you the best.”

“Barbara, please don’t.”

Instead of having anything else to say or giving in to his pitiful plea, with her head held high she turned and walked out the room.

26

Courtney opened the door to her home, a nervous wreck. She'd had lunch with Brandy, who'd told her just how much Lake's family was looking forward to meeting her next weekend. Great! That was all she needed to hear. Lake had been the one to hold out the longest, preferring to seek out his own woman. What if, after meeting her, his family thought she hadn't been worth the hunt?

"Hello, sweetheart."

She swirled around. "Lake!" Dropping the packages in her hand, she raced across the room, and he caught her into his arms. He had left a few days ago to attend a business meeting in Boston and she hadn't expected him back until tomorrow.

"I missed you," he whispered close to her lips, and then he was devouring those lips in a kiss that sent sensations sizzling all through Courtney. She had accepted a while ago that Lake had a scandalous way of kissing her. She liked it, and most of the time couldn't get enough of it. Like she could never get enough of him. He was everything she ever wanted. Everything she would ever need.

When he released her mouth moments later, they were both pulling in deep, heavy breaths. He looked at her. "Take off your clothes."

She stared at him. "What?"

"I said take off your clothes."

She blinked. "Now?"

He gave her one of his decadent smiles. "Yes, now. Right this minute."

She could feel her nipples growing tight and sensitive against the fabric of her blouse. "You sure you want me to do this?"

"Positive."

A long edgy silence encompassed them, and then she took a step back and pulled her blouse over her head and tossed it aside. Next came her skirt, and she saw that he was staring, not missing a thing, when her hand went to the zipper to ease it down.

She studied his expression, saw the hot look in his eyes. "You're enjoying this, aren't you?"

He didn't waste time mulling over a response. "Yes. More than you will ever know."

She had an idea. Well, more than an idea when her gaze lowered from his face to his crotch. He was big and growing by the minute. The second. Leaps and bounds. "Am I going to get something for all my trouble in doing this?"

He gave a smooth chuckle. "Oh, yes, trust me. You're going to get something, all right."

Her gaze moved back to his face. He didn't have a poker face. She knew exactly what he planned on giving her. "There," she said, standing in front of him stark naked. And unashamedly so. Lake had taught her that when it came to them, nothing was too risqué. He liked thinking out of the box. "It's your turn, Lake."

He grinned and began unbuttoning his shirt. Then he was removing his shoes, socks, and his pants. Next were his boxers, leaving him naked. He met her gaze. "Happy now?"

"Are you?"

"I can show you better than I can tell you." And then he was crossing the short distance that separated them. He pulled her into his arms and kissed her again, and she automatically became lost in the feel of his mouth on hers and what his mouth was doing. But she did feel the moment he caught her by the bottom and lifted her up and widened her legs open to wrap around him. But not before his manhood unerringly found what it wanted and he entered her. Just as smoothly. Just as quick. They were locked together. Body to body. Flesh to flesh.

He threw his head back, pulled in a deep breath, and she knew he had taken in her scent. There was no way he could have missed it. She was hot.

And then with them still locked together, she felt him walking her backward and she wondered where he was taking her. It didn't take long for her to find out. It was the nearest wall.

As soon as he planted her back against it, he lowered his head and went for her breasts. "You don't play fair," she muttered right before she released a groan she couldn't hold back. With each pull of his mouth on her breast, she felt her inner muscles contracting, clamping fully around him, and when his tongue began tormenting her nipple, she gave in to the climax she couldn't hold back. The one he'd known would come.

And it seemed that's what he'd been waiting for. Her to come. He began thrusting in and out of her, stroking her deep, hard, and fast. She began crying out when another orgasm took over her mind the same way Lake had taken over her body. She could swear that she could actually feel her toes curl as he kept thrusting into her relentlessly. By the time she screamed out another orgasm, he was right there with her, going over the edge, storming the waves, drowning in pleasure.

"I love you." He whispered the words hotly against her mouth.

"And I love you." And she knew he was all the man she would ever want and need.

Later that night she went in search of her little black book. She found it in the bottom of her drawer buried beneath her panties. She opened it up and flipped to the next page, the one after Solomon Wise's name. She smiled when she saw Lake's name. It was there. So regardless, she would eventually have met him, but she was glad they'd met the way they had: on their own and without help from anyone.

She felt even more convinced that it was meant for them to be together.

She placed the book back in the drawer and crossed the room to slide back in bed with him. She felt contented when in sleep he instinctively pulled her closer into his arms. Smiling, she cuddled up close to him, thinking that she hadn't needed her little black book after all.

her little black book
discussion questions

1. Do you feel that, in the beginning, Courtney should have been more supportive of her parents' decision to save their marriage?

2. Knowing the animosity between his wife, ex-wife, and daughter, should Joe have brought Suzette to the wedding?

3. When Harper Isaac was arrested, should Courtney have used her funds to pay for an attorney or to do whatever was needed to help get Harper out of the trouble he was in? What about her handling of the other two guys from her little black book? Were her expectations too high?

4. Do you think that Ron really had any intentions of trying to save his marriage?

5. Should Barbara have been so quick to trust her husband again, judging by what he did to her in the past?

6. Could you understand Peggy's reluctance to date again, even when a nice guy like Willie Baker came along?

7. How do you feel about Ron taking Ashira to Hawaii with him and Barbara? Should Barbara have suspected something?

8. What did you think of Lake Masters's style of romancing Courtney? Did he move too fast? Too slow?

9. Considering the men in her life, did you understand Courtney's reluctance to take Lake at face value?

10. Knowing about Ron's health situation, should Barbara have stayed with him in the end? Was informing him of the divorce in the hospital a low blow?